"A date?" Hope shook her head.

She couldn't quite believe what she was hearing. "Are you asking me on a date—to The End Zone?"

Lucien frowned. "Is that such a bad idea?" He straightened his shirt cuffs. "I'd like to check out The End Zone's food and don't want to eat alone."

And wasn't that flattering? Not! "Well, uh, no, not a bad idea at all." Hope felt flummoxed. What was he up to?

She didn't know him at all, really, but one thing she was sure of. Lucien Durand always had an agenda. That agenda would always include him coming out on top.

She supposed she would find out his ulterior motive if she went out with him. She would not, however, make it easy for him. "I'd love to go with you. I can only take off Mondays, because the restaurant goes dark on Monday."

His eyes widened. "You're kidding me."

She nodded, enjoying his obvious befuddlement. "I'm the only chef. Okay, aside from Shane. I can't take a night without closing."

A shadow crossed his face at the mention of Shane. "Baker's so inept he can't handle the kitchen alone?"

"Of course he can handle the kitchen alone." What did Lucien have against Shane? "I just choose to shut things down on Mondays. My name's on the food, so I make the food."

He gave her a sharp nod. "*Oui*. I understand that." He took her hand. "How about next Monday, then?"

Okay, she'd bite. "Sure. I'll meet you there." She gave him a big toothy smile. "What time?"

A Taste of Hope

by

Doreen Alsen

At The End Zone Series

A Taste of Hope

Cover Art by *Tina Lynn Stout*

The Wild Rose Press, Inc.
PO Box 708
Adams Basin, NY 14410-0708
Visit us at www.thewildrosepress.com

Publishing History
First Champagne Rose Edition, 2015
Print ISBN 978-1-62830-900-3
Digital ISBN 978-1-62830-901-0

At The End Zone Series
Published in the United States of America

Dedication

To my pool ladies
for all the laughs, support, and friendship
with which you gift me.
I've got the best job in the world!

Chapter One

"Hey, Hope! Guess who's out in the dining room!"

Hope Monahan looked up from the order of short ribs she was plating. Some of the sauce sloshed out of her ladle and landed on her already splattered chef's tunic. Her usually calm hostess, Cleo, looked like she'd stuck her finger in a light socket.

"It's Lucien Durand! Here for dinner." Cleo's voice vibrated with excitement. She sighed. "He's even more handsome in person!"

Hope slid the short ribs under the heat lamp. "Renee, pick up!" She wiped her forehead with her sleeve then looked at Cleo. "You're kidding."

"No! It's really him." Cleo nearly swooned. "Why do you think he's here?"

"Probably to check the competition." A cold sensation shimmied up her spine, despite the heat coming from the ovens in the kitchen line. She shook her head. "I can't come right now, we're too busy. I'll visit his table once things slow down."

"Okay!" Cleo left the kitchen to return to the hostess desk.

Lucien Durand in her dining room. Well, well, well. Big shot chef from New Orleans opening a branch of his L'Enfer chain of restaurants in Addington, Massachusetts, thinking he could corner the market on elegant dining in the area. Show the yokels how food is

1

done.

L'Enfer at Addington. What a stupid name for a restaurant.

She supposed she should be honored that Durand saw her as competition. Well, yeah, okay, she did feel flattered. Lucien Durand was a world class chef and media darling.

What arrogance! So what if his New Orleans restaurant, the first L'Enfer, had earned a couple of Michelin stars. Forget the line of spice products with his name slapped on the label. Never mind he dated supermodels and movie starlets and was pursued by the paparazzi. Big deal; his black hair, night dark eyes, and the face of a fallen angel smiled from the cover of *People* magazine's Sexiest Man Alive issue.

Although that last bit took more time to forget, as well as the fact he had a body that could make the seraphim weep. It was a doggone shame he had to cover it up with those designer suits.

So, curiosity snuck up on her as she pulled the next order down the line. If he was still here when she finished cooking, she'd go out and introduce herself.

Priorities, Hope told herself. Food first, eye candy for dessert.

****

Lucien Durand breathed deeply as he took note of his surroundings. Hope's had a warm, homey atmosphere, very upscale country. Quaint. Muted light, soft Celtic music, fresh flowers and candles on each table. The restaurant welcomed the diners and put them immediately at ease, like they were in a good friend's home.

Him? Not so much. Friendliness was not on his

agenda for the evening. He kept his senses tuned for weaknesses he could use against his competition.

A glass with bourbon and ice appeared on his table. Renee, his server for the evening, was back, dupe pad in hand. "Do you have any questions about the menu, Mr. Durand?"

Of course she knew his name. His face had graced enough magazine covers. Lucien shook his head. He'd barely looked at the menu. "Not right now."

Renee smiled. "Well, just let me know if you have any questions."

As she left, he picked up the one page, handwritten on vellum, menu. There wasn't a whole lot of variety. Also, the menu noted exactly where each item had been grown or where Hope herself had foraged for the ingredients. She grew all the herbs and most of the produce, right down to the apples for that evening's pie.

By the looks of it, Hope Monahan appeared to be an updated female Daniel Boone with a dash of MacGyver thrown in. He'd heard she ran an earth-to-table restaurant, limiting her menu to what was fresh and in season. By the look of things, he'd heard the truth.

That would drive him crazy, those limits and restraints. He wanted what he wanted, when he wanted it. He had no use for this live-off-the-land crap. He wouldn't put it past her to name the cow who had given its life for the braised short ribs in the menu.

The ever helpful Renee approached again, with overeager stars in her eyes and a big sharky smile. As if Lucien was on the menu for dinner. He hoped she wasn't the kind of waitress to write her phone number on his bill. It happened often enough.

He ordered the beet salad and the braised short ribs, along with a glass of merlot from a winery in Truro, on Cape Cod.

Everyone spoke of her with awe and admiration. Addington was ground zero for the Hope Monahan fan club.

He'd see if the food lived up to the hype.

****

The kitchen slowed a bit, so Hope could move away from the line and check on her guest of honor. She pulled out a generous slice of her special apple pie, then dropped a small scoop of her homemade organic vanilla ice cream.

Glancing down at herself, she sighed. Okay, she wasn't the neatest chef. If she had a clean jacket to change into, she would, but she didn't. Oh, well. Besides, you got hot and sweaty while working the cooking line. *Monsieur Perfect* every-hair-in-place Durand should know all about that.

Unless he never sweated. Which, from his appearance, fell smack dab into the realm of possibility.

Hope moved into the dining room and liked what she saw. Efficient, friendly staff, diners smiling and having a good time eating her food. Peaceful. Restful.

Her skin prickled. She knew why. Lucien Durand had spotted her. She turned her attention to his table. He was better looking in person than in any glossy magazine photo. His hair styled to perfection, those dark, dark bedroom eyes, that body perfect in a light gray suit, paired with a light blue tie, how could any woman resist him?

She checked out his plate. He'd barely touched it. Jerk. The short ribs were killer. She knew that beyond a shadow of a doubt. He had to be messing with her head.

Hope itched to take Mr. Irresistible down a few pegs. It was a dirty job, and she was just the woman to do it. She smiled and walked toward him. He stood as she approached.

"I've brought dessert for you." She put the plate on the table, then stuck out her hand. "I'm Hope Monahan."

He shook her hand. "Lucien Durand." He motioned for her to sit in the other chair at his table. "Are you able to join me?"

Oh, that voice, low and rumbly, with the subtle accent, hit her *POW!* right in the kisser. Get a grip, Hope. Get a grip. "Oh, no thank you, I've got to get back to the kitchen. I just came out to say hello and bring you dessert—on the house, of course. May I have Renee get you some coffee? An espresso? We carry a wide selection of fair trade coffee roasts. They're delicious."

His eyes, the color of midnight, turned a bit more smoky as he studied her. "An espresso would be wonderful, *merci*."

She felt her mouth curl up in a smile. Maybe she could get Renee to add a little arsenic to the espresso. "How did you enjoy your meal?" The question she didn't want to ask, given the full condition of his plate, just flew out of her mouth before she could stop it.

"Everything was lovely, thank you."

Lovely, heh. It was double damn better than lovely. "Great! I'm glad." She motioned to Renee, who hurried over. "Mr. Durand would like an espresso."

Renee's smile turned brilliant. "I'll be right back."

****

5

Lucien watched Hope walk away. Though she wore baggy pants, a dirty chef's tunic, and an apron tied around her waist, he could tell by the sway of her hips that her clothes hid a trim waist and a sweet little ass. For sure, Hope Monahan was one pretty package.

And, *bien sûr*, not his usual type. He went for tall, cool, leggy blondes. On the short side, with hair the color of chestnuts, eyes parsley green, almost too fragile, like a fine bone china teacup, the chef walking away from him didn't fit his type or his original idea of Hope Monahan, granola queen.

She looked strong and competent, even though her jacket was covered in dribs and drabs of tonight's menu. Flour dusted her hair. His fingers tingled with the urge to touch her and brush off the flour.

But only because he deplored messy chefs. He ran his own kitchen with military precision.

However messy, her food tasted delicious and full of flavor, her plates beautifully composed. He had really wanted to clean his plate, but he had to stick to his master plan to get her head out of the game. He'd visited most of the restaurants in town. Hope Monahan looked like the one for which he'd have to watch out.

Nothing made Lucien Durand happier than a challenge, and Hope Monahan was the real deal.

Chapter Two

"This came for you," Ainslie Mason said, her voice tinged with the sing-song of the deep south, as she walked into Hope's office. She tapped the envelope in her left hand. Ainslie was Hope's very capable catering and special events coordinator. "Looks like it came from L'Enfer Addington. See?" Ainslie held up the envelope and waggled it from corner to corner. "See the logo?"

Hope put down the Cuban panini she'd made for her lunch without taking a bite. She gave the envelope a suspicious glance, then took it from Ainslie. "Oh, really." A rich cream color and heavy, the paper felt expensive. Classy. She examined the logo, a quasi art deco design associated with L'Enfer Worldwide. It epitomized taste and elegance.

"Well, are you going to open it?" Ainslie perched herself on the edge of Hope's desk.

Hope snorted. "Aren't you the nosy one."

"It's one of my better qualities." Ainslie grinned.

"Not from where I'm standing."

"Go ahead, open it." Ainslie looked puzzled. "What's the worst thing that could be in there?"

Really. Hope blushed at how foolish she must look to Ainslie. "Of course, you're right." She worked the flap open.

"As if there were any doubt I'm right." Ainslie

craned her neck, obviously trying to see what came inside. She would need a chiropractor if she didn't stop twisting her neck that way.

The envelope held a card with embossed black lettering and a crimson border. She had trouble pulling the card free.

You are cordially invited—

Well, that was *not* what she expected, but she should have seen it coming.

"So, what is it?" Ainslie pushed off of the desk and tapped her foot.

"It's an invitation to L'Enfer's grand opening."

Ainslie's eyes widened. "I've heard it's going to be a huge event."

Hope had heard that too. "I didn't expect to get invited."

"Pfft." Ainslie waved that notion away. "Of course he's going to invite the competition, so he can intimidate you and show off all at the same time."

"You think?" Hope looked at the invitation again to find some kind of an out. There really wasn't one. She did the only thing she could. She made one up. "I can't go that night, I have to be here." Pasting a big stretchy ol' smile across her face, she handed the invitation to Ainslie. "You and Dave should go instead." Dave was Ainslie's brand spankin' new husband.

Ainslie crossed her arms under her chest and wouldn't take the card. "You're the boss. You can manage to get away for the evening. You know you're curious."

Hope sighed. "No doubt he'll have a different approach to food from mine. L'Enfer is elegant, but it's still a chain restaurant. He sells his persona as well as food." All high gloss and shiny image.

"Maybe not this one. This is no big city like New Orleans, London, Paris, and Los Angeles." Ainslie shrugged. "He might have changed his approach for small-town Addington. Have you ever eaten at a L'Enfer?"

"No. I've never had the opportunity." Because she was terrified of flying. "I've tried a few of his recipes. They weren't my thing, and I didn't want to buy his spice blends. I prefer to make my own."

"Then how can you judge his cooking?" Ainslie shook her head. "I was at the opening of the first restaurant in New Orleans, by sheer happenstance. It was quite the event. The man knows how to throw a party." Ainslie brushed an imaginary piece of lint off her periwinkle blue blazer. "Right from the start, the food was world class. His take on jambalaya was outstanding. Memorable." She smiled. "You should go and get a feel for what he does."

Yes, she should. "I guess I'm being super lame by ignoring the invitation."

"I won't argue with you about that, sugar."

Hope's heart beat a little harder in her chest, and her spine prickled at the idea of going to L'Enfer and seeing Durand being fawned over by the media. Watching him with those supermodels hanging on his arm.

And why did she care about the supermodels anyway?

She just didn't know.

Looking out the French doors that led to her gardens, Hope realized she really wanted to go. She looked back at Ainslie. "What should I wear?"

Ainslie's grin split her face. "I thought you'd never ask."

****

Lucien tinkered with the final details of the menu for his grand opening. In general his preparation was meticulous to the nth degree, as he refused to leave anything to chance. That was just how he rolled.

But beyond that, the launch party had to be extra special, extra perfect.

From the polished light figures, the gleaming silverware to the splashes of yellow and red flowers on the snowy white tablecloths, he examined everything once, twice, three times. He had extremely high standards and you either met them or you didn't. If you didn't hit the mark, you were gone, *la fin*.

Some people called him ruthless. That didn't bother him at all. He embraced it.

He liked being a badass.

Lucien's cell phone vibrated in his breast pocket. He grimaced at the screen. He hated getting calls from the pinheaded pencil pushers who called themselves accountants, but they were a necessary evil. He tapped the phone screen as he put it to his ear. "Durand."

"Chef," the voice of his head accountant crackled from the speaker. "We've finished working out the income predictions for the first six months of the Addington store. We're faxing it to you. As I told you, the numbers don't look good."

"I don't care about what the numbers look like." The voice on the phone buzzed around his head like a pesky fly.

The voice wouldn't go away. "We also did a

comparison of what the figures would be if you opened in Boston. Of course, they're better, with a return on your investment six months to a year sooner than in Addington."

Lucien brushed that aside. "I don't care." And he didn't. "It's too late to turn back now, even if I wanted to." Which he didn't. He'd made the choices he had to and, dammit all, he could manage to stay here, no matter what it took, just to get his sister into college and set her on a different path, away from the users and losers who followed her around.

The accountant cleared his throat. "I think you still need to look at these charts and projections. I'll fax them to you right now."

Lucien turned off his phone.

His corporate staff thought him *fou à lier* to open a restaurant anyplace other than a major city. Perhaps he was crazy as a loon to open a branch in a small college town, but he didn't think so.

The more the business people objected, the more determined he became to prove them wrong. He'd bet his *grand-mère*'s entire recipe book—that's how sure he was of this decision.

Grand-mère. He had promises to keep. Miles before he could sleep, too many promises to keep.

He'd had to move Angelique here, get her into college, keep her safe. As far from his ex-mistress, Cäcilia as possible. Nothing else had more importance, not the business plan, *rien*. He would do it too. Failure wasn't an option, not when his sister's life and reputation were on the line.

A headache brewed behind his eyes. He tapped the pen he held on the clipboard filled with checklists, reminders, and notes to himself.

"Chef." Robert, Lucien's right-hand man, walked quietly into the dining room. "You asked to see the R.S.V.P. list."

Lucien turned to him. "Yes." He put down the clipboard in order to take the list. "Thank you." As he scanned it, his gut clemched until he found the one name that mattered.

Hope Monahan. And, *eh, là voyons*! She was bringing a date.

Bien sûr she was bringing a date. A woman as beautiful as Hope Monahan would not attend a party alone.

For that matter, why should Hope bringing a date matter? He'd dated many women, many of them more beautiful than Hope. Scores of glitzy, dazzling women from all corners of the globe, including the woman named the most beautiful woman in the world, the model so infamous she was known by only one name. Cäcilia.

His stomach soured. Cäcilia may have a beautiful face and banging body, but she had an ugly soul. He was well rid of her. Compared to her, Hope Monahan's wholesome loveliness was much more appealing.

Hope Monahan, who was bringing a date to his grand opening.

He scowled. Hope Monahan's love life was none of his business. He couldn't care less.

Chapter Three

"You clean up real good." Hope smiled at her date for L'Enfer's grand opening, Shane Baker, her sous chef. Tall, blond, and muscular, he resembled a Viking more than a chef. His large hands could probably wield a mythic super hammer as easily as a sharp-edged cleaver and the heavy equipment in the kitchen. "Did sunglasses come with that outfit?"

Shane smoothed his hand down the turquoise and orange Hawaiian shirt. "Hey! It's my best shirt."

"The banana yellow blazer is a nice touch." Hope shook her head. "You'll blind everyone within a five mile radius."

"What can I say? I'm a stylish guy."

"It's an interesting look. Not many guys could pull it off."

"True that. I am one of a kind." Shane grinned, all Cheshire cat-like. "You look pretty good yourself."

Hope dropped into a little curtsy. "All courtesy of my personal stylist." AKA Ainslie, who had talked her into a leaf green dress, sunflowers and foliage embroidered onto the skirt and straps. She's also talked her into moss-colored patent leather high-heeled sandals. To say heels weren't her usual style would be correct.

Hope picked footwear for comfort, not for torture, no matter how great her legs looked in stilettos. "Think there'll be a lot of people there?" For sure her feet would get stepped on.

Shane snorted. "Only everybody in town. People are curious. He's world famous after all." Shane shoved his hands into his trouser pockets. "Might be some movie stars and supermodels there." He waggled his eyebrows.

Hope rolled her eyes. "It's the opening of a restaurant, not a royal wedding."

"Right. Not too many of those around here, either." He snorted. "The guy's a real hound dog, when it comes to the high-maintenance arm candy companions, and there are also not too many of them in Addington. Makes you wonder why he's opening a restaurant here. Ow!" Shane winced when Hope slapped him on his arm, then shrugged as he pulled his keys out of his pocket and jingled them. "You 'bout ready to go?"

"Just a sec." Her nerves jangled along with Shane's keys. She checked herself out in a nearby mirror, added a little bit more lipstick, and popped the tube into her purse. "Do I look okay?"

"Killer. All those supermodels will be green with envy."

"Yeah, right." Hope linked her arm around Shane's. "Let's do this."

****

Cars packed L'Enfer's parking lot, making it difficult to find a space. As Shane maneuvered his Jeep around the rows of vehicles, Hope assessed the look of the restaurant. Durand rehabbed what once had been a decaying old mansion into a place that would fit into New Orleans' French Quarter like okra in gumbo.

All the other versions of L'Enfer epitomized sleek,

stylish, and urban. L'Enfer Addington did not reflect that style décor. Painted in a cantaloupe pastel with pale lemon trim, it looked like dessert. He'd added balconies to the second floor, exchanging old windows for French doors. Flowers cascaded out of planters attached to the white wrought-iron railings that rimmed the balconies in a riot of red, orange, yellow, and green.

Shane made a patch of lawn into a parking space. "Parking sucks." He cut the engine and hauled up the hand brake.

Hope smiled. "Limits the number of patrons he can fit in on any given night. Bad for business," she said as she got out of the Jeep. A heel sank into the ground, making her stumble. Could she be any more of a clod?

A Dixieland band pumped music out the windows and doors. It should have been at odds with the candy-box exterior of L'Enfer, but somehow the wail of a clarinet, the staccato thump of the drums, the cheerful percussiveness of a piano, worked.

They climbed a short staircase to the porch and Shane opened the front door and held it for Hope. "After you." She stepped over the threshold and into the lion's den. The scents of exotic spices reached out and wrapped themselves around her. Her mouth watered as she inhaled deeply in appreciation. Garlic, red pepper, and onion, for sure, mingled with paprika, dry mustard, and cumin. The tiniest hint of cinnamon and celery seed added another layer to the mix, finished with the tang of fresh grated ginger.

Subtle light glowed from teardrop lampshades suspended at different heights in the foyer. A couple of leather-covered chairs flanked a display of spice and sauce blends, the labels carrying Durand's face.

L'Enfer Cuisine at Home. How enterprising of him. Hope shouldn't be surprised. She'd seen them at the grocery store. Of course he'd hawk his wares in his own restaurant. Nothing wrong with that.

Lucien Durand stood near the door. What in the world was he doing in the reception area instead of back in the kitchen where he belonged?

No chef's togs for him. He wore a black tuxedo, custom tailored to perfection. The contrast of a snowy-white shirt not only contrasted with the elegant black of his jacket, but also with his tanned skin. He laughed with the beautiful woman at his side, revealing a bright, sexy smile.

The man knew how to make a good first impression. A good second impression too.

Okay, a lifelong good impression.

He swiveled his head in her—and Shane's—direction. Something lit in those gorgeous dark eyes of his that made her shiver. The last time she'd felt that kind of shiver, Cormac was still alive. She didn't want anyone, especially someone like Lucien Durand to bring that feeling back. She took a deep breath.

Shane squeezed her hand. "You okay?"

She nodded and let him push her along.

Lucien walked toward Hope "Ms. Monahan, *bienvenu* à L'Enfer."

She shook the one he'd extended. Her brain went fuzzy when he lifted it to his lips and kissed it. "Thank you." Her cheeks heated as a frisson of delight curled around her hand. "I'm surprised to see you here, instead of behind the line."

"I have a very well-trained staff." He dropped her hand and moved on to Shane. "I'm Lucien Durand." He shook Shane's hand.

"Shane Baker. I've been looking forward to meeting you."

"Well, here we all are." Durand swept his hand in an extravagant arc toward the dining room. "Please, go and enjoy your meal. Angelique will show you to your table."

A smiling Angelique stepped up. "*Bienvenu à L'Enfer.* Please come with me." She had a slight accent that created a sense of mystery about her. Immaculately dressed in turquoise silk, she walked around on black skyscraper heels with such ease, she'd probably burst out of the womb wearing them. Angelique exuded exotic, with her long dark hair, darker eyes, and a little beauty mark on the right hand side of her red-stained mouth.

"Wow," Shane muttered as his eyes glazed over.

Was that drool coming from his suddenly slack-jawed mouth?

Good grief.

She nodded at the amazing Angelique. "Thank you." She sneaked one last look at Lucien Durand and followed the hostess. Shane guided her with his hand at the small of her back, but he only paid attention to Angelique.

The room held more people than the yearly town meeting. Hope wasn't surprised about that either. But, wait a minute! In one corner, looking all romantic-like, sat Bobby Santos with his girlfriend, Spike. Bobby owned a sports bar called The End Zone. As far as Hope knew, Bobby *never* took a night off.

Scanning the rest of the dining room, she realized just about every chief cook and bottle washer in

Addington was there.

Isadora Costa from the Costa's Cozy Cottage? Check.

Sam Wilson from Esmeralda's? Check.

Alex Alden from the Pilgrim Steak and Rib House? Check.

And, of course, Theo Chalkias from Pizza Plus? Check, check, and check.

Had every other restaurant in Addington closed for the evening? Probably.

Everybody wanted to check out international superstar chef, Lucien Durand work his magic. A veritable warlock in the kitchen, adding layer upon layer of seductive flavor to his food. The image of sensual lights in dark eyes along with skilled hands adding exotic herbs and spices into bubbling pots and pans intrigued her more than it should.

Forget the eyes. She'd stick with the bubbling pots and pans, thank you very much.

Chapter Four

Lucien watched Hope and her date as they followed Angelique to their table. Shane held out the chair for Hope. She looked up at him and laughed. Even Angelique laughed with Shane Baker, the biggest idiot in all the land.

That shirt and jacket were ridiculous. *Sa c'est de la couyonade.* Grown men should not dress as clowns. He didn't care for the way Shane looked at Hope, and he certainly didn't like the way Shane looked at Angelique.

As if they were on his personal menu, just there for him to gobble up. He would make sure Angelique stayed far away from Shane Baker. Hope was another matter.

Lucien's jaw clenched. Where was a *gris-gris* when you needed one?

Hope looked absolutely lovely. He'd suspected she hid a slim, elegant body underneath her chef's uniform, but he hadn't realized how gorgeous she really was.

Not gorgeous as in over-the-top sexy. The word lovely really fit the bill in every sense of the word when it came to Hope Monahan. Creamy skin, silken hair, very shapely legs, especially in those heels. The dress she wore couldn't have been more modest, but on Hope Monahan it looked more—not sexy, but more appealing. Refreshing. Like lemonade on a hot summer

19

afternoon.

For the first time in a long time he resented the cooking scents wafting from his kitchen. They'd gotten in the way of him being able to check out Hope's perfume.

The bite of annoyance nipped at his temper. Angelique still stood laughing at the *imbécile's* foolishness.

C'est assez. He needed Angelique back at her post, away from temptation. He should send a wine steward or waiter to fetch her. Lucien looked around and all of his staff were slammed. He'd have to go get her himself.

He took a step, then stopped, pride slithering up his spine. No, he would not go himself. He would send one of the bus boys. Lucien Durand did not fetch anyone.

Ever.

****

"Well, enjoy your dinner." Angelique gifted Shane with one last smile before she left their table to follow a bus boy.

He couldn't take his eyes off her. Hope rolled her eyes.

"Easy does it, lover boy." The tinge of laughter in Hope's voice made him look at her.

"What?" Shane cleared his throat, took a sip of ice water. It did little to alleviate how poleaxed he felt. His synapses were firing at lightning speed—he'd never had such a reaction to a woman, like she was an angel sent from heaven just for him.

Her hair would probably feel even more soft and silky than the blue dress she wore. Speaking of that blue dress, it managed to accent every one of her amazing curves without being too revealing.

That full mouth of hers looked totally kissable, and the little beauty mark next to it drove him crazy. Crazy was a good word for how he felt. Dizzingly, breathlessly crazy.

"You might want to wipe the drool off your face before we order dinner." Hope opened her menu. "What looks good?"

"Ha, ha." He almost rubbed his mouth with his hand, because he couldn't be sure if Hope was kidding or not. He wouldn't give her the satisfaction. Cracking open his own menu, Shane tried to focus on the food.

No good. His gaze lifted from the Oysters Bienville on the appetizer list to peek over the menu to find Angelique.

She stood smiling up to a scowling Durand, her small hand lying on his left sleeve. Shane's blood pressure spiked at the sight.

Hope looked over her shoulder, then sighed. "What's wrong with you?"

Good question. "Think he's sleeping with her?"

Hope choked on a mouthful of water. "Who, he?"

"Durand. Do you think he's sleeping with his hostess? Uh, Angelique."

She blinked. "I have no clue. Besides—" she shrugged—"it's none of our business." Her mouth settled into a sour-looking line. "A better question is why isn't the great Durand sweating around in the kitchen. Does he do any of his own cooking?" She looked over the menu at Shane. "Are you getting the oysters?"

"Yeah, sure. That'll leave you to try the shrimp cocktail. He's got that secret spice mix for them."

Shane, his composure still a little shaky, got down to the business of food critic.

****

"How are the oysters?" Hope dotted her lips with her napkin. The tang of the spices seasoning her shrimp still buzzed on her lips.

Shane shook his head. "Not too impressed. He's got all the right components for a Bienville, but there's nothing special that sets it apart. Nothing popping up out of the expected spice boil. I expected more from the saffron. Here." He put an oyster on her bread plate. "How's the shrimp?"

She slurped up the oyster. Nice described it, not a word she used as a compliment. "The shrimp is pretty inspired, actually." Hope scrunched her nose. "Changing out regular cocktail sauce or rémoulade for a tomato-and-gin infused sour cream dipping sauce really works. And the spice mix is genius." Much as she hated to admit it, she'd loved it. She stabbed a shrimp on a seafood fork, dunked into the sauce and held it out for him to taste.

He crunched on the shrimp. "You're right. So he's got one plus, one minus." Shane craned his neck and searched the dining room. "I wonder when the entrées are coming."

"No one's coming with them until they clear the appetizers and bring the salads." Hope knew damn well Shane wasn't looking for any damn entrée. He was looking for the amazing, mystical Angelique.

Hope took her focus from her plate and the remains of the shrimp to look around to see how the other diners were doing with their food. She most certainly wasn't trying to catch a glimpse of Lucien Durand.

The band was taking a break, much to Hope's relief. The music made it difficult to hear your dinner partner's conversation, though her partner, Shane, didn't seem inclined to talk. If he didn't stop staring at Angelique, Hope would be forced to whomp him upside the head.

Hard. With a cast-iron frying pan.

Twice.

She sighed as their server came to clear the appetizers and deliver the salads. She sniffed while she peeked under the mixed greens. Pre-dressed. What if she'd wanted the dressing on the side? She should send it back and ask for a naked salad, just to make the point.

No, she wouldn't be petty. More's the pity.

"This is good," Shane said around a mouthful of greens. "There's something in there I can't pick out, but I can probably figure it out if I work at it. What do you think?"

She stabbed her fork into a tomato and popped it into her mouth. The taste of lemon exploded on her tongue, along with a mix of thyme and dill. "It *is* good. I like the lemon instead of vinegar and the dill is a surpise."

"I could try to figure it out. It shouldn't be difficult."

Hope shook her head. "No doubt, but I don't want to stoop that low. Every dressing we make is head and shoulders above this. We'll stick true to what we do, what works."

Shane swallowed, nodded. "That's the best plan. I think we can beat him without copying his recipes."

Hope grinned. "That's what I think too."

They toasted each other by clinking glasses filled

with a very interesting Chardonnay.

****

Lucien watched over his dining room and felt that distinctive stretching in his chest brought on by success. Service had gone without a hitch, the diners had enjoyed his food and the music. Things were winding down, with only a few people left in the place.

Angelique appeared at his side. "So, *mon frère*, I think we did well tonight."

"I think so too." Lucien's brow furrowed. "That Shane Baker stared at you all night."

She smiled and shrugged. "He is an interesting man, I think."

"Not for you, *'tite chatte*." He could not envision his little sister with that clown. He couldn't let her get involved with *any* man. He'd made a mistake not protecting her before. Never again, he vowed.

Angelique pressed her lips together. "I know that look of yours, Lucien. I'm a big girl. I know how to handle men. "

There. Another thing that made Lucien long for a scotch on the rocks.

He didn't have time to think about it, because Hope and that idiot Shane were on their way to the foyer. He wanted to take the heel of his hand and smash his stupid face in as he looked at Angelique. Lucien managed to make a grim, scary smile.

"I hope you both enjoyed your time here at L'Enfer," Angelique chirped.

"Our meals were lovely, thank you." Hope did the talking, most likely because that oaf Baker was brain dead.

"And you, Mr. Baker?" Angelique fluttered her

eyelashes at him.

Grrrrrrr.

But then, Hope Monahan was right there in front of him, holding out her hand to shake. "You have a marvelous place. I'm going to enjoy competing against you. You are competing in the Addington's Tables contest?"

His pulse jumped and jittered. "*Oui.* I think we will have us an interesting time."

She smiled as she nodded. "Come on, Shane. You've got to get me home before your Jeep turns into a pumpkin."

Shane cleared his throat. "Well, yes. Thank you both for a great time." He and Hope left.

Lucien watched them leave. He put his hands into his pockets. "Shane Baker looks very close to his boss."

"*Mais yeah.*" Angelique wrinkled her brow.

"*Il est un bonrien.*"

"A scoundrel?" Angelique laughed. "Really? You can tell everything about a man based on a two-second conversation with him?" She shook her head.

"He's quite taken with you, I think."

She shrugged again. "*Peut être.*"

"You need to stay away from him."

"Why would I want to do that?" She crossed her arms under her breasts.

Anger snapped at him. "You know very well why. I shouldn't have to remind you."

Her eyes widened. "I know what I'm doing."

"You do not. Do you remember the hoops we had to go through to take care of your last little adventure?"

She pouted. "Why do you have to remind me? I learned my lesson. I won't make a mistake like that again."

"Because you seem to need reminding."

"I do not." Angelique shrugged. "I learned my lesson."

He hoped so, he really hoped so. "I still want you to stay away from that man." From any man.

"*Pooyah-ee!*"

Good grief indeed. He glared at her, suddenly feeling really grumpy. "*Non.* I need all your attention on school. "

"*Tu as fouré ton nez y'ou tu avais pas d'affaire.*" She put her hands on her hips.

"I have every reason to stick my nose in your business."

"Lucien, *non.* I don't need a bodyguard."

Lucien harrumphed. "I won't let you near a man I know isn't good for you."

She smiled and placed her hand against his cheek. "Taking care of me is different than ruling every minute of my life."

Like hell. He was in charge. No one else. Just him. "I've got a bad feeling about that one." Lucien frowned. "You need to stay away from him."

Angelique sighed and pulled her hand out of his grasp. "Whatever." She turned on her heel and marched in the direction of the bar.

Obviously, she was going to sulk in order to make him suffer. *C'est dommage.* His little sister didn't know what was good for her. She had horrible taste in men. She couldn't tell a lion from a lamb. The badder the boy, the more she was drawn to him. It had to stop.

Lucien cracked his knuckles. It didn't matter what Angelique thought. He'd lay down the law and save her from herself. Nothing was more important than that.

****

"Do you want me to come with you to the competition kitchen tomorrow?" Shane slipped the Jeep into second gear as he maneuvered out of the parking lot to the street.

"No, I think I want to wander around and get a feel for it on my own. If it's any consolation, the adorable Angelique probably won't be there. She's his hostess, not his sous chef."

"You're making too much of this Angelique thing." Shane flipped the left blinker.

"Are you blushing?"

"Absolutely not."

Of course Shane was lying. Hope could see his red cheeks with her own two eyes.

"Look," Shane said. "She's a beautiful woman, and I happen to like looking at beautiful women. There's nothing wrong with that."

"Didn't say there was." Hope touched his arm.

Shane shook his head. "God, Hope, give me credit for having some sense. She's a pretty girl. That's all."

Angelique Durand was way more than a pretty girl, Hope worried. She looked like she could eat Shane up and spit him out for breakfast. But what more could Hope say? Shane was a grown man and would do what he was going to do.

Chapter Five

Hope took a good first look around the Addington's Tables competition kitchen. All those shiny stainless steel and state-of-the-art appliances. Man! Her hands itched to use them. The huge pantry held every ingredient a chef could wish for and some she'd never heard of.

When she'd signed up to compete in the upcoming challenge by the Chamber of Commerce, she'd had no idea how much she looked forward to the contest. She didn't think of herself as being exceptionally competitive, but she was. She really wanted to win the honor of having the best restaurant in Addington, Massachusetts.

Who knew?

Nerves danced with excitement as she turned in a giddy circle. Laughter threatened to bubble out of her. She couldn't wait to get cooking. The next six weeks couldn't pass quickly enough.

Five slow hand claps made her freeze. Lucien Durand stood in the doorway to the pantry. "I didn't know you're a dancer as well as a chef."

Hope ignored the jolt to her nervous system his presence gave her. "I'm full of surprises."

"I bet." Humor glittered in his gorgeous dark eyes. "I'm looking forward to learning what they are."

Was he flirting? Hope licked her suddenly dry lips.

"I hope I don't disappoint."

"I don't think you will." He leaned against the doorjamb. "This is quite a setup."

"They seem to have thought of everything."

"And then some." Hope smiled what she hoped was a relaxed you-don't-do-a-thing-for-me smile. He wore casual clothes, a smoky gray cashmere sweater over a white tee and jeans. Very well worn jeans that hugged his body in all the right places.

Who would ever suspect Lucien Durand even *owned* a pair of jeans?

She didn't like it. It made him look more human rather than a legend in his own mind. She had this solid image of him that floated around in her head.

It didn't include denim.

More's the pity, because his butt looked seriously delicious in those jeans.

She'd just have to add well-fitting jeans to that image.

While she'd seen those broad shoulders underneath his designer suit jackets, she hadn't a clue about how broad they were. The sweater fit more snugly and showed he had the shoulders of an Olympic swimmer and not a chef.

"Where's your *sous-chef*?" Lucien looked around the room, his expression blank.

"Who—Shane?" Where did that question come from?

"Is that his name?" Lucien shrugged.

Of course Lucien the Magnificent didn't remember Shane's name. "Yep."

"I just thought you would be here with your second in command." He looked right at her now, instead of beyond her.

Okay, seriously, why would Lucien care about Shane? Unless…he had a crush on him.

Boy howdy! Maybe all the glamorous supermodels were for show.

Why was it that all the best looking guys were either married or gay? Okay, since this *was* Massachusetts, they could be both married *and* gay.

She shook her head. The man practically dripped testosterone. No way he was gay.

"Well, would you look at this? I never thought I'd see a kitchen setup so fancy except on the television."

That gravelly, six-packs-a-day smoker's voice could only belong to Isadora Costa, chef and owner of Costa's Cozy Cottage, Addington's go-to place for local seafood and Portuguese cuisine.

Hope blinked and held her breath at the pungent scent of Isadora's perfume. Someone needed to tell her to lay off the Jean Naté. A little bit went a long way. Isadora wore enough to go to China and back. Twice.

Her relentlessly coiffed hair sat jammed like a pitch-black helmet on top of her head. She troweled foundation like spackle on her face. Instead of making her look younger, it just caked up in her trench-like wrinkles. She painted her thin lips bright red and her eyelids a garish bright blue.

She wasn't a universally liked person. She'd been a devoted gossip and didn't mind who she spread dirt on. She may be annoying, but Hope didn't mind that. Isadora was lonely, that was all.

Hope knew loneliness. When her Cormac died in that plane crash, she'd become the loneliest woman in the world. She'd gotten very used to being alone.

Solitary.

But, as for Isadora, she could cook amazing food and do all the old-time Portuguese recipes. Where else could you find fish tongues and cheeks, perfectly breaded and fried? Isadora had a gift.

"I'm not even sure I know what all those machines do!" Isadora glanced up at Lucien as she prattled on about the amazing kitchen. She would have to use a chair if she wanted to look him in the eyes.

Lucien's whole demeanor changed. There was no other word for it. Hope really didn't know the man, but it looked like a mask had just dropped over his face, a charming mask, but a mask nonetheless. It wasn't obvious, but his whole body language changed.

If Hope could see it, why didn't Isadora, who simpered and giggled up at him?

A sixth sense? ESP? Super-amazing people skills?

Sh—yeah. Like Hope was an expert on all things Lucien Durand, that rat bastard. Like he had special looks just for her.

She pulled in the reins on her delusions. The man dated supermodels. He wouldn't have special looks for her.

Better question. Why would she want him to?

****

Lucien left the pantry and strode to the cooking station meant for him. One thing for sure, the Addington Chamber of Commerce wanted this event to be big and launch the town as a major tourist destination.

He only cared that the money raised would go to regional food pantries. He'd been given a lot. He owed more than he could ever repay.

He turned the stove burners on and off, getting a feel for how they worked. Checked out the pots and pans, the grill, the oven. They had provided knives and other tools, but Lucien would bring his own.

The promise was to *Grand-mère* to take care of Angelique, to get her out of the big city and away from the fast crowd she'd called her friends. Get her back on track and out of the influence of her friends who did drugs and drank too much, the users Cäcilia had introduced her to, who took advantage of her.

Who had betrayed her in the worst way.

That piece of filth would never see the light of day again. Prison was too good for him.

Death was too good for him.

Get her into college and be the first of them all to get a degree.

Nothing meant more to him.

He heard Hope laugh from in the pantry. Addington did have some charm, some considerable charm, all wrapped up in the person of Hope Monahan. Adorable in jeans and a silky parsley colored top that matched her eyes, she looked like a million bucks.

Usually he dismissed the competition, but he couldn't quite dismiss her.

She cooked well and with imagination. Beautiful in a fresh, utterly honest way. He felt compelled to learn more about her. He'd figure out a way to do that.

He always got what he wanted. He made sure of it.

"This is some kitchen," a low voice growled from behind him. He turned and found Bobby Santos, owner of a sports bar. The guy was a walking wall, with hands the size of ham hocks.

If he couldn't beat a line cook from a hamburger

joint, then he needed to put away his knives and go back to the bayou. He turned to face Bobby. "It looks adequate."

Bobby gave him an "are you for real?" look. "Whatever. I had a good time at your restaurant opening. The food was pretty good."

Pretty good? What did this *emplate* know about food? "Thank you."

"I haven't seen you around The End Zone to try my food. You should come. My treat."

Treat. More like trick. "I shall have to fix that, *oui*?"

Bobby slapped Lucien's back with one of those massive hands of his. "Absolutely. And bring a date." He made a beeline to the pantry. A chorus of hellos and heys greeted him as Bobby walked into the room.

Take a date to a sports bar. The women he dated wouldn't be caught dead in a small-town sports bar. The women he dated wouldn't be caught dead in a small town, period.

The sound of Hope's laughter floated across the room. She was smiling at Bobby. Her face lit up when she laughed. She looked fresh. Wholesome. Totally girl next door.

He'd never dated the girl next door. An ordinary girl. Lucien Durand didn't do ordinary.

She looked like someone who would like to go out to a sports bar as his date. His nerves thrummed electrically through his body at the prospect.

It was wise to get to know your competition. *Utile.* Practical. He'd kill two birds with one stone: get to know Hope better and check out the food at The End Zone.

Chapter Six

"A date?" Hope shook her head. She couldn't quite believe what she was hearing. "Are you asking me on a date—to The End Zone?"

Lucien frowned. "Is that such a bad idea?" He straightened his shirt cuffs. "I'd like to check out The End Zone's food and don't want to eat alone."

And wasn't that flattering? Not! "Well, uh, no, not a bad idea at all." Hope felt flummoxed. What was he up to?

She didn't know him at all, really, but one thing she was sure of. Lucien Durand always had an agenda. That agenda would always include him coming out on top.

She supposed she would find out his ulterior motive if she went out with him. She would not, however, make it easy for him. "I'd love to go with you. I can only take off Mondays, because the restaurant goes dark on Monday."

His eyes widened. "You're kidding me."

She nodded, enjoying his obvious befuddlement. "I'm the only chef. Okay, aside from Shane. I can't take a night without closing."

A shadow crossed his face at the mention of Shane. "Baker's so inept he can't handle the kitchen alone?"

"Of course he can handle the kitchen alone." What did Lucien have against Shane? "I just choose to shut

34

things down on Mondays. My name's on the food, so I make the food."

He gave her a sharp nod. "*Oui*. I understand that." He took her hand. "How about next Monday, then?"

Okay, she'd bite. "Sure. I'll meet you there." She gave him a big toothy smile. "What time?"

Lucien blinked. "I'll pick you up."

"That's not necessary."

"Yes, it is." He'd pick her up, come hell or high water. "How's eight?"

"Perfect." For show, she made a big deal of checking her watch. "Oops! Gotta go!"

"*Je va't voir plus tard*. Good-bye." He gave her one more nod, turned and left.

She stood and watched him leave, enjoying the rear view.

And felt like she had just dodged a huge bullet.

****

Shane shook his jacket off his shoulders as he walked through L'Enfer's front door. He figured that Durand would be at the contest kitchen, thus providing him, Shane, an opportunity to get to know Angelique better.

He'd barely thought of anything else since he'd met her the other night. It was driving him crazy. Never, *ever*, had he been like this over a woman.

Look up pathetic in the dictionary to find Shane's picture there, next to it.

The lunch crowd, if there'd been a lunch crowd, had thinned, with only a couple of tables taken. Servers bustled around, filling salt and pepper shakers, rolling silverware into white cloth napkins or using the hokie to get the crumbs off the carpet around their tables.

"Hey, shoog, where y'at? Are you here for lunch?" Angelique the goddess appeared before him. His heart jumped into his throat.

"Uh." His tongue wouldn't work. He swallowed. "Shoog?"

"Sugar." She shrugged. "Where y'at?" She picked up a menu while giving a very condescending nod. "How are you?"

"Oh." Say something, idiot. "I'm good. How are you?"

"Just fine, *cher*. Are you here for lunch?"

He swallowed again. "Sure."

"Are you alone?" She cocked her head to one side. "Will Ms. Monahan be with you?"

Damn, the woman was beyond beautiful, with that cloud of dark hair, bright, sassy dark eyes and that totally kissable mouth of hers. Clad in a show-stopping purple dress that hugged all her curves, he had all he could do to just breathe. "Hope? No. She's at the competition kitchen getting the lay of the land before the big day." He wiped his sweaty hands on his pants.

"So is Lucien." Angelique picked up a menu. "Do you want a table or to sit at the bar?"

He glanced at the wait staff, busy with the clatter of side work, who were definitely *not* wanting a new table. "The bar is fine. Great."

Wasn't he a smooth operator?

"Follow me." Angelique smiled at him and melted his bones.

She gave that dazzling smile to everyone she passed on the way to the bar. She could have been a Disney princess, flitting through the room, spreading fairy dust as cute little singing animals followed her.

He was really and truly losing his everlovin' mind if he was thinking about Disney princesses and fairy dust.

"Here we are." She motioned to the cranberry leather padded bar stool, then went behind the bar. "What can I get for you?"

He pulled himself together and got his head in the game. "Don't worry about me. I can wait for the bartender."

She trilled a laugh. "He's on his break, *cher*." She leaned on the bar and whispered, "It's just you and me."

Just you and me? Music to his ears. He wanted her more than he wanted his next breath.

Of course, she was so beautiful a man would have to be dead to not want her. Shane was totally not dead.

She cocked her head to one side. "So, what's it going to be?"

"A Kaliber, please." He didn't need alcohol to muddy his mind any further. The non-alcohol beer would have to do. "I have to work tonight."

"Ah." Angelique put a menu on the bar in front of him. "I'll be right back."

Shane looked at the menu but didn't see the choices listed on it. What he really wanted was to find out about Angelique's relationship to Durand. But how could he bring the conversation around so she'd volunteer the information?

Here's an idea. Why didn't he just come out and ask her? No. He wanted to be all slick and smooth about it, not desperate and stupid.

She came back and placed an ice cold Kaliber alongside a frosted mug on the bar. "See anything you like?"

Hell, yes, and it wasn't on the menu. "What do you recommend?"

"The Oysters Bienville are very good today. So is the Crawfish Etoufée. Both are Lucien's specialties."

A tendril of hair had escaped from her upswept hairdo. His fingers itched to tuck the silky strands back into that bun thing she'd fashioned her hair into. "I'll try the crawfish, please."

She grinned. "You won't be sorry. Lucien's a genius with seafood." She wrote his order on a dupe. "I'll just put this into the kitchen." Off she went.

Lucien's a genius with seafood sing-songed in his brain. Of course Lucien was a genius.

Yet another reason to hate him.

He took a swallow of his not beer. Not knowing about Angelique and Durand drove him crazy. He just *had* to know.

Angelique floated on the breath of angels back to the bar. "Your Crawfish Etoufée will be up in a few minutes."

"Great." Shane practically melted as she smiled at him, her dark, heavily lashed eyes flashing with life. He took a deep breath. "So, how do you like Addington?"

"It's quiet." She shook her head and scrunched her nose. "Not like New Orleans, where there's always a party going on. Here they roll up the sidewalks at 8 p.m."

"It's not *that* bad. We've got lots of stuff going on."

"Such as?" She rested her elbows on the bar, bringing her hands together in front of her and resting her chin on her hands. "I'm all ears." She bat her lashes at him.

Ugh! "I don't know. What do you and Durand usually do?"

She stood and tapped a finger against her lips. "Hmmmm. Let me think." Lifting her eyes to study the ceiling, she made a show of thinking. "There are all the parties and openings. Of course, it depends what city we're in."

"Oh." Shane scratched at the label on the beer. A thought hit him. What the hell was Durand doing escorting all those supermodels when he had the amazing Angelique at his beck and call? How could he put her through that? "Why does he make you share him with all the models?"

She waved a hand and scoffed. "Oh, la! None of those women stay for very long."

His hand flexed around his beer bottle. He wanted to punch Durand in the neck. "Why do you put up with it?"

She shrugged. "It is the way things work. Always has been, always will."

"How long have you known Durand?"

She laughed and her mouth turned into a grin. "All my life, shoog. He's my big brother." She touched him under his chin and lifted his suddenly slack jaw. "Close your mouth, if you don't want to be catching flies, you."

His skin sizzled where she'd touched him. He so missed the contact when she took her hand away.

Her brother. Hot damn. He forced himself to breathe, four counts in, four counts out.

"I can understand your confusion, *cher*." She leaned against the bar. "Seeings as *mon frère* is so ugly, him. Now about your Hope Monahan? Is she *your*

39

sister?"

Angelique looked at him, laughter still in her eyes, with a whiff of something else much more intense.

What did *that* mean? She wanted to know about his relationship with Hope? She was jealous? Or, maybe it was just wishful thinking on his part. "No, Hope's my boss." That sounded kind of cold. "And a friend. We go a long ways back." He took a risk and put his hand over hers. "Just an old friend."

She looked at him so intensely, making him feel like a smear on a lab slide. She could have pulled her cool small hand out from under his, but she didn't. Science experiment or not, her momentary lapse of control gave him a shot of confidence.

Made him feel more sure of himself, absolutely like his usual self. He felt his mouth turn up into his best lady-killing grin.

"Well, if it isn't Mr. Shane Baker in my restaurant." Durand's voice sliced through the atomic-charged air between Shane and Angelique. "Harassing my help?"

Angelique's face turned a cute shade of pink as she pulled her hand out from under Shane's. "Lucien! How was the tour of the contest kitchens?"

"Very educational." Lucien focused on Shane. "What brings you here during the afternoon?"

Shane stood. "Lunch. You know. That meal that comes after breakfast and before dinner."

Angelique grimaced. "I'll go check on your Etoufée." Pointing at her brother, she said, *"Tu fermes ta guelle."* Smiling at Shane, she danced off to the kitchen.

"Good idea," Durand muttered. He turned to look

at Shane, hairy eyeball well ensconced.

Shane hated that look when his mother did it, but nearly jumped up and clapped to see the magnificent Lucien Durand be bothered enough to use it.

He'd pissed off Durand. Maybe even made him nervous. Without a doubt, someone needed to take the man down a few pegs. Shane figured he was the one to do it. Dirty job and all that.

"So, how are the competition kitchens?" Shane sat back on the barstool.

"Adequate." Durand rummaged behind the bar and pulled up a Perrier bottle, popped the cap and raised it to his mouth.

"Did you run into Hope?"

Durand swallowed and put the little green bottle down very slowly. "*Oui.*"

"Did she like the setup?"

Durand glared at him. "Why don't you ask her when you get back to the restaurant?"

"I will." Shane grinned. "I have to eat first. I hear tell the Crawfish Etoufée is your best dish."

"I don't make a bad dish." Durand downed his Perrier. "Ever."

Of course you don't. "Angelique recommended it."

"I'm flattered."

"Got to check out the competition, you know."

Durand slammed the bottle down on the counter. "What do you want?"

Your sister. "I told you. Lunch."

Durand glared at him. "Why do I think you want a lot more than lunch."

Shane grinned. "You're paranoid."

Steam started to roll out of Durand's ears. "I

usually wait until I know someone before I insult them."

"Okay! Here's your crawfish!" Angelique appeared out of nowhere with a small platter, which she placed on the bar in front of Shane. "Can I get you another Kaliber?"

"Sure, thanks!" Shane turned his attention to the beautiful vision in front of him. "It smells great." Which it did, fresh, briny with a hint of garlic, onion, and Worcestershire sauce.

"Then I'll leave you to your lunch." Durand gave him a grim smile. "*Bon appétit.*" He gave Angelique a stony look. "*Il est un imbecile, celui là. Ne l'encourage pas.*" He strode back into the kitchen.

Shane took one last lukewarm pull off his Kaliber as Durand stalked off. He was really going to enjoy his lunch. Smiling at Angelique he picked up an oyster. "This looks awesome."

Angelique smiled back, her eyes warm and filled with humor. "*Bon appétit.*"

Chapter Seven

"Turn left here on High Street," said Hope, playing navigator. Lucien had picked her up for their "date" at The End Zone. Always a little bossy, she was telling him where to go.

Lucien let her, even though he'd spent weeks learning all about Addington. It made Hope smile, and, bossy or not, he found that he liked very much to make her smile.

For some reason, when Hope smiled, she made Lucien smile. Very few people had that gift. He could count them on one hand.

He flicked his directional to indicate left and made the turn. "So, what's good at The End Zone?"

Hope smiled. "Bobby's got a very eclectic menu."

"Define eclectic."

"Oh, a little of this, a little of that." She pressed her lips together, like she was trying not to laugh. "Bobby's got a diverse clientele. Tonight's Monday, right?" She laughed. "Of course it's Monday, otherwise I'd be in my own kitchen." She put her hands together in her lap. "Monday night is gumbo night at The End Zone."

"*Quoi t'as dit?*" A high pitched buzz assaulted his ears and he shook his head to clear it. "What did you say?"

"Bobby usually has gumbo for the Monday special. It's pretty good." She checked out her manicure. "You should try it. Maybe pick up a couple of ideas."

Lucien choked. He opened his mouth and no words would come out. Probably good, because he had nothing good to say.

"You okay?" Hope asked. "You need CPR?"

"You're joking, *vrai*?"

"About CPR? I never joke about that.

He grit his teeth. "Not CPR, gumbo."

"No, I'm serious. It's pretty good. Lots of people like it."

Lots of people were idiots, but Lucien bit his tongue. What did this Bobby Santos know of gumbo? Nothing. "Really." *Le Bon Dieu mait la main*! No way could that man make a gumbo worthy of the name.

Hope shrugged and chirped. "Really! Take your next right."

He turned, even though his GPS screamed that right was probably not his best choice.

"It's a shortcut."

He turned to look at her. She looked as innocent as a newborn baby. Appearances could be deceiving, he reminded himself. Perhaps she was pulling his leg.

A car horn blared out of nowhere and Lucien had to swerve to avoid hitting him. His focus back on the road, he reminded himself that Hope Monahan was not his type.

No way. Pretty smile or not.

****

I'm a bad, bad girl, Hope thought as she watched Lucien try not to splutter. "I'm sure Bobby will want your opinion."

"Unh," Lucien grunted. "What does some Yankee know from gumbo?"

"You'll have to let him know."

Another grunt. "Where is the next turn?"

"Left at the first light." Hope watched his fingers tap on the steering wheel. He might as well wear a bullseye on his back when it came to teasing.

She shouldn't tease him, really. Not about food. But his ego was so huge, he needed to be brought down a few pegs.

For all his talent, Cormac had been so modest and self-effacing. It had been so easy to be with him.

The man gaving the car right now? Not so much. There was nothing easy about Lucien Durand.

Lucien slowed as the red neon goal posts screaming The End Zone came into view. "Absoslutely worthless. *Sa c'est de la drigaille*," he murmured under his breath.

She didn't know what he'd said, but it didn't sound good.

****

Lucien sucked in a breath as he helped Hope out of the car. *Salleau prie*. He did not want to feel any kind of attraction to her. But her small hand fit so neatly, so naturally, into his. No. He had to keep his eye on the prize. Beating her in the restaurant competition.

He couldn't afford to be distracted by Hope.

But, he was.

She cleared her throat. He should take his hand away from hers. He didn't want to lose the physical contact, so he moved his hand to her back, intending to escort her into the building.

"Thank you." Hope grinned. "Let's go on in. Gumbo awaits."

He shook his head. Something awaited them in

there, but it sure as hell wasn't gumbo. Of that he was sure. He opened the door, and the scents of grilled beef and french fries enveloped them, underlined with the tangy scents of cumin and coriander. He sniffed the air.

Nary a touch of filé powder. It confirmed his feeling that Bobby Santos wasn't making anything that resembled gumbo. Lucien's employees at his New Orleans restaurant collected sassafras leaves every September, then dried them in the sun and crushed them into powder. It was the only filé powder he used.

He sold packets of that filé at all his restaurants, including those in Paris and London. Even Gordon Ramsey used his brand when he bothered to make a gumbo. He respected Ramsey for that.

But not for much else.

"Hey, Hope!" A chirpy blonde with a tray of drinks stopped to greet them. "How you doin'?"

"Hey, Chelsea." Hope smiled at the waitress. "Real good. Got a table for us?"

"Yep." She tossed her head in the direction of the booths. "Take your pick."

"Great!"

"Gotta go! I've got some thirsty customers."

"No problem." Hope looked up at him. "Where do you want to sit?"

Anywhere but here. The bar at his own restaurant would work. "You choose."

She pursed her lips as she surveyed the wall lined with booths. "Follow me."

He did, and while he followed her, he checked out her cute little derrière. He was only human, *n'est-ce pas*?

She stopped in front of a corner booth. "This

46

okay?"

"Sure."

She smiled and shimmied that cute little derrière across the banquette seat. How could such a tiny woman be so much poetry in motion?

"Are you joining me or are you going to stand next to the table all evening?"

"I wanted to make sure you were comfortable before I sat." He could have kept on looking at her, but that was way too obvious. He folded his tall frame into the booth.

Booth seating was not tall person friendly. He supposed he looked extremely awkward scooting across the seat. He found his spot on the banquette, settled down and banged his knees underneath the table.

Merde.

That waitress, Chelsea, brought over a couple of menus. The sports-themed cover screamed tacky; the cartoon-colored graphics could put you off your food. No style at all.

"The special tonight is Bobby's homemade chicken and sausage gumbo. It's really good," Chelsea chirped. "Can I bring you something to drink? Bobby's got a new beer. It's his version of an Oktoberfest lager."

"Water's fine for now, thanks," Hope told her.

"The same, please." Lucian cracked open the menu.

"Awesome. I'll get your water and be right back."

"So, are you game to try the gumbo?"

He looked up from the menu to see Hope watching him. "*Mais non.*" He shook his head. "I want to see what he usually prepares."

"Okay," she sing-songed, "but you don't know

what you're missing."

Yes, he did know. He imagined he knew very well what he would miss if he didn't order the gumbo. She grinned at him. That mouth of hers was killer and he could absolutely imagine what she would taste like if he kissed her.

When he kissed her, he realized. No ifs, ands, or buts about it. "What is the house specialty?"

"Hard to say. Wings. Burgers, especially the Bobby Burger." She shrugged. "His loaded cheesy fries."

Loaded cheesy fries. Yum. Only not.

Chelsea came back to the table with their water. "So, do you know what you want?"

"I'm going with the gumbo." Hope gave her menu to the waitress.

"I'll have the wings, a Bobby Burger, and the loaded fries."

Chelsea scratched the order out onto her pad. "How do you want the burger done?"

"Medium rare." He handed the menu back to her. "And the Oktoberfest lager. It's brewed here?"

"Yep!" She narrowed her eyes at him. "You're that famous chef, right? The L'Enfer guy."

L'Enfer guy? He was Lucien Durand, world-reknowned chef. "I own L'Enfer."

Hope piped up. "Can I get the lager, too, Chelsea?"

"Sure! I'll tell Bobby you're here." She left.

"I'm guessing you're hungry," Hope said with a smile.

"It's good to know the competition's food, what he's passionate about." He frowned. "You really need to drink an Abita Amber with gumbo."

She pulled the paper wrapper off her straw. "Bobby's craft beers are local and seasonal. And, as you know, I'm all about the local and seasonal."

He shook his head. Some things were sacred. Abita Amber with gumbo was one of them.

But, then again, he didn't think Bobby Santos could make a gumbo worth the name.

"So, why did you decide to open a restaurant in our little town?" Hope put her lips around the straw in her glass and slowly pulled the icy water through it. She swallowed and licked her lips. He couldn't take his eyes off her mouth.

Suddenly very thirsty, he grabbed his own glass and gulped. She smiled at him. She'd asked a question. Right.

"I needed a change of pace." No he didn't. He'd had to find a place to protect Angelique and get her back on track. Get her someplace where no one was likely to see the sex tape the rat bastard of a photographer took without her knowing.

"I imagine you'll get bored here after a while."

"It's not like it's a prison, *chère*. I'll still need to leave from time to time to take care of business in my other restaurants. Logan Airport isn't all that far away."

A shadow flitted across her face, just momentarily, but long enough to make him curious. "Do you travel much?"

"No." She shook her head. "It's not an option with the restaurant."

"Are you afraid your *sous-chef* would not be up to the task of running the restaurant if you took a week off?" That idiot Baker would most likely burn the place down.

"Shane?" Hope smiled again. "He could run things just fine, but when it's your own name on the food, it raises the stakes. Like I think I told you, people expect food cooked by Hope Monahan when they come to Hope's."

"As long as you have talented people following your recipes to the last detail, without fail, then you could take some time and do some travelling." Lucien would go crazy if he had to stay in one place too long. He couldn't even imagine staying in one place longer than six months. A year, tops.

Chelsea came back to the table with a tray loaded with drinks. "Here are your drinks, and I'll be back with your food in a minute." She grinned as she put two beers on the table.

"Thanks, Chelsea." Hope lifted her glass. "Cheers!"

"*À votre santé.*" He took a sip of his beer. It was surprisingly good. Clean, a nice amber color, and an underlying sweetness lightening the tang of the hops.

"Very drinkable, eh?" Hope looked at him over the top of her glass.

"Surprisingly so." She had a little bit of foam at the corner of her mouth. "You've got, uh…" He motioned with his hand toward the corner of his own mouth.

"Oops!" Her tongue snaked out to lick away the trace of suds. "Did I get it?"

She had the most kissable mouth he'd ever seen. He picked up his napkin, reached across the table and lightly touched the corner of her mouth with it. Her green eyes widened and locked with his. "There. All better."

He fought the incredible sizzle that popped up

between them. His fingers nearly trembled as he pulled his hand away, but he couldn't take his eyes off her, not yet. He swallowed around a lump in his throat.

"Is it?" Hope looked as baffled as he felt.

"Here's your food." Chelsea appeared. "Your gumbo, Hope. And for you, chef, here's your wings, loaded fries and a Bobby Burger." She set down the food. "Can I get anything else for you right now?"

He cleared his throat. "No, *merci*."

"I'm good. Thanks, Chelsea." Hope's face had turned an attractive shade of pink.

"Great! Enjoy." She bopped off toward the bar.

"Mmmmmm. Gumbo smells yummy." Hope waved the steam from the bowl up to her face. "You've really got to try some."

No, he didn't, though it didn't smell like a total disaster. The okra looked a little slimy, but the sausage did look fairly good.

Lucien, of course, made his andouille fresh every day. Without fail. When the sausage ran out, there was no more gumbo that night.

He looked down at his sandwich. Topped with some lettuce, a thick, bright red tomato slice, a slice of red onion, a couple of slices of bacon, and what smelled like aioli. He supposed it was a step above the average burger, but it still came down to taste. He set the top of the bun in place, rolled up his shirt sleeves and grabbed it to take a bite.

Flavor exploded in his mouth. The sweetness of the tomato, the bite of the onion, saltiness of the bacon, and hint of garlic in the aioli sang together with the absolutely fresh, high quality of the beef. The lettuce was fresh and gave crunch to the bite. The meat was prepared perfectly, juicy and cooked to perfection. Iron Chef Bobby Flay couldn't have done any better. Small-town Bobby Santos was the king of the hamburger.

He should stick with that and leave the gumbo to the professionals.

"How's your burger?" Hope looked at him over a spoonfull of faux gumbo.

"It's very good." He shrugged. "A hamburger does not a chef make."

Hope grinned. "Man, you are a hard nut to crack." She slurped another spoonfull of soup. "You better get going on those fries. They'll get soggy pretty fast with all the stuff thrown on top of them."

"They create a very complicated flavor profile." If you were interested in chili, cheese, scallions, and sour cream. He popped a couple of loaded fries in his mouth and immediately spit them out into his napkin. He grimaced and pushed the plate away.

"Don't like them?"

"A mush of flavors. No nuances." He grabbed his beer and drank. "The chili is a disaster, the cheese is little better than the cheese product you can buy in a can, the sour cream is overkill, and the scallions do little to elevate this mess."

"Can't wait to hear what you think of the wings." She filled a spoon with gumbo and held it out for him to taste. "C'mon, have a little."

"You aren't going to stop nagging me about this, are you?"

Again, the radiant grin. "Nope! You might as well stop fighting."

He sighed. "*Eh, bien.*" He leaned across the table so she could slip the spoon into his mouth.

"Open wide!" She brought the spoon to his lips. It didn't smell bad. He took the plunge and took the bite.

Adequate. Could use a little more filé, which was the Zatarains version if he didn't miss his guess. And he'd probably added it too early in the cooking process. Rice wasn't as firm as he'd like it. The okra wasn't fresh and slightly slimy. He bit into the piece of sausage. Inedible. Absolutely inedible. He spit it into his napkin. "Inedible."

"What? The andouille?"

"*Oui*. This sausage doesn't deserve the name andouille. Where did this come from?"

Hope shrugged. "Ask Chelsea to ask Bobby next time she comes around."

He grunted, took a slug of beer, and turned his attention to his burger, the bright spot of the meal, apart from his dinner companion.

****

Hope kept a weather eye out for Chelsea. Lucien reacted the way she predicted about the gumbo, but he really surprised her about the burger. Guess he wasn't as close-minded as she thought. She watched him grab a chicken wing out of the wax paper basket liner. He shook some extra sauce off it, dipped it into the bleu cheese-filled ramekin then took a bite.

"So how is it?"

Lucien dropped the half-eaten wing onto his bread plate and wiped his hands on a couple of napkins. He pursed his lips. "Too much vinegar. No balance between heat and other seasoning."

She picked one up out of the basket and took a bite. He was right.

No way would she tell him that.

"How are things going here? Need anything else?" Chelsea swung by their table.

"Where does Bobby get the andouille sausage?" Hope nodded at Lucien. "Chef, here, wants to know."

"Oh." Chelsea blinked. "Okay. Anything else?"

Lucien motioned to the fries and the wings. "I'm done with these. You can take them back to the kitchen."

"Sure thing." Chelsea gathered the full plates of food. "Do you want me to box them?"

"No thank you."

"'Kay. I'll be right back." With a shake of her head, Chelsea toddled off.

Elbows steepled on the table and resting her chin in the palms of her hands, Hope studied Lucien.

"What?" Those wicked, black eyes turned to her. She shivered and resisted the urge to squirm in her seat.

She attempted to project casual when she felt anything but. "Nothing. I'm just surprised you didn't find anything wrong with the burger."

His eyebrows beetled together. "I'm not above admitting when something is well done. The burger was good. The other things weren't." He shrugged. "I don't know why that should surprise you."

"I guess I don't see you as the burger and beer type."

He sat back against the booth and flashed her a toothy grin. "There's a lot you don't know 'bout me. I got my start cooking at my *grand-mère's grocerie* on a little dock on the bayou. I flipped my share of burgers, and boiled more crawdads than you could imagine in your lifetime." He grinned. "I had to be good at it if I didn't want her to feed me to the gators."

"So, enlighten me. How'd a simple boy from the bayou end up being one of the world's most famous chefs?"

"Now that there's a long story, *chère*." He shook his head. "We could be here all night. Besides, maybe I want to save some of my secrets for later on."

She felt her face flush. "I've got time."

"Huh. Maybe I want to hear some of your secrets. How did a nice girl like you end up in a place like this?"

She felt a laugh bubble out of her throat. "I haven't been a nice girl in a long time."

"Talk about! This evening just got better."

"Okay, you can lay off the good ol' boy accent now. You've made your point."

She took a sip of beer. "I really want to know how you came to be Lucien Durand, international *chef extrodinaire*."

He put his hand over his heart, then sat up and rested his elbows on the table. "Tell me the story of Hope."

Her heartbeat pounded in her ears. "There's not much to tell. I'm not that interesting."

"I beg to differ. I find you very interesting." The overdone accent had disappeared, but the heat in his eyes hadn't. He nodded. "Very much so."

Chapter Eight

Hope grabbed her beer, took a long slow sip, and carefully put down the glass. The arousal smoldering in his gaze made her both tingly and squirmy. "I'm just a small-town girl who owns a restaurant."

"I see." He smiled. "I guess I will have to charm your secrets out of you."

Excitement skittled up her spine. If he used more charm, he'd charm her into a coronary. Her mouth opened, but no words came out.

"So how are things here?" Bobby had arrived at their table, the deep rumble of his voice dissipating the pull between her and Lucien. "Chelsea told me you had some questions."

Thank you, Bobby.

Lucien unfolded himself out of the booth and stood toe to toe with the man. "Yes," he said, his king-of-the-chefs persona set to blast. "Where do you get your andouille?"

"From the same place in New Bedford where I get my linguiça and chourico. They just started making the andouille."

"It's deplorable. You should find a new supplier. I can help you with that, if you want."

"That so?"

"If you'd like. I make my own in-house, of course."

"Of course." Bobby gave Lucien the ol' hairy eyeball. Testosterone oozed out of both men. This wasn't going to end well.

She had to do something. "Lucien really loved the Bobby Burger."

Lucien swiveled his head to look at her while Bobby grinned. "That so?"

Lucien zapped his attention back to Bobby. "It was adequate."

"He ate every bite and raved about the flavor profile."

"I never rave." Lucien crossed his arms across his chest.

"And the freshness of the ingredients."

Bobby barked out a laugh. "I'll put that testimonial on the menu." He offered his hand to Lucien to shake.

Lucien unfolded his arms and shook Bobby's hand. His smile was at half mast. A mere pretense.

Bobby nodded at Hope. "Nice to see you again, Hope."

"You too."

Bobby disappeared into his kitchen, Hope supposed, while Lucien worked his way back into the booth. He looked grumpy.

Even grumpy, he looked yummy.

Chelsea returned with a dessert menu and put it on the table. "Here's the dessert menu. Bobby's apple pie is not to be missed. Do you want some coffee?"

"Coffee sounds great," Hope said. "What about you, Lucien?"

"That does sound good. Espresso, a double shot."

"Sorry, chef. We only do classic coffee."

"Then, I guess I'll have 'classic coffee' Really

strong and black."

"I'll be back!" Chelsea went on her coffee run.

"What the hell is classic coffee?" he demanded to Hope.

"Just the usual. I think she was trying to be funny."

He picked up the dessert menu. "Is the apple pie good?"

"It's good, but not as good as mine."

He smiled. "Your apple pie is pretty good."

"Thank you! That's because I only use apples from the trees behind the restaurant."

"You really do take this earth to table stuff seriously."

"I absolutely do. I grow my own herbs and vegetables, also behind the restaurant."

Lucien looked at her for what felt like a silent eternity. "I'd love to get a tour of your gardens and fruit trees."

Um, wow. She tried for a casual shrug, even though her insides had gone all warm and melty. "I'd love to show you."

"When would be good? I'm really keen to see them. How does this week look?"

Um, wow. "I might have some time on Thursday."

"Thursday sounds great."

"It's a date." Hope grabbed the dessert menu out of his hands. "Ooh, look. Bobby's added pumpkin pecan cheesecake to the menu."

"Another pumpkin cheescake? Isn't that overdone?"

"I don't follow."

"It no longer shows any imagination. I wouldn't be surprised if McDonald's put a McPumpkin pie on their menu."

Sweet Jesus on a waffle cone. He really was an arrogant, judgmental SOB.

"I think that's an exaggeration."

Lucien's eyebrows lifted. "We obviously have a difference in opinion." He shrugged. "It happens sometimes. I usually end up being right."

Hope dropped the menu on the table and leaned back against the booth back. "You can really be a jerk sometimes."

He laughed. "I've been told that now and again. I think it's one of my better qualities."

She snorted and grinned. "Of course you would."

He reached across the table for her hand. Placing his over hers, his thumb lazily caressed her knuckles. "Come on. Admit it. You like me."

The heat coming from his hand nearly scorched her hand. "You're impossible."

"I'm irresistable."

Yes, he was, but no way would she let him know that. "I'm impervious."

"No, you're not. You like me a lot."

Hope reluctantly pulled her hand from under his. "In your dreams."

Lucien's gaze darkened, and his smile disappeared. "Dreams? I have a lot of dreams about you, *chère*.

Breathe Hope, breathe. She could barely hear him over her heart palpitations. "No you don't."

"I do. Do you dream of me?"

Not that she'd admit to. "No."

"Liar."

"So, have you decided on dessert?" Chelsea appeared at the table, coffee on a tray.

Talk about arriving in the nick of time.

Hope tossed her hair back. "I'm going to get the pumpkin cheesecake, please."

Lucien didn't take his eyes off of Hope. "I'll take the apple pie."

Chelsea set down the heavy cream pottery coffee mugs, nutty, fragrant steam rising from the hot liquid. "Do you want vanilla ice cream on that pie?"

"Yes, please."

"I'll be right back." Chelsea left.

Lucien lifted his mug and toasted her with it. He took a sip of the coffee and grimaced. "This tastes like dishwater it's so weak." He put down the mug, disgust written across his face.

Hope popped open a creamer and poured it into her coffee. Picking up a spoon, she stirred the cream in, then took a sip. "Mine's just right, Goldilocks."

"What did you just call me?"

"Goldilocks. You know, as in this coffee is too strong. *This* coffee is too weak. *This* coffee is *juuussssstttt* right."

"I've got specific standards about food." He drummed his fingers on top of the tabletop. "There's nothing wrong with that."

"In your own restaurant. Do you ever kick back and relax?"

He frowned. "I do. Of course I do."

"What do you do?"

"I cook. When I get the time, I go back to the bayou and go fishing."

She slapped her hand on the table in delight. "You fish."

"Sure. What's wrong with fishing?"

"Nothing! I just can't picture you doing it."

"I'll just have to bring you to the bayou someday so you can watch me."

Well, that wasn't happening. Ever. "Maybe."

Chelsea came back with dessert. "Here you go! Enjoy!" After putting the plates on the table, as well as clean forks and napkins, she left.

Lucien took his fork and flaked up the pie crust before he took a bite. "The crust is too dry and the ice cream is unremarkable. Yours *is* better than this."

"I'm glad you like my pie. Do you want to try some of this cheesecake?"

"No thank you."

"You should."

"I gave in to the gumbo. I refuse to try that pumpkin atrocity."

Now that made her laugh. "Pumpkin atrocity?"

"Whatever. Look. Let's get out of here." Without giving her a chance to say anything, he signaled for Chelsea.

"I haven't finished…"

"I don't care." He wagged his fingers, catching Chelsea's attention. Reaching into his pocket, he liberated his wallet and pulled out a pile of cash then tossed it onto the table. "Let's go."

He practically yanked her out of the booth, nearly bumping into Chelsea. "We're leaving—I've left money on the table, keep the change." He tugged on her wrist as he headed out the door.

Hope stumbled along after him as he pulled her across the parking lot, under the leaves into the semi-privacy of a big maple tree. "Hey, slow down!"

He stopped so abruptly, so she bumped solidly into

him. He wrapped his arms around her, yes, to stop her from falling. He should let go, but he didn't care about what he should do. He always did what he damned pleased.

"You can let go of me now." Hope raised her face to look at him.

"Not until I do this." He lifted her chin with one finger then leaned in to kiss her.

Chapter Nine

Her lips were softer and sweeter than he'd imagined. Intoxicating, like the finest champagne. He could taste the pumpkin cheesecake, but on her it tasted delicious and fresh, scandalously so. He wanted to devour her, but he forced himself to take his time to savor the moment.

To make it last.

Hope voiced her agreement in short hums of desire from back in her throat and opened her mouth under his. His tongue slipped past her lips to fully taste her, to coax her to open up for him. Needing more, he tightened his grip around her, hungry to feel her body against his.

She melted in his arms, like butter on a hot griddle, right on down to that certain sizzle between them. Her arms twined around his neck as if that was the only way she could stay upright. She was soft and supple, and so responsive to his kiss.

He was more than happy to hold her. He could do it all night.

Preferably naked.

The wind whispered past them carrying the scent and chill of fall. Their mouths broke apart, came back together, just a touch then separated. Hope rested her forehead on Lucien's chest and sighed.

Her sigh rippled right over his skittering heart. He

pulled her closer because he couldn't get his arms to let her go. He rubbed his hands up and down her back.

She pulled away. "Would you take me home, please?"

"I think we should talk about this." Women always wanted to talk about their feelings, as if just enjoying a kiss wasn't enough. He'd learned a long time ago that being willing to listen to the female of the species always earned him some brownie points.

"No, we shouldn't." Hope shook her head. "Please just take me home."

She didn't want to talk? No feelings to explore? To justify? He should be relieved, but oddly didn't feel that way at all. Just the opposite. "Sure. Let's go."

****

Hope slipped into the car while Lucien held the door. "Thank you," she murmured. She could barely catch a breath. Her lips still tingled from Lucien's kiss.

Lucien was the first man to kiss her since Cormac died.

And she'd liked it. Dear lord, how she'd liked it. She wanted to do it again.

And again.

Swamped with guilt, buzzing with desire, she felt diced into a million pieces.

Lucien got in and started the car. Thankfully he didn't say anything. Hope looked out the window as they passed through downtown Addington. He'd rocked her world. How could everything still look the same?

"We'll have to talk about this at some time." Lucien's face held no emotion. He didn't look at her, just out the windshield to the road.

"I don't know if I have that much to say. It was just

a kiss. No big deal." Liar, liar, pants on fire. She pitched one shoulder up in a shrug. "I'm a big girl. I've been kissed before."

Lucien cleared his throat. "As you say." His voice sounded very formal. "Just a kiss."

"Right." She looked back out the window.

"When do I get a tour of your garden?"

"Tour?"

"*Oui.* You promised a tour of your gardens."

"Oh, right." She sighed. "I've set aside Thursday morning for some gardening. Getting it ready for winter, that kind of thing. How does ten o'clock sound?"

"Sounds great. It's a date."

She chuffed a laugh. "I wouldn't necessarily call it a date."

"What would you call it? For whatever it's worth, what would you call tonight?"

How the hell would she know what this thing brewing between them would be called. "Two colleagues out to check on the competition." There. That sounded good.

"I don't usually kiss my colleagues after checking out the competition." He pulled the car into the parking lot of Hope's restaurant. "This was a date." He turned in his seat to face her. "I called it a date from the very beginning."

"You were teasing me."

His eyes glittered. "I never tease. Let me prove it to you." He put a big warm hand behind her head and pulled her toward him. "This is a date," he whispered, bringing his face closer to hers.

She couldn't breathe; she couldn't hear over the

pounding of her heart. He kissed her. Not gently, but like he was staking a claim.

Then she wasn't thinking any more. She was kissing him back, totally giving herself up to her desire he stoked in her.

He broke off the kiss. "Now tell me this wasn't a date. I dare you," he murmured.

She pulled back and grabbed the door handle, wrenching the door open. "Thank you for dinner. I'll see you Thursday morning." Hope practically leaped out the car, making a run for it. She scrambled up the stairs leading to the terrace outside her apartment over the restaurant. Opening the door, she ran into the safety of her space.

After she turned on a light, she couldn't help but notice the photo of her and Cormac at their wedding. She put her hand over her mouth as she wandered to the picture. Kissing her fingers, she placed them over Cormac's beloved face. "I'm sorry," she whispered. "I'm so, so sorry."

It felt like good-bye.

****

Lucien watched her run away and sighed. It should not be so difficult to seduce Hope Monahan, but it was.

He liked it. He always enjoyed a challenge.

He backed the car out of her parking lot and decided to go to L'Enfer to check on things. It didn't take long to get there. The parking lot was still fairly full, even at this hour.

L'Enfer was hopping, just the way he liked it.

"Hi, Helen," he said to the woman greeting people at the door. He looked around. "Where's Angelique?"

"She couldn't come in tonight." Helen moved

behind the reservations desk.

"Did she say why?" Lucien scowled.

"Some last minute lecture at school. She said she couldn't miss it."

"Thank you for covering."

"No problem."

Lucien scratched his temple. Something about this didn't feel right. Why hadn't she called to tell him directly? He pulled out his cell phone to check for a text or a voice mail. None.

Curiouser and curiouser. He punched in her number. And went straight to voice mail.

He looked at Helen. "Everything running smoothly tonight?"

"Absolutely. Lots of happy customers."

"*Bien.*" He smiled. "That's what I like to hear. I'm heading home. If Angelique comes by, tell her I'm waiting at home."

"Yes, chef."

He didn't like this, not one bit. She just couldn't duck out of work at short notice. He relied on her. However, if the lecture was important, then she had no choice.

He took the time to look over some sales figures for the L'Enfer Cuisine at Home. The third quarter looked good. Should he expand the number of offerings? Frozen dinners? No. Too gauche. Perhaps he should—

The door opened and in flew Angelique. She stopped when she saw him. "Lucien! I thought you were out for the evening."

She was windblown and brought the chill and scents of autumn, smoke from fireplaces wafting up chimneys, and the woodsy aroma of falling leaves. She'd curled her hair into some fancy hairdo, and she wore more makeup than a model at Fashion Week. Another consequence of his *mésalliance* with Cäcilia, who'd taught Angelique to apply makeup with a trowel.

She did not have the appearance of a person who had spent the evening in a dusty lecture hall.

As she shrugged off her coat and threw it over a chair back, he realized he hadn't seen that dress before.

"A new dress for a last-minute lecture?"

She twirled around for him. "Do you like it?"

"It's pretty." He put down the papers he was reading. "How was the lecture?"

She grimaced. "Oh, you know. Just some dry, boring professor droning on about French poetry." She wrinkled her nose.

"He must have had a lot to say. It's pretty late."

"I went out with some friends, you know, to unwind." She stepped out of her skyscraper heels, picked them up, and dangled them from her right hand fingers.

"I wish you had called before dodging work tonight."

"*Pfffffft.*" She waved the shoeless hand dismissively. "You hired the best people. And Helen wanted the hours. She's saving for a trip to Rio during Mardi Gras. I told her she should go to New Orleans, but she speaks Portuguese and wants to go there."

"I didn't know that." He wouldn't let her distract him. "What was the lecture about? I'm sure your professor, uh, what's his name, had a good reason for requiring you to attend."

"I don't want to bore you."

"I would never be bored. I'm living vicariously through you." He had one regret in his life: not going to college. "Please. Tell me all about it."

"Well, about poetry. From the Renaissance. I can't understand half of it. The French was ancient, so different."

"The lecture was in ancient French?"

"No, no. The poetry was." She rolled her eyes as she plopped herself onto a leather couch. "I have to take the class to graduate."

"You don't like poetry?" He loved poetry. He knew just as well that Angelique didn't. "It's very romantic, *n'est-ce pas?*"

"Well, there's romance and then there's *romance.*"

"*Vraiment?* I am a stupid male creature, totally missing the romance gene. Enlighten me."

"You're being *fou* right now and I'm too tired to explain it to you." She yawned, like a silent movie star overacting. "I need to go to bed."

"Leave me your notes from the lecture. I'd love to read them." He picked up a pencil and tapped it on top of his desk. "And you never told me your professor's name."

She got up off the couch, her face blank. "Um, Dr. Ross. I'll get the notes for you later. *C'est trop tard. Bon soir, mon frère.*"

"*Bon soir.*" Lecture his ass. She was lying, *bien sûr.*

He turned off the lights in the living room and sat there thinking. Angelique had always been impulsive. That's why a sleazy photographer had made a sex tape featuring his sister. The thought still chapped his ass. But tonight?

There was more to this story.

He'd bet the next year of his New Orleans' restaurant's profits that Shane Baker was front and center in whatever his sister was up to. He would check it out on Thursday morning when he visited Hope's gardens.

Chapter Ten

Hope dropped a basket of Eastham turnips onto the counter, next to where Shane was whistling and cheerily chopping celery, carrots, and onions for *mirepoix*. "You look chipper this morning. You're not usually a morning person."

He grinned and shrugged. "Guess I just woke up on the right side of the bed."

"Right." She studied him a moment longer. "You got lucky last night."

"Hope! You know I'm not the kind of guy who kisses and tells."

"Hmm. Do I know her?"

"I'm not talking. What do you want me to do with the turnip?"

"Cut it into little pieces and cook it so we can mash it with some parsley root and potatoes."

He winked at her. "Gotcha." He went back to work on the *mire-poix*.

Something didn't feel quite right. She couldn't put her finger on it. She'd figure it out sooner or later. Or Shane would end up spilling his guts. He wasn't good at keeping a secret.

If he didn't stop whistling, she was going to conk him in the head with a cast-iron skillet.

Truth be told, she hadn't been able to sleep at all, remembering Lucien's kiss.

And not able to remember Cormac's.

Hope moved to a cabinet and pulled out some organic wheat flour and raw sugar, then to the walk-in fridge and got some butter. Pie crust. She needed to think of pie crust, otherwise there would be no dessert for tonight's menu.

She settled into the rut of one of her favorite routines. Measure the flour. Dump it into a bowl. Mix the sugar in. Cut the cold butter in gradually and cut it all together into a dough.

All the while she struggled with her feelings for Lucien. She liked him, even though he could be a real jerk. She liked him a lot.

She liked kissing him. A lot.

It had been so long since she'd been kissed. So long since she fully joined and shared a kiss. Had stoked its fires. Had craved a response.

Her first kiss with Cormac had been innocent and so very, very young. They'd been children. They'd come to their wedding bed as virgins.

Nothing about that kiss with Lucien had been innocent. He'd kissed a lot of women in his life.

How many women had he slept with?

She felt her lips turn down into a frown. According to the tabloids, he was a total man slut.

She sighed. The man had totally messed with her head.

Shane stopped whistling. Good. She wouldn't have to kill him.

"Hey," he said. "How did it go last night at The End Zone with Durand?"

Okay. Take that back. She would have to kill him. "Fine."

"Did his highness find the food to his royal liking?"

"He liked the Bobby Burger. Gushed over it, actually. Wasn't crazy about the wings and the loaded fries."

"Really." Shane leaned against the counter where she was still cutting butter into the flour.

"Hated them. Sent them back to the kitchen practically uneaten. And of course he hated the gumbo, or at least the andouille Bobby uses."

"Of course he did. So he just liked the burger?"

"Yeah. He wouldn't even take a taste of the pumpkin cheesecake—no imagination, he said." She smiled. "He did say that my apple pie is better than Bobby's."

"Your apple pie is better than just about anybody's." Shane shook his head. "I'm going to get a bottle of water from the bar. You want one?"

"That'd be nice. Thank you."

"No problem." Shane left.

She finished with the dough and took it to the fridge to chill, while she made the apple filling. Apples from her own trees, organic cranberries, brown sugar, cinnamon, and nutmeg. A touch of clove and a whiff of allspice. More butter.

None of it took one Lucien Durand off her mind.

****

Shane sat in a far corner of the bar and punched some numbers into his cell phone. It rang a couple of times before the person picked up.

"Hey, gorgeous." He kept his voice quiet, but couldn't hold back the smile that spread on his face as he listened.

"Good morning, shoog. Where y'at?" Angelique's faintly accented voice caressed his hungry ears.

Everything about Angelique Durand made him hungry. "I'm thinking about you, baby."

"Me, I'm thinking about you too."

"All good, I hope."

"You know it is." She chuckled, the sound so sexy.

"When can I see you again?"

"Right now, if you want."

He held back a sigh. "I'm at work."

"And ain't that a shame, *cher*. I've got class this afternoon. Then I've got to show at the restaurant. Lucien was not happy I called Helen to cover for me."

"Did he give you a hard time?"

"Nothing I can't handle. Hey! Did your boss say anything about her and Lucien?"

Shane frowned. "Not so much. Just about what he thought of the food." But he thought Hope'd been distracted. He didn't like that much. "He said her apple pie was the best he'd ever eaten."

"Must be one hell of a pie." She laughed.

"It is." Lord, he loved to hear her laugh.

"Look, I have to go. I'll try to call, but definitely text you later on."

"Awesome." Was it too soon to say I love you?

Probably. But he did.

He did love her. Truly, crazy, madly, head-over-heels-at-first-sight love.

"*A bientôt*. I can't wait to see you again."

And the typical male response. "Me too." Why couldn't he say more? He hated being a cliché, but what could he do. She scared the shit out of him.

It made him want her more.

He sat there a few minutes after she hung up, just to get his bearings.

He couldn't. He didn't have any more bearings. So he went behind the bar and snagged a couple bottles of water.

Shane wondered how he could balance his love-at-first-sight adoration of Angelique Durand with his instant hate for her brother. Maybe he'd never be asked to.

And maybe pigs *could* fly.

****

Hey! Sorry I'm late." Hope rushed into Esmeralda's and to the table where her friends sat. "I had to deal with a last-minute liquor delivery." She pulled out a chair and sat while she grabbed a notebook out of her bag. "So, catch a girl up."

"We think we have a great idea," Ainslie, the event coordinator of Hope's catering business, said in her thick Southern drawl.

"Ooh, good!"

Andi, a long, tall, elegant, pearl-wearing blonde with a remarkable likeness to Grace Kelly, said, "It will tie into the Addington's Tables, if we can make it work."

"Turn a benefit for End Hunger into a ballet benefit? I don't see how that will work."

"The key to it is tables," Andi said. "We'd like to commission artists to create and donate tables that will be auctioned during the cook-off. The ballet would take twenty-five percent of the table auction, giving End Hunger twenty-five percent of the rest of the auction price. The artist would get fifty percent. We wouldn't take any of the money the cooking competition

75

generates."

"What do you think?" Gina picked up her water glass. Her red hair was a riot of curls. She was hugely pregnant.

"It sounds good in principle, but I don't have enough clout to help make it happen."

A waitress came to the table with her friends' food. "Here we go. Hey, Hope. What can I get for you?"

"The cobb salad, please. And an iced tea."

"Great! Be right back."

"This could also bring more people to the contest. More people to taste and donate to End Hunger." Gina picked up her spoon and scooped up some creamy New England clam chowder.

"Very true," Ainslie agreed.

"I think we need to get all the chefs on board before we do anything else." Hope drummed her fingers on the table.

"We can get started on that right away." Andi nodded toward the kitchen door. "Here comes Sam, bearing your salad if I'm not mistaken."

Hope turned around. Sam Wilson, owner of Esmeralda's, was on his way to their table.

"Hey, Hope." He put the dish in front of her. "When I heard you were here I had to come out and see if the rumors are true."

"What rumors?" Her stomach rolled over.

"Well, someone saw you and Lucien Durand outside The End Zone, lip-locked in the parking lot."

Oh crap. "I don't know what you're talking about."

"One of Bobby's servers went out to grab a cigarette and said she saw you two." Sam had a big grin on his face.

"Who?"

"Sandy, and she is never wrong."

True that. Hope sighed. "Okay, yeah. He kissed me. No big deal. Listen." She really wanted to wipe that grin off his face. "The committee here thinks it might be a good idea to combine their fundraiser with the Addington's Tables contest." She explained it to him.

"Might work." Sam shrugged. "I guess I wouldn't mind. But the big decision lies with the competition committee." A crash in the kitchen made him wince. "Looks like I need to go."

She turned back to the table. Three shocked and stunned faces greeted her, eyes wide, jaws dropped.

Great. Just great. She grabbed her fork and stabbed a hunk of crisp, tart apple. "This looks really good."

"Hold it a second, girlfriend." Gina put her spoon down. "Lucien Durand kissed you?"

"It's not a big deal."

"I beg to differ." Ainslie's eyebrows nearly flew off her head. "Lucien Durand is a very big deal."

"It was just a kiss." She stuffed the apple chunk into her mouth and chewed.

"There's no such thing as just a kiss with you." Andi pointed out.

Gina shook her head. "We want details! Did your toes curl?"

"You can stop now. It's not what you think."

"Was it any good? He looks like he's a really good kisser." Of course Gina wouldn't let go.

"I'm not saying."

Gina frowned, then brightened. "Just rate him on a scale of one to ten, one being sloppy and drooly, ten being you saw stars and swooned."

"Stop it." Andi punched Gina in the arm. "It's no crime if he kissed, you. And, here's the thing. It didn't upset the time space continuum if you kissed him back."

"I liked it a lot. I did kiss him back."

"You say that like it's a bad thing." Andi smiled gently. "Don't be ashamed of your feelings."

"I feel like I'm betraying Cormac." Hope's eyes misted. "I promised to love him forever."

Ainslie placed her hand over Hope's. "It's not betraying Cormac. You need to move on. That's what Cormac would want. He'd want you to be happy."

Hope used her napkin to wipe away the tears. "He wouldn't want me to date some international food superstar."

"Why not?" Ainslie asked. "He was an international Irish music star."

Her mouth opened and closed a couple of times. She couldn't come up with an answer. "I don't know. He just wouldn't."

"Nobody's saying you have to marry him." Gina waved a hand. "Nobody's saying you even have to fall in love with him. Just have some fun. You deserve it. Take him out for a test drive. Kick the tires, so to speak. Check out how smooth the stick shift moves."

Hope face-palmed. "Oh my god."

Gina wasn't done. "Seriously. He was one of *People Magazine's* Sexiest Men Alive and he wants to engage in mutually hot lip-locks? No brainer."

Andi laughed. "I'd let him kiss me."

"Me too," Ainslie chimed in.

Gina raised her hand. "Yes, please."

"You're all married."

"And your point is?" Gina picked up her soup spoon and pointed it at Hope. "It's time to come back to life, Hope. I knew Cormac, and I know how much you two loved each other. He wouldn't want you to be alone for the rest of your life. And Lucien Durand? He's probably not a forever kind of guy, but what a way to re-enter the dating world."

"Just relax and enjoy it. He's hella hot and that accent is to die for." Andi grinned at her.

Hope chuffed out a little laugh. "He is hot." And funny and interesting and compelling. And sexy. Don't forget sexy. "I suppose you're right. It just feels a little scary. But, how do I know if he is just pretending to be interested in me because he wants to get me off my game and win the competition?"

None of them said anything for a moment. "So you keep your eyes and ears open," Gina said. "Don't let him distract you. You're right on top of everything." She tapped her right temple. "Keep your eyes on the prize."

"Of course it's scary," Ainslie said. "I was scared to death when I started dating Dave. But it was so worth it."

Gina just rubbed her belly. "You know how I feel about it."

"He's coming by the restaurant to get a tour of the gardens."

"Is he now?" Andi's eyes sparkled. "Sounds like fun."

"And if it turns out to be a lot of fun?" Gina asked. "Take pictures so we can fully appreciate his fineness."

Hope stuck her tongue out at Gina. But they'd convinced her.

She would go for it, but be smart. She wasn't going to let him sidetrack her from the contest. She'd take a shot and go for it all.

Chapter Eleven

"Hey, Hope! You look great today. What's going on?" Shane watched Hope as she entered the kitchen. "You got an appointment with the bank or something?"

She arched a brow. "I don't look great every day?"

"You know what I mean. You're wearing makeup, which you hardly ever do, and you've done something more than a ponytail with your hair."

"I felt like it, that's all." Of course, it had nothing to do with Lucien's garden tour later that morning.

He sniffed. "Are you wearing perfume?"

"Is wearing perfume a federal offense now?"

"Hunh," he grunted. "No. It's just that it's kind of a waste when you'll be behind the line tonight. What's on the menu?"

"Cranberry glazed duck breasts, potato leek soup, apple and butternut squash puree, parmesan, wild mushroom risotto with cauliflower. I haven't decided on dessert."

"Salad?"

"I'll grab some watercress from the hydroponic garden and we'll do bacon with some kind of vinaigrette."

"Gotcha. I'll start on the soup." Shane loped off.

Hope sat on a stool and put a hand over her churning stomach. She glanced at the clock. She had an hour until Lucien showed up for his tour.

Gina and the girls said to go for it; just the encouragement she needed. She really hoped she wouldn't make a fool of herself.

****

Hope grabbed a few sweet basil leaves. Lucien would be there any time now, and she wanted to get into the garden before he did. She most definitely didn't want him and Shane to cross paths.

Hope raised her face to the sun as she headed for her garden. She loved it, remembering the happy hours she'd spent in the summers on Granny's farm in Ireland, while her Doctors Without Borders parents went about healing the world.

And ignoring their only child.

They still did. Whatever.

"Hope." Lucien stood at her garden gate. She knew it without looking. Her stomach lurched, then got the butterflies.

She swivelled. "Lucien, come on in."

He did. "This is a very impressive garden."

"Thank you. I'm just getting started."

He wandered to the brick path separating one section of plants from the other. "Your herbs smell delicious."

She plucked a leaf off a sage plant, rubbed it and handed it to him. "Smell this."

He took the fragrant leaf. "Very nice."

Hope beamed. "I've got to get the perennials ready for the winter before the first frost. Then I'll pull what's left of the annuals to dry. I had a lot of basil this year, so I'll be making and freezing a lot of pesto."

Lucien looked particularly yummy today in a pair of old jeans that hugged his butt, as well as other places, and the white shirt underneath an unzipped L'Enfer hoodie. The dark stubble on his chin made him look dangerous. His midnight gaze made her heart flutter.

Dammit. If he kissed her again she would go for it. Maybe that would take care of the attraction she felt for him.

"Come on, let me show you around."

She took him to all the little plots ripe with the multi-colored heirloom tomatoes, tender leaves of spinach, the sweet orange mini pumpkins. Hope took off her gloves.

She thought she was being smooth as she found ways to touch him, brush up against him. Innocent contact, nothing overt.

They reached the fruit trees, the summer fruits gone, but the plums, pears, chestnuts, and apples still hung low on their branches. "The apples are heirloom varieties. They have such a different taste to them."

"Heirloom apples?" Lucien raised his eyebrows as he plucked a plump red and gold apple.

A shaft of warm fall sunshine caught him in its light as a soft breeze ruffled his hair. No fallen angel had ever looked so good.

"Yep."

He gently squeezed the fruit. She *so* could imagine those gentle, skilled fingers massaging her breasts. Her heart beat a little faster.

He polished it on his shirt. "What kind is it?"

She swallowed so she could speak. "A Baldwin."

"Hmmmmm." He inspected the newly shined fruit. "Like Alec and his other brothers?"

Oh, that voice, low, rich with the spice of its Cajun

accent, slipped over her like dark silk. It made her want to do all sorts of crazy things.

Sinful, delightful things.

Ahem. Apples. He wants to know about heirloom apples. "No. These go way back before Alec Baldwin started punching out paparazzi."

He barked a laugh.

Okay. She did walk into that one. "Well, for one thing, they've got a statue in Wilmington marking the first tree found growing wild." Dear Lord, Lucien Durand was one gorgeous man. "In 1740."

He smiled. "They know the exact year the tree was found?"

"Well, yeah, I guess. At least, that's the date on the statue."

"Then it must be true." He gave the apple a measuring eye. "Looks tasty." He took a big bite out of it.

What she wouldn't give to take a big bite out of him.

"Mmmmm. This is good." He punctuated his comment by waving the fruit in front of him. "Nice and firm." He licked his lips.

Oh my. "It's got a reputation for being hard. Sometimes people call it the woodpecker." She felt her face flush. God, what a dork she was.

He threw his head back and laughed, the sound husky, as if he didn't laugh very much. "You're kidding!" It totally transformed his face.

His happy smile was irresistible, so she smiled back. "Would I kid about heirloom apples?"

"Absolutely!" His eyes sparkled. It made him look younger, less worldly. Less jaded. "I'd go somewhere and start talking about woodpecker apples and look like *un imbécile*."

"You'd do the same to me in a New York minute."

"You think I'd try and fool you?" He shook his head. "You are unfoolable, you."

"I'm totally foolable." She shouldn't admit that, but the charm of his genuine smile had her on the ropes.

He tossed the apple up then caught it when it came down. "Want some?"

She tossed her hair back. "Trying to tempt me?"

"Maybe." He held it out to her. "What are you afraid of?"

"Nothing." She was a lying liar who lied.

He took a step closer. "Then take a bite."

Her hand trembled a bit as she reached out and pulled the fruit out of his warm, strong hand.

"Go ahead." He moved in another step. "*Je te défie*." He made his voice a whisper. "I dare you."

Lord, he smelled so good, like sunshine and fresh air. Her eyes locked with his as she brought the juicy, fragrant fruit to her mouth and took a bite.

The skin cracked against her teeth, and the tart juice trickled from the firm flesh of the apple on to her tongue. She couldn't look away from him.

"It's good, *oui*?" He lowered his head as he plucked the apple out of her hand and dropped it on the ground.

She swallowed with some difficulty. "Yes," she whispered.

"This will be better." He kissed her, a gentle brushing, testing of lips, tasting of tart apple and sweet dreams.

He lifted his head. "You're trembling, *pichouette*,"

he whispered. "*Ça me plait.*"

She couldn't speak. He touched her under her chin and lifted it. "*Encore.*" Dipping his head, he captured her lips again.

This was no gentle, tentative brush. He settled his mouth over hers and took possession. His tongue teased her lips open while he framed her face with his warm, big hands.

She kissed him back; she couldn't stop herself. She didn't want to stop.

How long had it been since she'd been kissed like this? Forever. Maybe never. Something thawed, opened, and bloomed inside her, a place long neglected, opening up to the devil magic of this man's wicked, *wicked* mouth. Her heart hammered against her rib cage in short staccato bursts. Dear Lord, she'd missed this, missed it so much.

Lucien ripped his mouth from hers, took a step back and stared at her. He ran his hand through his hair. "*Merci Dieu.*"

Goose bumps raised on her arms as the autumn air cooled her skin. She couldn't take her gaze off him. Touching her lips with her trembling fingers, she tried to come up with something sophisticated to say, but her voice wouldn't work.

"Hey, Hope? Is there any more butternut squash for tonight's—whoa!" Shane stumbled into the garden. His eyes narrowed as he looked at Lucien and Hope. "Chef Durand," Shane practically growled. "I didn't know you were here."

Lucien's face turned cold as he turned to look at Shane. "I didn't know I needed to run my schedule by you."

Yikes! "Lucien is here to get a lesson on Baldwin apples."

"Really. That's just what it looked like." Skepticism dripped from Shane's voice.

Like a crown prince dismissing a peasant, Lucien gave Shane one ice-cold shoulder. "Hope, thank you for showing me your garden. I learned more than I thought I would." He held out his hand for her to shake.

What?! Something about this felt, well...wrong, even though it was professional.

And, for real? He learned more than he thought he would? Jerk.

She shook his damned hand, though she'd rather choke than do so. No reason to not be polite. "You're welcome."

"I'll leave now. I'm sure you have a lot of prep work to do."

"She does." And, of course, Shane picked that moment to channel his inner caveman.

Lucien shook his head, turned and left, taking the warm sunshine with him.

Shane kept his mouth shut until Durand was out of hearing range, then scowled at Hope. "What the hell did I interrupt?"

Hope frowned. "Nothing."

Shane snorted.

"Okay," Hope said. "Nothing that's any of your business."

"This guy is totally a player. He collects models like squirrels collect acorns." He watched Hope blush and look at the ground.

"Nothing happened. He just kissed me." She looked Shane in the eyes. "That's all."

"Hope, don't take this the wrong way, but the only guy you've ever kissed was Cormac. I can't stand back and let Durand hurt you. I won't stand back."

"Oh, please." Hope turned her back to him. "Stop speaking to me like I'm a child. I'd like to have some fun. I'm moving on."

"Is that what you're doing? Moving on?"

Hope shrugged. "Would that be so bad?"

"No. Not at all. Just don't move on with Lucien Durand."

"Why not? He's attractive, available, and we share a common passion."

"Passion? You mean food, right? Or something different?"

"Maybe both. At any rate, it's my business."

"Has it ever occurred to you that he's trying to get you off your game for the contest?"

Of course it had. "Are you saying he wouldn't be attracted to a woman like me?"

"No, not at all." Shane stepped back. "He's just got this reputation for rolling over people to get what he wants."

"I won't let him."

"If he hurts you—"

"If I get hurt, it's on me. I'm a big girl."

"Hope, I love you like a sister. You know I only want what's best for you. This guy is bad news."

She turned to face him. "Shane, leave it alone, okay? I don't need this right now." She gave him a quick hug before she left the garden.

"I'm going on record as being really against this."

"So noted. If you're done, I'd like to get back to work."

She turned and headed into the kitchen. Eye on the prize, girl. Eye on the prize.

Chapter Twelve

How could he get to see her again, Lucien wondered, without scaring her? Without making her run away.

After his visit to Hope's gardens and their kiss in the warm sunshine he needed to see her again. He craved to see her again. To taste her.

He obsessed about it, which was ridiculous. Women fell at his feet. It should be no problem to romance Hope. He only had to pick up the phone.

His mouth thinned into a tight line, and he tapped his pen on the ledger in front of him. He caught a glimpse of the promotional flyer for the Addington's Tables competition. Dropping his pen, he picked up the flyer. It listed all the restaurants in the competition. He hadn't eaten at some of them yet. He needed to rectify that.

So he pulled out his phone and tapped her number into it. Funny that he knew it by heart already. He needed to add her to his contact list, he thought absently.

It went to voice mail. "Hope. It's Lucien. I wonder if you'd like to accompany me on Monday night to dinner at the Pilgrim Steak and Chop House. I'm still trying to taste all my competitors' food. We can label it research. Please get back to me and let me know. *À bientôt.*"

After throwing the phone onto his desk, he leaned back in his chair and brooded. All he had to do was wait for her to call him back.

He hated waiting. He hated things being beyond his control. He liked being the man with a plan.

Hope Monahan didn't figure in any of his plans. If he didn't take care, he'd be off his game at the competition and would not dominate all the other chefs.

Anything less than first place was unacceptable.

If he could be distracted by Hope, perhaps she could be distracted by him.

Total win/win. He would have the pleasure of her company and make sure he won the competition. And, by the time the contest was over, he'd be off to another challenge. Their romance will have run its course, and they'd part as friends.

Lucien pushed himself out of his chair and went to stand in front of his office window. Looking out at the tree leaves starting to turn from green to vivid red, gold, and orange, he took in the view, marveling at the beauty of a New England autumn.

He'd miss it when he left.

****

"Who called?" Shane stood at the sink washing kale.

Hope frowned, then put her phone back into her pocket. "None of your business. You're so nosy these days." She had no intention of telling him. "It's not a very good look on you."

He shrugged. "Hey, I'm just looking out for my friend."

"Oh, please." She slapped his arm. "I don't need looking out for."

He muttered something she couldn't catch.

"Don't you have some work to do?"

"It was Durand, wasn't it?"

She rolled her eyes. "So what if it was?"

He looked at her, his eyes serious. "You know where I stand."

"I certainly do. And I'm not having this conversation with you again." Annoyance sparked along her skin. "I am neither a fool nor a child. I'll see whomever I want, when I want. I don't need to run my dates by you for approval."

"Jesus, Hope. I'm not trying to insult you." Shane shook his head. "Cut me some slack."

"So, cut me some too. I know what I'm doing." Her story and she was sticking to it.

He stuffed the kale into the salad spinner. "And for the record, you barge into my business all the time."

"I do not." Well, maybe. Kinda, sorta.

Shane shook his head. "I hope you know what you're doing."

"Go away."

He did. She looked at her phone and listened to the voice mail again.

You know, it was pretty high-handed to leave a voice mail asking her out and telling her to call him back, like she was some love-starved teenager who would blindly jump whenever he beckoned.

You know what? Too darn bad. She was busy next Monday night, doing what she didn't know. It didn't matter. The only thing she knew for sure? She wasn't going to dinner with Lucien Durand at the Pilgrim Rib and Steak House.

And she wasn't going to ring him back. She'd let

him stew about it, and if he really wanted the pleasure of her company, then he could make an effort. She might be late to the whole dating thing, but she was no doormat.

The sooner he learned that, the better off they'd get along.

****

Hope still hadn't phoned back, Lucien worried as he came out to welcome guests in the reception area of L'Enfer. He never worried about a woman returning his calls, because they always did.

It really pissed him off that she made him wait.

Angelique came back to the reservations desk after seating a party in the main dining room. "We're nice and busy tonight."

"Yes." He fiddled with his cufflinks. Of course they were busy. Every L'Enfer worldwide was busy every night.

He felt Angelique stiffen beside him, so he looked up. A short but well-built, stunning, and very pregnant redhead walked into the lobby with a studious looking man. He wore wire-rim glasses, khaki pants, and a blue button-down shirt. He topped it off with a tweed jacket that had seen better days. He might have had chalk dust on his fingers. He guided the redhead into the room with a hand at her lower back.

Angelique moved forward to greet the pair. "Professor Ross, how wonderful to see you here."

"We just had to check out the new restaurant," Professor Ross replied in a crisp, upper-class British accent. "My wife, Gina, wouldn't let up until I brought her here."

"I've heard so much about you." Mrs. Ross had a

wide smile on her face. Lucien sighed inwardly. Women always smiled at him.

"All of it good, I hope." He shook Ross's hand. "How do you know my sister?"

Ross smiled. "She is in my French Renaissance Poetry seminar."

"Really." Wasn't that convenient? Time to get some answers. "Angelique came home last Monday after your special program. I tried to get her to tell me all about it, but she was very vague."

Ross's brow knit. "You were there?" he asked Angelique.

"Of course I was there," Angelique jumped in. "I signed the attendance sheet."

"Right. Sorry."

"Let me take you to your table." Angelique grabbed a couple of menus and the wine list. "Follow me."

Ross nodded to Lucien and offered his hand to shake. "Nice meeting you."

Lucien shook Professor Ross's hand. "I hope you enjoy yourself. *Bon appétit.*"

Something smelled off. Angelique could have ducked into the lecture and signed the attendance sheet, then hared off and gone somewhere else. How high school. Lucien felt disappointment wrap around him. He'd hoped she was beyond all that infantile behavior.

He had to be canny. Clever. Angelique was slippery and hard to pin down. Sooner or later she'd make a mistake and he could pounce on her and get the truth.

A complimentary bottle of wine for Professor Ross and his wife was a good start. Oh, wait. Mrs. Ross was clearly pregnant. No wine. Dessert. Chocolate dessert.

He found chocolate always worked with women. Better than flowers. All those starved supermodels swooned over chocolate, but wouldn't eat it, at least not while he looked. Ridiculous females. They looked good on your arm, but he much more preferred a woman who liked food. Who appreciated food.

Like Hope.

The phone in his inner jacket pocket felt like a lead weight against his chest. His fingers itched to pull it out and call her again.

He was *fou*. Ridiculous. Women accommodated him, not the other way around.

Angelique returned to the reservation desk.

"Your French professor looks very professorial."

"Must be the accent." She reached under the desk and pulled out the box of complimentary breath mints and filled the cut glass candy dish.

"I'm going to send them dessert."

She gave him a sideways glance. "That's very nice of you."

"I have my moments."

"I'll take it to them when they're ready. Never hurts to make brownie points with your professor."

"No, I'll do it." Lucien looked at the couple. Mrs. Ross kept staring at him. *Eh, bien.* "I'd like to get to know your teachers."

Angelique shook her head. "I'm not five. It's not like you need to interrogate my teachers about how I'm doing."

"I'm not going to interrogate your teacher. It's just dessert." He shrugged. "It's good for business to get to know people in the community."

"You've never done that before."

"I've never opened a restaurant in a small town before. They're different than the cities we already have restaurants in."

She gave him a suspicious look. "Whatever."

A new party entered into the foyer and grabbed Angelique's attention. Actually, she looked pretty eager for the distraction.

He decided it was time to take a stroll around the dining room. As he walked, his phone vibrated in his pocket. His heart hitched a beat in rhythm with his phone. He pulled it out and checked the display. Not Hope.

Deflated, he stuffed the phone back into his pocket.

What on earth was the matter? Women always called him back. They usually called him first. Well, he wasn't chasing after her. It'd be a cold day in hell before he did.

****

"I hope you enjoyed your dinners," Lucien walked over to the Ross's table as their server cleared their entrée settings.

Mrs. Ross still stared at him with this big wide smile. "Everything was wonderful, thank you."

Lucien put down two dessert menus. "I hope you've saved some room for dessert. I stole my pastry chef from Gordon Ramsey's Paris restaurant, and he's never forgiven me."

Mrs. Ross's eyes widened. "I don't know if I can eat another bite."

He opened the menu he'd put in front of her. "Georges is a genius and just tonight composed a *petit gateau au chocolat avec lentisques*."

"*Lentisques*?" she asked.

"Pistaschios," her husband answered. He looked at Lucien. "How did you know she'd been craving them?"

"I had an inkling." He gave a benevolent smile. He'd had no idea, so this was gravy, so to speak. "Shall I bring a *gateau* for *madame*?" Okay, he was laying it on thick, but the ends justified the means if he could get info on Angelique.

Mrs. Ross lit up like a roman candle. "Yes, please!"

Lucien smiled. "I'll be right back. Would you like Sarah to bring you some coffee? Tea?"

Professor Ross nodded. "Yes, please. Tea for both of us, herbal for Gina."

Gina stuck her tongue out at her husband, then sighed. "I hate herbal tea."

Ross patted her hand. "It's good for you and the baby."

"I'll let her know. We have a wide variety of herbal teas." Lucien had them right where he wanted them. "Let me know if there's anything more I can do for you."

"Thank you," Ross murmured.

"Well, really, I should be thanking you. Angelique really enjoys your class." Lucien straightened his shirt cuffs.

"Really? I'm so glad." He took off his glasses and used his tie to clean them. "She's very quiet."

"Oh, really." Lucien chuckled. "That's not my experience with her."

"Oh, well." Ross put his glasses back on. "I suppose she's different in class."

"I try to get her to talk about her studies, but she

doesn't share much. I'm very interested in her French poetry class."

Professor Ross perked up, which was just what Lucien wanted. "Who is your favorite poet?"

"Several, really." Which was the truth. "Baudelaire. Verlaine. Especially *Mandoline*." He shrugged. "Victor Hugo."

Ross shook his head. "None of them are my specialty, but they are wonderful poets. *Mandoline* is beautiful. So many composers have set it to music. My specialty is the Renaissance, though."

"I would love to learn more." Again the truth. "But let me get your *gateau*."

He left the table confident he'd created a rapport with Angelique's professor. Some days it was good to be a charming, and an honest SOB.

****

"Do you think I can clock out now?" Angelique looked at her watch. "I have some things I have to do."

"What kind of things?" Lucien leaned against the reservation desk. The dining room was clearing out. They'd just said good-bye to Professor Ross and his wife.

"School things."

"What kind of school things?"

She breathed out a gusty, annoyed sigh. "I've got to get to the library before it closes, so I can get a book I need. For a test tomorrow."

"Professor Ross didn't mention a test."

"He's not my only teacher, you know. So—" she smiled up at him—"can I leave work early?"

He studied her face for any telltale signs of a lie. He couldn't tell, but she was a good liar. "What time does the library close?"

"Eleven. I'll probably stay there and study."

"Wouldn't it be better if you brought the book home?"

She jammed her fists on her hips. "I am not a child, Lucien. And you're not *Grand-mère*. And what if I need to get another book? I don't want to make a second trip."

"Okay. Go clock out."

"*Merci*!" She went up on tiptoes and kissed his cheek. "I'll see you later!"

Lucien watched her walk to the kitchen and debated whether or not to swing by the Barrett University Library on his way home.

****

Shane felt his phone vibrate in his coat pocket. He left cleaning the grill and walked to a corner in the pantry. Pulling the phone out, he smiled as he opened the text message. Angelique had gotten let off work early and wanted to meet him in the parking lot of Barrett U's library.

He shook his head. He didn't like the sneaking around, but Angelique just tied him up in knots. When he was with her, he couldn't think straight. He'd do anything she wanted.

He'd always thought love at first sight was a crock, but then it happened to him.

Shane looked at the mess on the grill and sighed. He'd better finish cleaning up in record time. He had to meet his girl at the library.

Chapter Thirteen

Hope rolled her shoulders. After working in the garden all day, her arm and back muscles ached. Still, a Monday spent in the garden always soothed her. Just like Granny, she liked growing things. Even more, she liked to cook the things she'd grown.

So she hobbled to her personal kitchen above the restaurant, filled the kettle with water, and set it to boil on the stove. That done, she pulled out dill, beef short ribs, beets, and the rest of the fixings for borscht.

Soon the soup was under way, filling her apartment with the rich, complex scent of the fall taste profile she wanted to get. She'd try it with the staff tomorrow and tweak it before she put it on the menu. Maybe it was competition material.

She could have spent the evening going to dinner with a very handsome, very charming man. Maybe she should have called Lucien back.

This dating stuff was hard. She couldn't remember what few rules she knew long ago before she married Cormac. Still, if he really wanted to take her out, wouldn't he have called again?

She grabbed some carrots and took the peeler to them. A little carrot cake was always a good idea. She grated and chopped with abandon.

Okay, him not calling again because she'd been considering having a fling with him confused her.

Whatever the hell "fling" meant.

Maybe she could fling him back to New Orleans. She giggled as she pictured him landing on his big ol' arrogant head.

The kettle whistled. Hope pulled it off the heat, used some of the water to warm the teapot and sprinkled some decaf green tea into the mix.

She really wished dating came with a rule book. Or that men came with an owner's manual.

Most likely, Lucien Durand would break all the rules in any book he wanted.

She grated some fresh nutmeg, along with some cinnamon to the carrot cake mixture. Maybe it needed some coconut, even though that broke her eat-local rule. Why not take a walk on the wild side?

Like call Lucien back.

Maybe invite him to dinner herself. The Pilgrim Steak and Rib House would still be there next Monday.

Or maybe have dinner in. Was it too soon?

She had no clue.

Irish soda bread. She should make a couple of them too. Try out a gluten-free version.

She sighed. Maybe she should ask Ainslie. Ainslie had rubbed elbows with the rich and famous once upon a time. She knew how they thought, how they worked. Ainslie would help her buy a clue.

****

"Toni, pick up!" Lucien swiped at his forehead. He was working the line, something he hadn't done in a while.

He needed to do it more often. His staff had gotten lazy and haphazard.

In fact, they were well nigh incompetent. That

simply would not do. He pushed the button for her beeper. "Toni!"

"Sorry, chef, I'll get these right out." Toni flew in from the dining room.

"About damn time." His blood pressure spiked at the sight of the waitress. "The sauce is nearly ruined."

"Yes, chef." She grabbed the plates and skuttled off.

He ripped a dupe off the line. "Manny, two Shrimp Étouffée. They better go out looking perfect this time."

"Yes, chef." Manny had panic in his eyes.

Good.

"Joe! Two filets, one medium rare, the other rare. I want to check those before they go out." Lucien had decided he'd check everything the kitchen put out that night.

"Yes, chef." Joe nodded before throwing the two steaks on the grill. They hit it with a satisfying sizzle. At least the grill was up to temperature.

Lucien turned his attention to a waitress about to take out a bowl of gumbo. "Mary! Your underliner is dirty. Get a new one." He pointed a cleaver at her. "Never, *ever*, take out a messy plate."

"Yes, chef. Sorry!" Mary squeaked, then scrambled to do what he said.

He put down the cleaver. Another waitress came in and punched her dupe. Lucien pulled it off the line. "I need three blackened snapper, two barbequed shrimp, and one lobster creole."

"Yes, chef." Both cooks answered together.

Lucien turned to the stove and started the Bearnaise sauce for the filets and wondered what the hell was more important for Hope Monahan to do than go to dinner with him. His hand clenched around the whisk he used to stir the roux. If he whipped it any harder, he'd turn it inedible.

Dammit.

"Joe! Are those filets ready yet?"

"Just plating them now, chef."

Lucien turned a sour eye to the plates Joe worked on. "Don't take all day at it. The sauce is going to turn."

"Yes, chef." Joe slid the plates down the line.

Lucien rearranged the potatoes Joe had plated with the steaks, then sauced them. "Mary! Pick up!"

Manny, working as sauté cook, put two plates of blackened snapper under the heat lamps, and, *Dieu*, the plate looked like a dog threw up on it. He felt his blood vessels explode. He picked up one of the plates. "Manny! Is this a presentation worthy of L'Enfer?"

Manny opened his mouth, then closed it again.

"Cat got your tongue? Well, I'll tell you!" Lucien emptied the plate into the garbage, then threw the plate to the floor. "That was garbage. Do both orders over." He motioned to a dishwasher. "You. Over here and sweep up this broken plate."

Manny slinked back to the stove, while the dishwasher scrambled over with a broom and dustpan.

Did he have to fire everybody and start over again? Lucien guessed he'd simply have to spend more time, at least for the time being, back in the kitchen. Angelique would have to put in a few more hours and run the front of the house herself.

At least as long as it took to fix the mess in his kitchen.

****

"Well, this is awkward," Ainslie said. "You just

103

want to call him out of the blue and ask him to dinner?"

"Well, no, not quite." Hope frowned. "Okay, yeah, that's what I want to do, but how do I do it without looking like a total doofus? Or fickle?"

Ainslie and Hope sat in the bar of Hope's, chatting over coffee and gluten-free soda bread. Golden morning sunlight filtered through the windows that overlooked Hope's gardens. The two women usually met there once a week to discuss upcoming catering events.

Finding Ainslie had been a godsend. She was the queen of planning events and took so much pressure off of Hope. As the restaurant took off, Hope had less time to devote to that side of the business. She hired Ainslie on a hunch and never looked back.

Ainslie was also the most excellent of friends.

"You could lie and say you didn't get his message until today." Ainslie picked up a piece of warm, butter-slathered soda bread. "God, this is good. I can't believe it's gluten-free."

"So it's a keeper recipe?"

"Yes," Ainslie said around the bread in her mouth.

"I don't want to lie. I hate lying."

"Then tell him the truth."

"What? That I didn't call him back because I was miffed that he assumed I'd drop everything and go on a date with him?" Hope took a sip from her coffee. "It sounds so junior high."

"Well it does if you put it like that. But you should start out as you want to go along. If you don't want him to treat you as an afterthought, then you should tell him he needs to take you seriously."

"So do I do that when I call him?"

Ainslie shrugged. "I'd wait to tell him in person.

It's easy to blow someone off if it's on the phone." She brushed crumbs off her blouse. "As you well know."

"So, what next?"

"You could take off early one night, like say, tonight, and go over to L'Enfer for a drink. I guarantee he'll be interested in what you have to say. He won't be able to resist."

Hope chewed on that for a second. "But what if he does resist? I'll make a total fool of myself."

Ainslie laughed. "Honey, his ego won't let him resist. He'll need an answer for why you didn't return his call. And why you're there in person."

"The potential for humiliation is off the charts."

"No guts, no glory."

"That's easy for you to say."

Ainslie shook her head. "Remember when I first started dating Dave? I was terrified. But I took that leap of faith. Now look at us, married and happy."

"Anyone would be a fool not to trust Dave. He's the most reliable man I know. Lucien Durand is a well-known player." Hope took another sip of her coffee.

"Remember you're not looking for Mr. Right. You're looking for Mr. Right Now."

Hope nearly choked on her coffee. "Ainslie!"

"Well, it's true, isn't it?"

"I suppose."

"The potential for humiliation has just shrunk exponentially."

Hope mulled that over while she grabbed a piece of bread. "Tonight?"

"Why not? You've got all afternoon to plan your attack."

Hope sighed. "Why not."

****

"Hey, Luce! Guess who's sitting at the bar waiting to talk to you?"

Lucien peered over the shelf in front of the line. Angelique looked back at him, a huge grin on her face.

He was sweaty and he was annoyed. He'd spent another evening whipping his incompetent kitchen staff into shape. And now in no mood to play a guessing game with his sister. "Who?"

"Why, Hope Monahan, shoog."

Hope? "What's she doing here?"

"I don't rightly know, but she seems to be lookin' to pass a good time at the bar."

He shook his head. "Come again?"

"You heard me. Hope's at the bar hopin' you'll come and talk to her."

"Hmmpf." Lucien grabbed the handkerchief from out of his pocket and swabbed at the sweat on his face. Why the hell was she here? "I'll be out in a minute."

Angelique's grin grew wider. "I'll let her know."

"I just bet you will," Lucien said to her retreating back.

God help him, Angelique just laughed. Little sisters were a pain in the ass.

He really should ignore Hope. Let her stew the way she'd made him stew. Damn female. How dare she play him for a fool. He'd show her.

He'd show her…what?

Hell.

He looked around the kitchen, evaluating the carnage his kitchen crew could make while he was gone. "I'm taking a few minutes," he said to the room at large. "Don't screw up."

He wouldn't lie to himself. He really wanted to find out why she was here. He travelled to the front of the house, though he hated moving through the dining room in his chef's attire.

Eh, bien. There was no help for it.

Entering the bar, Lucien spotted her. His prey.

Hope.

Even in jeans and a long-sleeved tee she looked cool and collected, like she hadn't spent the evening behind a stove. He knew she had, because this was Tuesday, and she always worked on Tuesday. Every day except Monday, when she let her restaurant go dark.

Lucien shook his head at the very idea of letting L'Enfer go dark for more than one day of the year. Christmas. *C'est assez.*

Hope turned on the bar stool, almost as if she felt his presence. Her hair was up into a ponytail and she couldn't have looked more like the girl next door if she had tried. Face devoid of makeup, she didn't look old enough to sit at a bar.

She sure was old enough, though. That he knew for sure after kissing her in her garden. She was all woman, soft curves and sweet-tasting mouth. He wanted to taste her again.

"Hello," she said as he got to the bar.

"Hello."

The bartender came with a glass of white wine for Hope. "Can I get you anything, chef?"

"A coffee, please, Roland."

"Sure thing."

Roland pulled a bowl filled with mixed nuts from under the bar and put it between Hope and Lucien. "I'll be right back with your coffee."

"Well…" Lucien slid onto the bar stool next to her. "Angelique said you wanted to talk to me."

She cleared her throat and looked up. Her eyes appeared wide and luminous in the dim atmosphere of the bar, studded with pinpricks of the muted lights dancing on their surfaces and fringed with long dark lashes.

"I guess I want to, to, uh, explain."

That was cryptic enough. "Explain what?"

She sighed and looked him in the eyes. "Why I didn't call you back."

Oh really? "And why was that?"

"I thought…I got annoyed. It sounded like you were just expecting me to drop everything because you left a message on my voice mail."

He hid a smile. She looked so miserable.

He was feeling a lot better. "So you didn't call me back to teach me a lesson?"

"Something like that," she grumbled.

He felt a grin spread across his face. "And you want to reschedule for next Monday?"

"Maybe. Look. I've been out of the whole dating thing for a long time. I don't know what the rules are." She angled her head up in a so-what're-you-gonna-do attitude.

"I don't think dating comes with a rule book." He chuckled. "If it did, I'd throw it out anyway."

"You know what I mean." She wrinkled her nose at him. "Are you laughing at me?"

"Absolutely not." Lucien tried to erase the smirk he knew was on his face, but it wasn't happening. He let out a bark of laughter and quickly stifled it.

"I'm not staying if you're going to laugh at me." She rummaged in her bag for her wallet.

"I'm sorry." He laid a hand on her shoulder. "Please stay. I'd love to go to dinner with you next Monday."

"Great." Hope looked him over. "You've been working in the kitchen. I thought you only provided the star power when guests came into the restaurant."

Roland showed up with Lucien's coffee. "Here you go, chef. Can I get you anything else? Hope, do you want a refill?"

Lucien was relieved at the interruption. He'd rather crawl naked over broken glass than admit to Hope Monahan that his kitchen was currently a disaster. "Yes, please top up Ms. Monahan's glass. I'm fine right now, *merci*."

"Thank you," Hope said to Roland.

"Enjoy." Roland moved off to serve another couple at the bar.

Lucien raised his coffee cup in a toast. "*À votre santé.*"

Hope raised her glass. "*Slainté.*"

He raised his eyebrows. "Gaelic?"

"Yes." She sipped her wine. "This is a very fine Riesling."

"I suppose with a name like Monahan it makes sense. The Gaelic, I mean."

"My husband was a Monahan. But you're not too far off the mark. My maiden name was Murphy. I'd spend summers with my grandmother in Ireland when I was in high school."

"Really."

"Really. It was great, because Granny lived on a

109

farm and that's where I got my passion for cooking. Speaking of which, you were working the line tonight. Isn't that unusual for you?"

"I was showing the kitchen some new recipes." He crossed his fingers behind his back.

"Ooooh," Hope said. "Are they for the contest?"

"Wouldn't you like to know."

"I would." She flashed him a saucy grin.

"Too bad." He reached out a finger and tapped the tip of her nose.

"A girl can try." She took a sip of her wine. "Where does this come from?"

"A little winery on the Mosel river in Germany. They sell exclusively to me."

Hope raised her eyebrows. "Wow. It's very good. But I wonder? Better than a Riesling from the Mosel?"

"Is this a trick question? Mosel Rieslings are the best.

"Just wanted to make sure."

"Of course. I wouldn't serve anything but the best." He popped a handful of nuts into his mouth.

She swirled the wine in her glass. "So, do you want to go to the Pilgrim on Monday?"

He swallowed, then drank some of his coffee. A flash of victory ran through him, though he didn't know whether it was due to pleasure or victory. "I would love to go with you."

Hope smiled. "Great. It's a date, then." She watched him with those big green eyes of hers. "Don't you need to get back to the kitchen?"

Probably. "But not before I do this." He slid off the bar stool and framed her face with his hands. She gave a little *eep* of surprise just before he touched his lips to hers. She tasted sweeter than the wine she'd been drinking. She opened, softened in his hands and he used his tongue to explore every exquisite, sensitive place in her mouth.

Slowly, with great reluctance, he broke the kiss and laid his forehead against hers. It cheered him to see that Hope was breathing as heavily as he was.

"Lucien!"

He lifted his head and looked at Angelique. Her timing sucked. "*Oui?*"

She stood with her arms crossed in front of her. "They need you in the kitchen."

Why hadn't he killed her when she was a baby? "I'll be right there."

"I should go, anyway." Hope hopped off her bar stool and pulled out her wallet. "How much for the wine?"

He reached out and touched her hair. "It's on the house."

"Thank you, then." She tucked her wallet back into her bag. "See you on Monday."

"It's a date."

She gave him a sweet, angelic smile and left.

Speaking of angelic, he turned his attention to his sister. She stood smirking at him.

"This better be an emergency," he growled.

Angelique stood her ground. "I'm sure it is."

He glared at her as he moved past her to the kitchen. If there wasn't an emergency, heads would roll.

****

After Shane finished cleaning behind the line, he hopped over to the bar for his shift drink. Before he could sit down, his phone buzzed. He smiled when Angelique's face appeared on the screen. "Hey, babe."

"Guess where your boss was tonight."

"Where?" he asked, though he was afraid he already knew the answer.

"Why, right here, shoog. Sitting at our bar, asking my big brother out."

"What the—" He frowned.

"He must have said *oui* because when I came to take him back to the kitchen, they were playing what looked like an epic game of tonsil hockey."

"Tonsil hockey?"

"They were kissing like it was their job."

He shook his head. He didn't like that, didn't like it at all. "Is Hope still there?"

"*Non*, she left. I think this is a very good thing for us."

"How would that work?"

"She'll distract him, keep him too busy to pay too close attention to me."

"Ah." More time with Angelique without looking over his shoulder for Lucien Durand carrying a shotgun was made of good.

But, it might not be a good thing for Hope. "He'd better not break her heart."

"He never does. All his ladies stay friends with him after it's over."

"Hope is different."

"Stop worrying. You're acting like an old lady."

"I'm sorry if I care about my friend." Smoke started coming out his ears.

"Oh, please. Everyone is so careful of St. Hope's feelings. She's a big girl. She looked more than willing to kiss my brother."

"Your brother has a reputation of being an international playboy."

"Yeah, and he eats pretty little girls for lunch."

"Hope's had a rough few years. Really rough years." Shane ground his teeth together.

"You sound like you're in love with her yourself." Angelique's voice held a twinge of jealousy

He hoped. "She's a good friend, that's all."

"You've made that clear as glass."

"What do you want me to say?"

"Whatever you want to say."

Yeah, right. Shane knew that tone of voice. You didn't win an argument with a woman when she sounded like that. "I don't want to argue with you."

"Then don't. It will all work out, you'll see. Oops! Here comes Lucien. I'll call you later." She clicked off and his screen went black.

He stared at his phone for a second. He guessed he needed to make a choice between protecting Hope and keeping Angelique happy.

There was no choice. He'd do both.

Shane knew Hope thought she knew what she was doing, but he wasn't so sure. One thing she would not like was him interfering.

So he just had to find a way to keep tabs on her without her noticing.

Sounded like a plan.

Chapter Fourteen

"I feel pretty, oh so pretty—"

"Since when are you a musical theater fan?" Shane
scowled at Hope as she warbled over a marzipan filling
for her merlot poached pears.

"I feel pretty and witty and bright!" She waltzed
over to him, grabbed his hands and tried to get him to
dance with her. "And I pity any girl who isn't me
tonight. Deedle la ti deedle ay!"

She did not suceed. "Don't be such a grouch,
Shane."

He pulled his hands back and crossed his arms over
his chest. "You can't sing."

"You're telling me, a Murphy, that I can't sing?"
She tsk-tsked. "All Murphys can sing."

"Except you. You couldn't carry a tune in a
bucket." His eyes narrowed. "There's a reason Cormac
never let you warble along with his recordings."

She waited for the inevitable spear of grief to slice
her at the mention of her dead husband, but it didn't
come. Instead a slice of a humorous memory. He'd
teased her endlessly about her tin ear. "Everyone's a
critic."

"So what has you singing *West Side Story*?" He
attacked the carrot with a peeler.

She wondered what bug had wandered up his butt.
"I'm just feeling good today."

Shane grunted and grabbed another carrot.

"Seriously. What's going on?" Shane was never in a bad mood. "Are you having woman problems."

He stopped mutilating the carrot. "No. Why does my mood have to be caused by a woman?"

Whoa! "Sorry. I'm not used to you being in a bad mood is all."

He stood as still as a statue. "I guess you don't know everything about me."

"I guess I don't." Whatever. No one was going to rain on her parade today.

Especially not Shane. She'd listened to him a million times as he maneuvered his way through all the available women in town.

"If the reason for your good mood is Lucien Durand, you can take it to the bank that he's playing you, so he can get you off your game for Saturday's elimination round in the competition."

That thought did niggle around in the back of her brain. "I can separate the two. I don't trust him as far as the competition goes." And maybe she didn't trust him on a personal level either.

"Just be careful. I'm going to finish prepping this soup." He turned his back to her.

"Whatever." Dang. Hope went back to her prep work. Let him sulk. She wouldn't let him spoil her good mood.

The Pilgrim Steak and Rib House was a traditional place. It would be fun to dress up, do all that girl stuff you did to get ready for a date.

If she bought a new dress for the occasion that was okay. She really didn't have anything that was in style now. And she didn't have anything sexy, anything that screamed man-bait. Time to rectify that.

She finished the marzipan mix and started filling the pears. She'd make cookies to go along with them, delicate, lacy tuiles that snapped when you bit into them. Place them on top of a *crème Anglais.*

She glanced back at Shane who was done murdering carrots and had started attacking celery, chopping it very fine. She hoped he got over this little snit soon.

****

The next Monday Lucien pulled his car into a space behind Hope's, got out and bounded up the staircase that led to her apartment. Not that he wasn't jazzed about going to the Pilgrim. No. He felt something he hadn't felt in a long time.

He felt happy. Happy to see Hope. He didn't question it, he just ran with it.

Were his palms sweating? He wiped them one at a time on his slacks then hid the blush-colored rose behind his back.

After taking a deep breath, he knocked on her door.

"Hello." Hope smiled. "Why don't you come in for a minute?"

He pulled out the rose. "This is for you. Though it's not nearly as lovely as you."

Which was true. She looked amazing in a dark green turtleneck dress which clung to every curve and ended up well above her knee. Mile-high stiletto heels in a matching green made her legs look very long indeed. She wore no jewelry except for a watch and emerald earrings that brought out the vivid green of her eyes.

She took the flower from him. "Oh, how pretty!

Please come in while I put this in water," Hope crooned.

He stepped in and closed the door. "The color reminded me of your skin, creamy and tinged with pink." Where had that come from? "You look beautiful tonight."

She dipped into a little curtsey. "Thank you, sir. Make yourself at home and I'll be right back."

He admired the way her *derrière* moved as she left the room.

Her home looked feminine and cozy. Lace curtains covered the windows. Pastel-hued floral fabrics in cream, green, light pink, and what he supposed was rose covered her furniture. The walls were painted in a darker, soothing rose. Bowls of dried flower petals and candles stuck in crystal candlesticks competed for space on a couple of small tables and some bookshelves. Mingling scents of cinnamon and vanilla in the air told him she'd obviously baked that day.

His mouth watered.

"This is so pretty!" Hope brought the rose in a fragile cracked glass vase. "It's been so long since anyone has given me a flower." She lifted the bloom to her nose and took a sniff, then put it down onto a doily-covered end table. "I love the scent of roses."

"Someone should bring you flowers every day." He cleared his throat. "They obviously belong in here."

"I guess the décor is a little overkill with the roses. What can I say? I like flowers." She grinned. "After being one of the guys all day it's nice to take refuge in a totally feminine space."

"I can understand that." He liked it.

And, he liked the challenge of making her feel

totally feminine, totally a desirable woman. "We should go. Do you have a jacket? It's pretty chilly out."

She wrinkled her nose at him. "Not for a New Englander, Southern boy." She grabbed a silky wrap off a chair it'd been draped on and held it up for him to see. "All set."

Lucien took it from her and held it out for her to slip it on. Her hair also smelled like vanilla along with some other exotic, intoxicating spice. After he helped her with her shawl, he took a step back before he gave into the temptation to run his fingers through her hair and mess it all up. "Now you're all set. *Allons.*"

He hoped he survived the night.

****

The Pilgrim Steak and Rib House had the honor of being the oldest restaurant in Addington. It stood in the heart of the town, on Main Street tucked next to an antique shop on one side and a book store on the other. It's clapboard shingle walls were broken up by French windows fronted by flower boxes filled with cheery russet and bright yellow mums. Since the Pilgrim didn't have a parking lot, they had to cruise around the block to find a spot.

Hope studied Lucien as he slipped the car into a space. Her heart had started beating a little faster the moment she'd opened her door.

His presence in her dollhouse of an apartment had loomed large, dark, and potent. Masculine.

Thrilling.

She'd lapped up the comments about her appearance like a starving kitten in front of a bowl of fresh cream. For the first time in years she felt pretty. Desirable. Sexy.

Which was what she had been going for when she dressed. Nice to know she could still bring it. Lucien was already out of the car and opening her door. He offered her his hand to help her out of the low-slung black Porsche Carrera Turbo, and she took it eagerly. The car may be fast and new, but the old-fashioned romantic gesture really grabbed her heart. "Thank you," she murmured as he helped her out.

"*De rien.*" He rubbed his thumb over her knuckles.

She felt her face flush, and she knew he'd see it, given the pale Murphy skin she'd inherited from her Irish ancestors. "That's sweet of you to say."

He steered her down the sidewalk toward the Pilgrim. "It's nothing more than the truth."

The evening air held the crisp scents of fall, of wood fires and chill air. The sky was cloudless and the stars started to pop out, blink, and shine along with a bright sliver of moon. "It's a lovely night."

He looked at her and smiled. "Absolutely gorgeous."

Oh. My. He had no business looking at her like that. Like he wanted to gobble her up in one big bite.

"Are you warm enough?" Lucien slipped his hand under her elbow.

Oh, yeah. "Absolutely."

He shifted his arm so that he was no longer cradling her elbow, but her arm was entwined with his. His body exuded heat. He smelled good, of soap and cloves.

She wanted to nibble on him. All over.

Ahem.

Stepping into the Pilgrim Steak and Rib House brought you back a few generations. The décor, colonial with heavy maple furniture upholstered in a deep maroon Naugahyde and a pot-bellied stove off to one corner of the room, made the dining room resemble a living room from the seventies.

All it missed was a braided rug.

Alex Smith, one of the owners, greeted them at the reservations desk. Her gaze zeroed in on Lucien. "Chef Durand, how wonderful to see you here. Welcome to the Pilgrim."

Exuberant and friendly, Hope'd always admired Alex's easy way with people. She always projected such positive energy. Granted, too long in her company with all that energy could give you a headache. But she had a good heart.

"And Hope, so good to see you." Alex gave her an air kiss on each cheek. "Are you two together?"

"Yes." Lucien straightened out his coat sleeves. "A table for two."

Alex's eyes sparkled with interest. She picked up two menus and the wine list then scanned the room. "Right this way."

Lucien put his hand to the small of Hope's back and led her along behind Alex. It sizzled where he touched. "There you go!" Alex smiled. "Betty will be over shortly."

Lucien pulled one of the chairs out for Hope and helped her into her seat. She looked up at him as she sat. "Thank you."

"*De rien.*" He slipped into his own seat and cracked open the menu. "So what's good here?"

Hope picked up her own menu. "They're famous for the baby back ribs. Alex does a special spice rub and sauce. It's pretty good."

Lucien sniffed. "I'll be the judge of that. What else?"

"They say the twice baked potatoes are made from an old family recipe." She shrugged. "People like them."

"But you don't."

"I didn't say that."

He chuckled. "It's written all over your face."

"You got me." She laughed.

"Hmmmmmm." He reached across the table to touch her hand. "I wonder. Do I have you?"

Lord have mercy. "We'll see." She smiled. "If you behave yourself."

"What if I don't? I can tell you, *chére*, you'll have a lot more fun if I misbehave."

Hope could very well imagine that, yes indeedy do. "You sure know how to make a girl's head spin."

"I do my best." He winked at her.

Winked!

She grinned and winked back at him.

He laughed out loud. "Oh, *chére*, you and me, we're going to pass a good time for sure."

****

Lucien smiled as Hope listened to Betty, their server, as she rattled off the night's specials. He needed to stay on his toes if he meant to keep her distracted enough to keep her off her game when the first round of the contest began.

No one else would be that much fun to defeat.

Certainly not the Pilgrim Steak and Rib House.

The menu hadn't been updated since the 1950s. The décor wasn't something to write home about. But it had the most lethal thing on his checklist for a good restaurant, the one thing that made it a travesty.

It had a salad bar.

A. Salad. Bar.

With iceberg lettuce on it.

Given the option between soup or salad bar, he took the soup. He felt fairly safe since there was little to do that would ruin it. He hoped he didn't regret his choice.

He noticed Hope also ordered the soup. "You didn't opt for the salad bar."

She wrinkled her nose. "I don't know where that produce came from. It's certainly not local."

Of course. "I should have known." He toasted her with his water glass.

She picked up her glass and grinned. "I guess I'm pretty predictable."

"Not at all, except for food. Your opinions on that are well known."

"I can pull out a surprise or two when the need arises." She sipped her water.

"I'm intrigued," he said. "Might the need arise on the competition cook-off?"

"Maybe I might. You'll have to find out when everybody else does."

"I can keep a secret."

"I don't trust you as far as I can throw you. You're cut-throat when it comes to beating the competition."

"I do like to win."

Hope snorted. "You like to demolish."

He barked out a laugh. *"C'est vrai."* He pointed a finger at her. "But you should admit that you like to demolish too."

"Not everybody. Just you."

"I should be flattered, I suppose." The mischievous sparkle in her eyes enchanted him.

Hell, the whole package that was Hope Monahan enchanted him.

Which was the reason he had to be vigilant and not let her distract him.

Didn't mean he couldn't distract her and have fun doing it. "Are you prepared for the first round of the contest?"

She opened her napkin and put it on her lap. "Absolutely! Get ready to bow down before me, because I will beat you."

He chuckled. "I think not. You have yet to see the master at work."

"Hmmmmm." Hope narrowed her eyes. "Most likely because I don't check myself out in a mirror when I cook."

She looked amazing in the dim light of the dining room. The mischievous sparkle in her eyes, the saucy toss of her head, and the challenging smile on her face did more to enchant him than all the seductive poses of every model he'd ever dated. "We should have a contest to see who's the undeniable master in the kitchen."

She scrunched her face. "Aren't we already competing against each other?"

"This would be a *private* competition." The more he thought about it, the better he liked it.

Her eyes filled with suspicion. "Private? What do you mean by private?"

"A competition just between you and me." He reached for her hand across the table and rubbed his thumb, light as a whisper over her knuckles. He smiled when she jolted under his touch. "By ourselves."

"By ourselves?"

"No one else around. Just the two of us."

Angie showed up with their chowders and a basket of bread. "Here you go."

Not good. Their drinks hadn't even come yet. "And our wine?"

Angie blinked. "I'm sorry. I'll get it right now." She rushed away.

He cleared his throat. Back to distracting. "Where were we? *Oui.* A little competition between the two of us."

"Okay," Hope said. "I'll bite. What do you want to cook? What are the stakes?"

"Let's see. Our best, our favorite meals." He leaned back in his chair and let his imagination run wild. "Our most seductive meals."

She laughed. "Really." Could she say it with more sarcasm?

"What? You're afraid of me seducing you?"

"Puh-leeze." She spooned up some of the creamy chowder. "I can reduce you to a mound of quivering jelly."

He watched her put the spoon between her soft lips. His body reacted. Maybe she could bring him to heel.

That might be fun. No might. That would be fun.

Memorable, even.

What was he thinking? Nobody could bring him to heel. "You could try."

Her tongue snaked out of her mouth and licked those sweet lips. "I certainly could. How would we know who wins? What are the rules?"

"When it comes to romance there aren't any rules." He grinned at her. "Haven't you heard? All's fair in love and war, *chère*."

She raised her eyebrows. "That's what they say. Seriously..." She cocked her head to the right. "How are we going to do this?" She motioned to his bowl. "You should try that while it's still hot."

He picked up his spoon and stirred the chowder. Good clam to potato ratio. Creamy consistency without being like wallpaper paste. He sniffed it before he put it into his mouth.

Good balance of flavors. So far, so good.

And why the hell was he going on about soup when he had a beautiful woman to seduce? How had he let her distract him? That couldn't happen again.

"So, how is it?" Hope asked.

"Adequate." He leaned back in his chair. Get back to the point. "Here's what I propose for this wager between us. We each prepare a romantic dinner for two at our homes—no restaurant kitchen advantages. Each course can earn so many points. The one with the most points, wins."

"That won't work. We're each going to give our own meals full points." She leaned her forearms against the tacky table cloth. "Maybe a bet, instead of a contest."

"You're right. It needs to be more personal." He flashed her his patented lady-killer grin. "More intimate."

"Intimate?" She licked her lips. "Okay, I'll bite."

He reached for her hand again. "I most certainly hope you will."

"Will what?"

"Bite."

She chuckleds and grabbed her hand back. "I guess that's for me to know and for you to find out."

"Don't worry, I will." The sound of her endearingly musical laugh wove itself around his heart and entranced him. "So, here is how I think it should go."

She slapped her hand against her chest. "Be still my heart. I'm not sure I'm ready to hear this."

"Believe me, you're plenty ready. Here's what we're going to do." Lucien knew exactly how to make a bet like this work to his advantage. "I cook you a meal, you cook me a meal, we let things take their course and see how, uh—"

"Turned on?" she offered, her face the picture of innocence.

He cleared his throat. "That's one way to put it. *Oui*. No matter who cooks, we should both be able to get some satisfaction."

She snorted. "I'm not sleeping with you."

"You say that now. Do you really think you can resist me?"

"Oh, please, get over yourself." She spooned up some chowder. "Humility is a very attractive character trait." She sipped soup and swallowed. "Very sexy."

Yes, Hope was. Very sexy. Even with a soup spoon full of chowder in her mouth. Especially when that pink tongue of hers zipped out to catch the last lingering taste.

This aphrodisiac dinner challenge was a stroke of brilliance, genius, *sans doute*.

Win-win all around. He had no doubt he'd have her eating out of his hand, so to speak.

To that end. "I've always found humility overrated."

"You would. So listen," she said, "here is how I think we should make this work, if we're going to do it."

"Believe me, we're going to do it."

"Hush. Don't interrupt. Next Monday, I make dinner. Monday after that, you make dinner. Everything is on the table, and I don't mean just food—ambiance, appearance, music, all that."

"How do we know who wins?" After the initial shock of Hope shushing him, Lucien sat back and let her take the lead.

"First, we're honest about our reactions and opinions, I guess you'd say our feelings. Then we let the evening proceed."

"Okay, let me see if I got this." He held up one finger. "We each make our most romantic menus." He held up a second finger. "We pull out all the stops to set the *mood*." He waggled his eyebrows up and down on the word *mood*, then held up a third finger. "We let nature take its course."

She laughed. "Was that a joke? Because I'm not sleeping with you. That is totally off the table. If you're good with that, let's go ahead next Monday. I'll start."

He wasn't, but he thought he could change her mind. "Works for me."

Their server appeared at their table bearing a bottle of wine. "I'm sorry it took so long." She presented the bottle to Lucien. "Shall I open it for you?"

Lucien nodded. "Yes, please." He caught Hope's gaze. "I think we might have something to celebrate."

Chapter Fifteen

"So, was the Pilgrim the last place you needed to check out?" Hope asked as they walked from the restaurant to Lucien's car.

"No. I still need to eat at Costa's Cozy Cottage. I've never been able to find the time when they're open."

"Isadora keeps odd hours." Hope thought Isadora was just plain odd, period. "If you want to catch a dinner service, you need to get there on Thursday, Friday, and Saturday."

"That makes no sense." Lucien shook his head.

"I think it's a staffing thing. Usually Isadora and her sister run the place and dinner all the time is beyond what they can pull off without hiring an extra waitress. Isadora's granddaughter comes in from Boston to help on the three days they do serve dinner."

"How does she stay in business?"

"You won't find any better Portuguese food outside of New Bedford, Fall River, and Provincetown."

"I see. I will definitely have to get there. Too bad there is no dinner service on Mondays. I'll have to go alone."

"I'm sure you'll survive."

They'd reached his car and he opened her door. "*Madame*, your chariot awaits."

She slipped into the car. "Thank you."

He smiled as he shut the door. It was only a matter of seconds before he slid into the driver's seat. She watched him as he put the key in the ignition. He turned and faced her. "I've been thinking about doing this all night." Leaning in, he lightly placed his palm under her chin and kissed her.

Her eyelids fluttered down. She trembled underneath his gentle mouth. She couldn't breathe because he literally stole her breath away. He broke that whisper of a kiss and pulled away in slow motion. Her eyes blinked open but it took a moment until her gaze focused.

Lucien watched her, his eyes darker than usual. They beckoned her to fall into them, to drown in them. It would be so easy to lose herself, to dive into his gaze and never surface ever again.

But she was made of stronger stuff. Hope dragged her wits about her and slapped a grin on her face. She needed to gain the upper hand here, or else she'd always be in the passenger seat, so to speak. "That all you got?"

His eyebrows lifted. "*Chére*, I can make you beg if I want to."

"What's stopping you?"

"I'm thinking the front seats of my car are too small and a little too public right now, but when the time and the place are right, you'll see all I've got."

She bet he'd got a lot. "You can try."

He laughed and turned the key. The engine roared to life. "Buckle up, sugar. It's going to be a bumpy ride."

She grabbed her seat belt as he stepped on the gas.

It was going to be a bumpy ride.

Of that, she had no doubt.

****

Lucien pulled the Porsche into a spot next to Hope's Prius. He mentally shook his head. A Prius. So wrong on so many levels.

Hope was unsnapping her seat belt; she gave him a saucy little smile. "Thank you for a lovely evening."

What? Lucien had other plans for Hope tonight. Their date was over when he said it was, dammit. He put his hand over hers. "You just wait right there." Bounding out of the car, he rounded to her door and opened it for her.

She took his hand and let him help her out of the car. Then, standing on tiptoe, she pressed a chaste kiss on his cheek. "Thank you, again."

Dieu. Did she really think he was letting her go with only that stingy peck on the cheek. She'd better think again.

He pulled her close and went in for what could definitely be called a real kiss. Though sorely tempted to crush his mouth on hers, he held himself back and just rubbed his lips on hers, waiting to be invited in to take what he wanted. He didn't have long to wait.

Her arms came up and twined around his neck. She opened for him like a rose in the summer sun. She hummed back in her throat. He took it as a sign she wanted more, so he deepened the kiss, using his tongue, lips, and teeth to make her crazy.

Hell, he was making himself crazy at the same time.

He broke the kiss and dragged in a breath, then laid his forehead against hers. Hope's breathing was ragged and noisy. Good.

"Invite me in for coffee." Time to take this to the next level.

"Coffee?"

"*Oui.* Invite me in."

She took a step backward, away from him. "I don't think that would be a good idea."

"Why not?" What was she thinking? Of course it was a good idea.

"We've got this little bet going, remember?" She shook her head. "We don't want to put the cart before the horse."

Of course they should put the cart before the horse. Why make them both suffer? "I think we're ready now," he said.

"Well, I'm not so sure. Let's do these two dinners and see how things go."

"You're really going to make us wait."

"If we get together now, it spoils the whole anticipation thing."

"Anticipation is overrated. I'm not good at it, I don't like it."

She had the gall to laugh. "Now, don't sulk. I think we'll get there soon enough, if we play our cards right."

He *couldn't* get there soon enough. He wanted now.

"Remember, the bet was your idea." Her eyes sparkled. "I'm going up now. Thank you again for the lovely evening. I had a great time." She started up the steps leading to her door.

"Wait," he said. "I'll walk you up."

"You don't need to."

"I want to." He motioned to the stairs. "After you."

If she went first, he could at least enjoy the sight of her *jolie derrière* as she climbed. She had such a sweet ass. He couldn't wait to see it in the flesh.

Hopefully that would happen soon. Maybe within the next hour.

A soft light from an outside lamp illuminated the way to her porch. They climbed the rest of the way in silence. When they got to her landing he demanded her keys.

"I can open my own door, Lucien."

"I'm sure you can." He held out his hand. "Give me your keys."

She gusted a heavy sigh as she dropped them into his hand. "*Merci.*" A second later he pulled open the door. "Are you sure you don't want any coffee? Dessert?"

She cocked her head to the side. "Are you begging?"

Had to give her that one. He shook his head. "I never beg."

She laughed. "Good night."

He stepped into her space and framed her face with his hands. "One more for the road," he said, right before he stole a light kiss, then another one, then one more. "Good night." He started down the steps.

"Hey, Lucien."

He turned to look at her. Had she changed her mind? "*Oui?*"

"You've still got my keys. I kind of need them."

Pooyah-ee! He was *fou*. "Here. Catch." He tossed them.

"Got 'em. Good night." She turned on an inside light, then closed the door.

He descended the stairs wondering why he'd thought that bet was a good idea.

****

"Would it really be so bad for your brother to know about us?" Shane pushed himself against the headboard of his bed. The amazing, incredible, beautiful, totally naked Angelique sat up. The sheet covering her perfect breasts dropped to her waist.

He lost all power of speech at the picture she made. He always did. Maybe someday that would change.

Probably not.

"Lucien is not so easy to manage. It just will take some time." She didn't look at Shane as she said this.

It was starting to get a little under his skin. "How much more time?" Shane really wanted to claim her as *his* for the rest of the world to see.

Angelique Durand was a force of nature. He'd adored her from the first time he'd seen her. He didn't see that changing anytime soon. "How much time?"

Her mouth turned down into a pout and she pulled the sheet up over her breasts. "I don't know. He's got this idea I can't go to school and date at the same time." She raked her hand through her dark hair. "I don't want to go to school. It's just a waste of time. It's not like I'm ever going to be this big smarty pants, *ennuyant* person who knows all the answers to the questions no fun person is asking. I want to be a model."

He'd heard this before. The thought of her leaving Addington and going all over the world and getting her picture taken while she was half-naked sent him into a panic. "Why can't you do both? Finish your degree then go do the model thing."

"Because I'm not getting any younger." She sighed

133

impatiently. "One of Lucien's lady friends, Cäcilia, says she can get her agency to represent me, but I'm almost too old now."

Of course Lucien would date the supermodel Cäcilia. Shane dismissed the idea of rolling his eyes as too girly. "That's crazy. You're only twenty-one. You've got plenty of time before you're too old."

"Not for modeling." She shook her head. "It has to be now. Cäcilia said so, and she should know."

"So you'd chuck school, just like that?" He snapped his fingers.

"I can go to school after I'm done modeling. Maybe by then I'll know what I want to study."

Again, a familiar refrain, as she said it often. Like, in nearly every conversation they had. So he said what he always did. "Something will hit you, grab your interest."

She laughed and pressed herself against him. Snaking her hand down his body, she stroked him. "Maybe I'll grab this. I think it's *très intéressant*."

His breath caught in his throat, and his eyes crossed. Fifteen minutes ago he would have sworn he needed a little more time to recover and, uh, rise to the occasion, but Angelique had magic hands and fingers.

An hour and a half later they were getting dressed and ready for Shane to take her to her car, which was parked in the lot in front of Barrett U's library. If he felt uneasy, the buzz in the aftermath of fantastic sex masked it and pushed it away.

So he took her to her car. "Text me when you get home, okay?"

The drive from there back to his apartment was a little lonely. He opened the door and realized how cold and empty it felt without Angelique. He went to the kitchen and got himself a beer. He sat at the kitchen table in the dark, not drinking it, waiting for a text to keep him company.

Chapter Sixteen

"So many choices, so little time," Hope muttered as she jotted some notes and listed ingredients for Monday night's dinner challenge with Lucien. Many of the tried and trusty aphrodisiac foods were out of season or, even worse, predictable.

She'd settled on the entrée, honeyed duck breast with dried cherries, and the dessert, flower petals in white chocolate. She loved the romantic flair of *Oeufs à la Neige Aux Roses*, but her roses were nearly done and she didn't want to use flowers from the florist. The appetizer course stymied her. She could go for grilled scallops with basil and lavender essence, or roasted ginger and butternut squash soup.

Oysters were obvious. God forbid she serve something obvious to Lucien.

Thankfully, she'd had the foresight to dry a variety of edible flowers and cherries. Although, it wasn't foresight. She did it every year.

Hope glanced at her list of sexy foods. Honey, check. Flower petals, check. Basil and rosemary she could put in risotto for the starch. Still, she needed an appetizer and a first course.

Smoked salmon mousse with the usual accoutrements would work for the appetizer.

So, it came down to ginger in the soup or the seafood with basil and lavender for the first course. She wasn't crazy about the soup idea.

Grilled scallops with basil and lavender essence it was.

She went to her refrigerator and pulled out a bottle of her special supply of New York state Rieslings. A Hosmer Riesling, to be exact. She extracted the cork, which made a very satisfying pop, then inhaled the scent. Enjoying the sound and the bouquet, she poured the wine into a glass.

She wished, not for the first time, that you could get shipments of New York wines in Massachusetts. For now she had to content herself with wine trips to the Finger Lakes.

This wasn't a bad thing. Not really. Yeah, she had to close the restaurant for a week once a year, but the wine made it all worth it.

The question of the hour was, should she stay subtle or go for some traditionally romantic notes. She wanted to stick to her guns, to be a purist. She had a point to prove to Lucien, after all.

All you needed were fresh, seasonal ingredients. She moved from her kitchen to her desk, dropped her butt into her office chair and sighed.

She asked herself, not for the first time, why she'd gotten herself into this bet. Sure, she could chalk it up to her competitive nature and her desire to prove herself the better chef.

Okay, yeah. She wanted to wine and dine Lucien.

No...more. She wanted him to want her. Did she believe in aphrodisiacs? Absolutely. Food could accomplish anything. Carefully thought out and perfectly executed food could rule heaven and earth.

And stubborn, egotistical chefs who thought they

knew it all. That they were gods.

Lucien Durand topped that list.

She admired him for that. Truth to tell, she admired him a lot. She hadn't expected to. But now that she knew the man, she liked him.

He would think "like" wasn't a passionate enough word. He was all about passion.

Did she have the passion to match him? She liked comfortable. Home. Roots.

He was a citizen of the world, at home anywhere he put those itchy feet of his. Frequent and sudden travel made up a big part of his life. Still, that didn't mean she didn't have passion. She had tons of passions. Skads of passion.

She'd been saving it all up. It could explode out of her any minute now.

She conked her head on her desk. Why had she put the stupid condition of no sleeping together as part of the bet?

Crazy. All that pent-up passion made her insane.

She needed to talk to her friends. She pulled out her phone and got to work rallying the troops.

****

"You want me to go to dinner with you on Thursday?" Angelique looked at Lucien as if he had just grown another head.

"*Oui.*" Lucien sat behind his desk in his office at L'Enfer.

"*Pourquoi?*"Angelique shoved her hands into the pockets of her magenta sweater.

"Why? Can't I want to have dinner with my little sister? It's time we caught up on what's going on with you."

"Are you sick or something? Like only having a couple of months left to live?"

He sat back in his chair. "I'm just a guy who loves his little sister and wants to know how her school career is going." He watched Angelique carefully. "After all, I'm paying for that school career."

Angelique rolled her eyes. "My school career is going great. You have nothing to worry about."

"I'm interested in what you're studying."

"Then *you* should take the classes," Angelique sputtered. She squinted at him. "Besides, I don't think for one minute you want to go to dinner with me. I'm just your back-up because Hope Monahan won't go on a Thursday."

Okay, she had a point, not that he'd let her know. It didn't change the bottom line. He needed to spend time with Angelique. "I need to check in with you, and I need to check out Costa's Cozy Cottage." He smiled. "I can't trust just anyone to have a knowledgable palate. You're on a very short list."

"You've never listened to anything I've had to say about food."

"Of course I have." There had to have been one time."

"No, you have not. Remember the time I made red beans and rice? You took one bite, made a face and spit it out." She shook her head. "You only have one opinion that matters to you—yours."

"Look. I want you to come with me." Why were sisters so annoying? "So, you'll come with me."

"Do I have a choice?"Angelique pouted.

"*Non.*"

The pout turned into a lethal glare. "Can I go

now?"

"Sure." He winced when she slammed the door.

Maybe he *should* go alone. Angelique would make every effort to get under his skin and ruin his evening.

He'd bite the bullet. He hadn't been paying very much attention to her lately. She could go off course very quickly.

He turned back to his computer and logged in to check his e-mail. First to pop up was a message from Cäcilia, which he deleted without reading it. He had no patience for her drama anymore. There seemed to be a problem brewing in the New Orleans' L'Enfer that he'd have to go down to fix. Travel wasn't a good idea right now.

Eh, bien. That's what he paid people lots of money, to handle things he didn't have time for.

A year ago he would have hopped on the first plane. Now? He had to ride herd on Angelique.

He had to win a cooking competition and seduce Hope Monahan in the process.

He could win the contest with one hand tied behind his back. He needed both hands for the conquest of Hope Monahan.

He wanted both hands all over Hope Monahan.

Smiling, he picked up a pen and tapped it on his blotter. He always got what he wanted.

Chapter Seventeen

"Whoa, this is trouble waiting to happen." Shane grinned at Gina, Andi, and Ainslie as Hope brought a plate of cookies to the table where her buddies sat.

"You know it." Hope put the plate in the middle of the table, which she'd also set with Granny's Trellis Shamrock Parian tea set. "So scram. I hear some turnips in the kitchen screaming to be chopped."

"Yeah, yeah, I know when I'm not wanted," he said. "Behave, ladies."

Gina stared at Shane as he left the room. "God, he's seriously adorable." She looked at Hope and Ainslie. "I don't know how you two get anything done when you have all that hotness in the kitchen."

"It's a tough job, but someone's got to do it. And I don't get into the kitchen much." Ainslie grabbed a cookie. "So. What's up?" She took a bite. "Mmm. Are these made with the flour from that guy who grows and mills heirloom grains over in Vermont?"

"Yes. I think it gives them a nuttier flavor." Hope sighed. "You're going to think I'm crazy. I kinda, sorta got into a bet with Lucien."

Gina frowned. "That's the Addington's Table thing, right?"

"No. A different bet. A private bet."

Andi leaned forward to get her own cookie. "A private bet? Sounds interesting."

"Yes," Gina said. "We must have details."

"You know we went to the Pilgrim last Monday, right?"

They nodded.

"Well, one thing led to another and we started talking about aphrodisiac dinners and who could make the more seductive meal."

"Oh, ho!" Gina patted the top of her incredibly huge pregnant belly. "And what's the prize for that bet?"

Hope felt her face flush warm. "Not what you think."

"And what do I think?"

"I made a hard and fast rule. No sex."

There was a long beat of silence. "Then what was the point of the bet?" Andi wanted to know.

"I'm not really sure." Hope felt embarrassed to admit that. She shrugged. "I guess to prove who can put on the best romantic dinner."

Andi lifted her eyebrows. "You say romantic. What does he say?"

Gina swallowed a chunk of cookie. "I doubt he's calling it romantic."

"Yeah, I figure. I'm sticking to my guns, though."

"What are you making?" Ainslie asked. "Can we get the recipes if they work?"

"Sure."

"Sounds like an excuse to spend time together in a more…ahem, intimate fashion," Andi pointed out. "Which is great, if that's what you want."

"I think the no-sex rule is awesome," Ainslie said. "Keeps the mystery going."

Gina nodded. "Like how Christmas Eve is so much

more fun than Christmas Day. All that anticipation."

"It's that whole anticipation thing that's killing me." Hope moaned.

"Nah." Gina waved Hope's whine away. "It'll bring him to his knees, 'cause you know he's gonna be wanting you bad."

"Here's one of the most eligible bachelors in the world, and you'll have him on his knees in front of you, pleading for a chance with you." Andi toasted Hope with her cup of tea.

"You think?"

"On. His. Knees." Andi put down the cup and adjusted the pearls around her neck..

"Mmm hmm," Gina agreed.

"That's easy for you all to say. You've all had sex in the last ten years." Hope scowled. "Me, not so much."

"You made the no-sex rule," Andi said. "You can break it."

Ainslie shook her head. "She can but she shouldn't. He's used to things coming easy for him. Believe me, I know that kind of man." Ainslie's ex-husband was in jail for all sorts of white collar crimes. "Trust me on this. He does not think he can lose."

"I already figured that out about him." Hope took a big crunchy bite of cookie.

"I think you're worrying too much about it," Ainslie said. "You know it's going to happen at some point." She pointed at her. "When you want it to."

"And when it does happen, don't forget we want all the details," Gina added.

****

Details were important, Hope mused as she set out

apricot-colored candles. Orange was the color of the second chakra, the one that ruled over sexuality and desire. She had also put on her amber earrings and necklace, amber also linked to the second chakra.

Did chakras work? She believed in them absolutely. No question, no hesitation. She'd gone on a quest to find new meaning in her life after Cormac had died.

She'd studied the beliefs that kept her closest to the rhythms of the earth, air, water, and fire felt the most comforting to her, along with the constant cycle of life and death and rebirth. She'd found a new way to live her life and had jumped into the pond with both feet. Well, she hadn't jumped into all aspects of new life so enthusiastically. She'd only now dipped her toe into the part of the pond having to do with men.

And that was about to change. Big time.

Granny's grandfather clock toned six bells. Lucien would be there soon. She padded to her kitchen to check on the food.

She'd changed her mind about the dessert. There were just enough pale blush- colored blossoms left in her tea rose garden. It hadn't been a big leap to add some pink and green to connect to the fourth chakra— the one that ruled the heart. To her mind, there needed to be affection in seduction.

Not that she would cave on the no-sex clause in their bargain. She wasn't. You could take that to the bank. Still it wouldn't hurt to stir up some good old-fashioned desire.

Nothing wrong with that at all.

She grabbed a pair of scissors and snipped some red, yellow, and orange blossoms off her hanging basket of nasturtiums. The peppery flowers would look pretty against the deep, jewel red of the cherries and make a nice balance to the sweet elements of the honey on the duck.

She lifted the lid off the pan of duck and enjoyed the rich, sweet, thick scent of the honey glaze. Smiling, she replaced the lid, pleased.

She was ready for the dragon to gobble up her tasty dishes. All of them. However, she'd make him wait first.

Heh.

A vigorous knock on her door let her know Lucien had arrived. She took off her apron, then looked down to make sure she didn't have food splattered on her cashnere sweater. She fluffed her hair up a little and smacked her lips.

Perfect.

She made the short trip through her parlor to the door and opened it.

Speaking of wanting to gobble up.

Lucien leaned against the door frame holding a bottle of wine and a clutch of flowers, an explosion of dark pink zinnias, pale painted daisies, magenta roses, and purple freesia. He'd dressed all in black, a cashmere V-neck sweater topped with a tailored blazer. He gave her a slow, ladykiller grin. "Hi."

"Hi," She nearly stuttered. "Why don't you come on in?"

"Why don't I." He crossed the threshhold and held out the flowers. "These are for you."

"They're lovely." She buried her nose in them and inhaled the delicate scents.

"At the risk of being a cliché, not nearly as

145

beautiful as you."

"That's okay. You can be a cliché anytime you want to give me compliments."

He gifted her with a lopsided smile. It made her heart palpitate at rabbit speed. "I also brought some wine. A nice little Bordeaux from this very small vineyard in the *Côte d'Or*. I use them exclusively at my Paris restaurant."

She took it from him. "How thoughtful. Why don't you make yourself at home while I put the flowers in water."

"*Bien*. Why don't you open that bottle and decant it. By the delicious smells coming from your kitchen, I think it will go well with the duck."

How did he know she had made duck? What was she thinking? Of course he knew. It would serve him right if she didn't use it, seeing as he was being so high-handed, but then she caved. She wanted to try the wine. She'd use the Riesling she had chilling for the scallop course.

She arranged the flowers in one of Granny's Waterford vases and turned around to take them out to the parlor and nearly bumped into Lucien.

"I thought I'd watch the master at work."

"Really." Okay. She'd put on a show. "Just let me take these out to the parlor and I'll teach you a few new tricks."

"You can try." He bent his head to give her a sweet brush of a kiss on her lips. "I've picked up an awful lot of tricks over the years."

"I just bet you have." She stepped out of his reach. "I'll be right back. Don't touch anything."

He laughed. "You're so fierce, *pichouette*. Me, I'm

so scared."

"You better be scared. I'm tougher than I look."

"I just bet you are."

She made short work of taking care of the flowers, went back into the kitchen, and caught him looking into the pan of duck. "Hey, no peeking."

"Just a little bit, *chère*. It looks good." He leaned against the counter and crossed his arms over his chest. "What else is on the menu?"

"You'll just have to wait and see." She handed him the bottle of Riesling and a wine opener. "Why don't you open this? There are some glasses on the coffee table in the parlor."

He took the wine and opener. "Don't take too long. I'll miss you too much."

She sighed and pushed him toward the door. "Scram."

He toasted her with the wine bottle. "You sure about that?"

She bit her lip. His gaze latched onto her mouth, bright and avid, as if he wanted to take a bite out of her.

"Just go take care of the wine, and I'll be right out."

"Your wish is my command, *chère*."

"Don't I wish," she shot to his back.

Lucien let loose with a wicked chuckle as he left the room. The seductive sound made tingles race up her spine She shivered, then shook her head. Hope picked up some cheese straws she'd made with her new favorite flour and goat cheese.

Lucien stood at her mantel studying the family pictures. He turned to her and smiled. "Let me help you with that."

"I've got it." She placed the basket filled with the straws on her coffee table. "Thanks for opening the wine."

He picked up the bottle. "Shall I pour?"

"Yes, please." She sat back in her seat and watched him do the honors.

He splashed a small sip into one wine glass. Holding the glass to the light, he swirled the liquid. "Bright. Good color." He brought it to his nose and sniffed deeply. "A hint of citrus."

"Taste it."

He turned that lady-killer grin of his on full blast. "I'm getting there. Some things can't be rushed."

Now, didn't that sound promising? Her heart beat a staccato, heavy rhythm.

Lucien had finally decided to taste the Riesling. He rolled it around in his mouth before he swallowed. "Not bad." He poured wine into both glasses.

Not bad? "It's way better than not bad," she muttered as she took the glass he held out for her.

"You're really cute when you're annoyed." He took a sip of his wine. "*Très jolie.*"

Hope took a deep breath. "I bet you say that to all the girls."

"*Mais non, cheri.* Just the pretty ones."

She felt her face flush and damned, not for the first time, her Irish complexion. She imagined she'd turned the bright red of a lobster just pulled out of boiling water. "Here, try a cheese straw and let me know what you think." She knew he would have no trouble giving his opinion.

He took one of the twisted sticks out of the basket. "No greasy feel, good." Then he sniffed it. "Nice aroma. You used goat cheese, *oui*?"

Hope nodded. "Yes."

Lucien took a bite. "Good crunch, but not dry at all. Beyond the goat cheese, there are some real low notes I can't place."

"I've been playing around with some different flours. For this, I used a stone ground, heirloom grain flour from a farm in Vermont."

"It certainly adds something exotic and complex to the flavor profile." He finished off the cheese straw. "Very nice. And pairs very well with the wine."

Even though she knew he was telling the truth, she still thrilled at the compliment. Lucien Durand didn't hand out compliments often. "Thank you."

"And the ambiance is seasonal without being kitschy."

Hope scrunched her brows. "Seasonal."

"Well, *oui*, with pastel orange tones all around the room. Most people would go for Halloweeny, with pumpkins everywhere." He shuddered. "But you are much more subtle."

Hope smiled. Little did he know of the method behind her madness. "Nary a Jack-o'-lantern in sight."

Lucien toasted her. "You have taste and a good eye for what works. It's very present in your restaurant as well as your home."

Three compliments in the space of a couple of minutes. Must be a record. He had to want something from her.

Oh, jeez. What could that be?

Three guesses and the first two don't count.

"Why don't you wait here while I get the first course ready?"

Lucien grabbed her hands and pulled her out of her chair. "Why don't I go to the kitchen with you and watch you work?"

Hope tilted her head to the right. "Okay."

He rubbed his hands together and grinned like a pirate. "Let's get to it."

Absolutely. "Follow me, grasshopper."

"Grasshopper?"

"You know, like that old show?" She looked up at him. "Kung Fu—David Carradine?"

"We didn't have a TV, *chère*, growing up." Lucien shook his head. "*Grand-mère* couldn't afford one."

"Oh." Lucien looked and acted like he was manor born with that proverbial silver spoon in his mouth. No one would ever guess he grew up poor in the back of beyond. "Looks like we have that in common, being raised by our grandmothers."

He shrugged like it was no big deal. "*Grandmère* was a great lady. Taught me the value of hard work." Lucien smiled. "Encouraged me to go after my dreams. But most of all, taught me the value of family."

"That's why you're so protective of Angelique."

"She is high-spirited." Lucien said. "And stubborn. She's given me more than my share of gray hairs."

On an impulse, she touched his hand. Immediately she felt a zap, a tangible jolt of electric connection that went straight through her body.

Straight up through to her heart.

Looking down to where Hope touched him, he cleared his throat, a sexy baritone rumble. "What are we making?"

She pulled him with her into the kitchen. "Scallops."

He flashed one of those sexy smiles of his. "*La coquille St. Jacques.* And how shall we prepare them?"

She turned on the grill on her range top to heat up. "I'm going to grill them. You are going to do the heavy looking on."

"Yes ma'am." He saluted her. "I like to look."

Her eyebrows nearly flew off her forehead. "Oh really?"

"I like to watch all sorts of things. Like how your eyes mist over after I've kissed you." Lucien pulled her against his body. "I like to kiss you." He bent his head to hers so he could kiss her.

She couldn't breathe, she couldn't think. All she could do was cling to him and kiss him back.

Boy, could that man kiss. He took his time, coaxing her mouth with gentle nips of his teeth and light sweeps of his tongue to open up to him. She melted into it all like butter in the summer sun.

"*Si doux.*" He said in a husky, gravelly voice as he broke the kiss. "So very sweet." Lucien was short of breath, just as she was. "I could eat you all up in one bite, but I think I'll take my time, so I can enjoy every taste and flavor." He kissed her again.

Hope was glad he embraced her so closely because she didn't think her legs could hold her upright.

This time his kiss was more playful, more devilish. Teasing. Wonderful.

When their mouths broke apart, Hope sighed. She felt tingly all over. "We better stop this, or I'll never get the scallops done."

"Would that be a bad thing?" Lucien wasn't letting her go.

She took a step back and held her hands in front of

her. "Yes. I've got a bet to win."

He threw his head back and laughed. "That's my girl, keeping her eye on the prize.

She cocked an eyebrow at him. "Your girl? I'm nobody's girl. It's best you learn that now."

"So fierce, *pichouette*," he chuckled.

"I'm tougher than I look." She moved to the refrigerator and grabbed the scallops and the basil-lavender mixture. She hip-checked the door closed. "What does pee-shou-ette mean?"

He grinned. "I think I won't tell you."

She put the scallops on the cutting board and grabbed a paring knife. "That means I won't like it."

"I never argue with a woman holding a knife."

"Good idea." She turned her attention to the scallops, but she was hyper aware of him there. In fact, he had leaned against the counter and watched her. It was difficult not to be aware of him. He emanated heat.

Heat and sex.

"So the woman holding the knife wants to know what pee-shou-ette means." She turned her attention to the cutting board. She surgically cut a small slit into each of the scallops.

"Perhaps later." He moved next to her and lifted the plastic wrap from the bowl she'd taken out of the fridge. "What is this? I smell basil." He sniffed again. "And something floral."

She slapped his hand away from the bowl. "You have to wait."

"You are a cruel woman, *chère*."

"You better behave, then."

His eyes glittered. "And if I don't? What are you gonna do—spank me?"

Hope snorted. "In your dreams, buddy."

"I've been dreaming about you a lot." He smoothed down a lock of her hair. His voice grew husky, scraping along every nerve ending she had.

Hubba hubba. Was it getting hot in here?

Wake up, girl. Lucien was so full of it. "You don't dream about me."

"Wanna bet, *chère*?" He leaned in and kissed the top of her head. "I've been losing a lot of sleep, me."

A vision of a naked Lucien rolling around on his bed wanting her nearly gave her palpitations. She needed to get her hormones under control or else she was toast. Her hands needed to get busy cooking and not itchy with wanting to give Lucien some palpitations of his own. "We already made a bet, which means I really need to get to work on this appetizer."

The man had the gall to chuckle.

Jerk.

She stuffed each scallop with the basil and lavender pesto. "Let me get these scallops on the grill."

"Scared of me, Hope?"

"*Pfffft*. You wish." She didn't dare look at him.

"I'm wondering if you wish for the same things I wish for. I bet you do."

"It depends. I wish for a lot of things." Hope shrugged in an effort to fake nonchalance. "A cure for cancer. No more war." She grinned and traced a circle with a finger in the air. "Whirled peas."

His eyebrows beetled together over his eyes. "Aren't world peace and an end to all war the same thing?"

"Sorry. Bad joke. I was talking about pea puree. Trying for a little food humor." Now she felt silly.

153

He stared at her for a second. She could see the wheels turn in his head. Then he smiled. "That's a very bad joke."

It was her turn to shrug then focus her attention on the food. "I think it's time to put these babies on the grill." Each scallop landed with a satisfying sizzle. The kitchen filled with a clean, briny aroma, followed by the rich after-notes of the basil and lavender.

They didn't talk as she finished and plated the dish. She arranged some lavender sprigs and sprinkled some pistachios over the scallops, then stood back and smiled. Beautiful.

Hope picked up the plates and looked at Lucien. "C'mon. Let's go eat some dinner."

Chapter Eighteen

"Just sit back and relax while I get dessert ready." Hope gathered the dirty entrée dishes.

He enjoyed the view of that cute *derrière* of hers as she took the plates away. He couldn't wait to get his hands on her. This whole no-sex rule with their bet was *fou*. He had to plan and play his cards right. If he pushed too much tonight, it would prove her food won the day. No, he had to wait until they ate his aphrodisiac-inspired dishes and drove her crazy and got her into bed then.

A challenge. There was nothing he loved better than a challenge. It made the victory taste that much sweeter.

Speaking of taste, Hope rocked in the kitchen. The meal so far exceeded all his expectations. He shouldn't be surprised. Hope was a fine chef.

Eh, bien. He didn't have anything to worry about. He had an agenda all worked out.

When Lucien Durand planned a seduction, he didn't leave anything to chance. He wanted to rub his hands together in glee. Like taking candy from a baby.

And what a pretty baby, what a pretty little morsel Hope was. He could eat her up in one bite. But he wouldn't. He'd savor her. Make the pleasure last.

Drive them both crazy.

Not yet. After the dinner he would create. Then

he'd win both games, both the food and the seduction. Again. Candy from a baby.

Life was good if you were Lucien Durand.

He hadn't always thought so. Not back in the bayou. And what crazy impulse had made him confide in her about how poor he'd grown up? This made the second time. Something about her made him want to open up, to tell her his secrets.

He needed to cut that out right now. He didn't want to give her anything that would give her an advantage. She was just so damn easy to talk to. Words fell out of his mouth when he talked to her. He needed to fix that, *tout droite*.

He didn't want to speculate as to how she got him tied up in knots. He decided that it was just something about Hope. Her fault.

Unsettled, Lucien stood and moved to the mantel to study the photos again. So many faces smiled at him, a middle-aged couple in scrubs, and stethoscopes hanging around their necks. An elderly woman in an apron grinning for the camera as she pounded bread dough. A laughing, young Hope next to an equally young man, who draped his arm over her shoulders. He had the biggest smile on his face that Lucien had ever seen. Happiness, giddiness, hung around the couple like a bright, sparkly cape.

Pure joy.

It made Lucien feel like a voyeur, an intruder into something private and sacred. A dull ache prickled uncomfortably in his chest, right underneath his heart. He didn't like it.

Hope bustled back into the dining area carrying a small china bowl and a bottle. "Almost ready. Take this." She handed him the bottle of chilled champagne. She sprinkled rose petals she pulled out of the bowl across the table. "Be right back."

He looked at the pale pink petals, then at the champagne. His hands automatically started to peel the foil top and wire cage off the cork. He spared one last glance at the picture of teenage Hope. She'd been a pretty girl with a lot of promise. Now she was a beautiful woman, promise fulfilled.

She came back carrying a fanciful fluted dish that smelled of roses. "Let me put this down here," she said as she reached the table. "I'll get the plates."

"Do you have glasses for the champagne?" Lucien asked.

"Oh, yes, of course. There are a couple of crystal flutes in that curio cabinet over there." She nodded her head in the direction of the cabinet.

"*Bien.*"

When he turned back to the table, his breath caught in his throat. The serving bowl was filled with raspberry-colored custard. Floating in the custard were four poached meringue "eggs."

Sprinkled over the whole thing were candied rose petals. The whole thing smelled like hot-house flowers.

"*Dieu.* You have really pulled out all the stops." What would he have to do to top this?

She grinned. "This is one of my favorite desserts. I hope you like it."

He set the glasses on the table and picked up the champagne. "It smells like a garden in full bloom." He worked the cork out of the bottle with a satisfying pop, and filled the glasses with the fizzy wine.

"Well, sit down and let me serve." She took an

antique silver ladle and put first some of the custard, then floated two of the meringue balls on top of it, followed by a plethora of the sugared rose petals. "Here." She set the dish in front of him and repeated the process in another bowl.

Though the dish looked delicate, it packed a hell of a punch. The custard had a slight berry aroma that mingled well with the rose-tinged meringue and sugared blossoms. It needed to be eaten slowly, savored. "This looks really good." Presentation-wise, he had his work cut out for him.

It turned him on. Big time.

She beamed at him. "Thank you."

Her smile was warm, like the sun coming out after a torrential rain. It made him happy.

Happy. Huh. Such a simple word. Uncomplicated.

Had he ever really felt happy before? Not that he could remember.

Never mind. Right now he was going to eat an amazing dessert with a beautiful woman. He needed to go with the flow. Then he looked at Hope, and all his resolve to take it slow went out the door. He wanted her, more than he wanted any other woman.

He broke out into a cold sweat. This wouldn't do.

"Are you going to try it or have I stunned you into submission?" Hope asked.

"It's so pretty, I don't think I should eat it."

"Oh no, don't give me that. You're afraid it's going to be better than any dessert you've ever eaten." She smirked at him. "Or made."

"Are you calling me chicken?"

"Ba-bwauk."

"Lucien Durand is no *poulet*." He broke off a

chunk of the meringue egg, then spooned up some of the custard, trying to catch one of the candied roses in the bite. He held her gaze as he popped the spoon into his mouth.

It was amazing, enough so that he wanted to close his eyes and chase down every single flavor. The subtle tang of raspberry in the custard, the wisp of fragrance from the roses along with the exotic taste of rose permeating throughout. The slight crunch of the poached meringue. Perfection.

Seductive, especially with Hope watching him eat it.

"Is it good?" she purred.

He swallowed with difficulty, not because of the dessert—that was sublime—but because of the sandy lump of emotion stuck in his throat. "This is one of the best desserts I have ever eaten."

Hope glowed. Literally, she lit up like an angel touched by God.

Twice.

She nodded, the picture of graciousness. "Thank you, sir."

He didn't think about it. He put his spoon on the table, got out of his chair, and marched over to Hope. Her eyes widened as he pulled her out of the chair, hauled her up into his arms and kissed her. Her mouth was soft and pliant under his, yet eager. Supple.

He came up for air, then dived back in for a deeper taste. He raked his fingers through her silky hair, which smelled of the flowers she had cooked with.

Hope twined her arms around his neck and rose on her tiptoes to press even closer to him. Arousal pooled his groin, tightening his genitals in the pleasure/pain of desire. He ran his hands down her back to her pretty ass, squeezed it and pulled her even closer.

Urgency spurred him on as he snaked one hand under her sweater to cup her breasts. He had to see her, taste her, learn the shape of her, the warmth and softness of her skin. He craved it.

Craved her. *Bon Dieu*, how he wanted her.

He'd been waiting for so long for this woman. For Hope. Where the hell did that come from? And what the hell was he doing?

This was not going according to plan at all.

Hope pulled her mouth from his and put her hands between them, pushing away from his embrace. "Maybe we should put on the brakes a little."

Her face flushed pink, her lips puffy and red from his kisses, her hair messy from his fingers, her eyes unfocussed, Hope looked beautiful. His. He didn't want to take it slow, particularly *son bandeur* wanted to continue on.

But no meant no. He took a step back and lifted his hands.

Her hands shook as she tugged on her sweater. "We said no sex."

He went back to his side of the table and chugged his glass of champagne. Then he poured himself another one and downed it in two swallows. The bubbles were a welcome burn in his throat.

She smoothed her hair then slipped into her seat. She dipped her fingers in her water glass and splashed her face.

He threw her a jaundiced look. "You are a cruel woman, Hope Monahan."

"It's part of my charm."

He grunted.

"Besides, I didn't say stop. I go slower." She sighed. "We had terms we agreed to."

"That was stupid." He shook his head. "We made the terms, we can break them." Why was he going on about this? Wasn't his plan to make sure they didn't make it to bed after her meal, to arrange it so it happened after his meal so he would win the bet?

He looked at the reason for his deviation from his course. She watched him back with those pretty green eyes of hers. He took a deep breath.

"You probably want to finish those meringues before they go soggy."

Yeah, like he cared about soggy meringues right now. "You know we're going to end up in bed."

"I'm looking forward to it." She took a slow, deliberate swallow of champagne.

He knew he shouldn't ask, but did anyway. "Why wait since we both know where this is headed?"

"Waiting will make it better."

He snorted. "For whom?"

"Both of us, I hope." She pushed a meringue egg around in the rose and raspberry custard. "Or at least that's my plan."

"You've got a plan?" He felt a spark of temper. Never mind he had his own plan.

"Don't you?" She slid him a sly, slow smile.

Well, yes, but it had gone to hell. Not that he'd admit it, to himself or to Hope. "I guess I'll just have to make my dinner so you can't resist me."

"I'm stronger than I look." Hope flexed her arms to show off her biceps. "Made of sterner stuff."

Lucien thought of the photos of a young,

incandescent Hope on her mantel. For some reason, he wished he'd known her then. Of course, she'd belonged to someone else.

He knew it was totally unreasonable to be jealous of a dead man. But, of course, he wasn't jealous. Frustrated. He was frustrated.

Really frustrated.

It was a new feeling. He didn't like it. Time to get control of the situation again. "Sterner stuff, eh?"

"You know it." She moistened her forefinger and picked up one of the sugar rose petals with the tip of it. She slowly brought the confection to her mouth and, like a kitten, licked it off her finger.

His mouth went totally dry. His water glass was empty so he reached across the table to grab hers.

"Do you want me to get you some more water?" She held up the empty bottle of Cristal. "More wine? Or do you want some coffee?"

Hell no, he didn't want any damn coffee. He had a few ideas about that tongue of hers and where he wanted her to use it. How he wanted her to use it.

It was just a matter of time.

But suddenly he didn't feel confident that he could call all the shots, at least with the physical part of their relationship.

Relationship? Holy hell. He didn't have relationships; he had dalliances.

No matter. He'd thought that seducing Hope and winning this bet would be like taking candy from a baby?

He began to think that maybe he was the baby and Hope was doing the taking.

Chapter Nineteen

"So, what do you think about Colcannon potatoes with the pheasant?" Hope asked Shane. Hope and Shane spent the morning brainstorming what to make for the entrée part of Addington's Tables. She hoped he had good suggestions.

"You mean the roasted pheasant with apples and Calvados?"

"Yes. I think Colcannon with brussels sprouts instead of cabbage would be a nice counterpoint to the sweetness of the apples." Hope tapped her pen on the pad of paper next to her elbow.

"Add some bacon?" Shane looked hopeful.

Hope laughed. "Bacon makes everything better."

"Damn straight." Shane's phone vibrated in his shirt pocket. He pulled it out and checked the screen. His eyes widened.

"Put that down. You can answer the text when we're done."

"Uh, sure." He definitely looked distracted as he repocketed the phone. "So, what's next?"

"Why don't you enter what we just decided into your tablet, and then we'll talk appetizers. I don't have to tell you not to let anybody see our menu plan."

"Of course not. I'll guard it with my life." He shook his head. "I want to win just as much as you do. It'll be great to take Durand down a peg or two."

"Yes, it will." She moved to the sink and filled a kettle with water for tea. She set it on a burner and turned up the heat. "What do you think about individual pomegranate cheesecakes for the dessert?"

Shane looked up from his tablet and frowned. "That would be a lot of work."

Hope shrugged. "It's only the three official judges."

"Doable, I guess. But there's that pesky time factor."

"We'll play with the recipe and do a few trial runs to perfect the timing."

"You're the boss."

She moved away from the stove to the coffee and tea station. "I am." She pulled down a tin of loose Irish breakfast tea from the shelf over the coffeemaker. "But you know how much I value your opinions and ideas. You're my partner in crime, buddy."

Shane stood and stretched. "No worries." He rubbed the back of his neck with one hand. "We can cut out some time if we make them smaller." His phone vibrated again. He plucked it out of his pocket. A big grin creased his face as he looked at the screen. "I'll be right back." He walked away.

A niggle of a worry crossed Hope's mind. With the contest two weeks away she needed all Shane's attention. She couldn't have him distracted.

Distracted, huh. She'd bet all her money that Angelique was the author of the texts Shane had gotten. Usually Hope didn't think about Shane's love life, but she sensed this thing with Angelique was different.

Shane was the brother she'd never had. One of Cormac's good friends, he had been there for her when

Cormac died. He helped her get through the darkest time of her life. She probably owed him her life.

She had the horrible feeling that Angelique would break Shane's heart, and there was nothing she could do to stop it. It wasn't that she didn't like Angelique because she did. At least what she did know about Angelique she liked. She suspected Angelique kept a secret or two.

Then there was the way Lucien kept her on a short leash. Overprotective? Maybe.

He did like to control everything.

She smiled, remembering watching Lucien's control unravel a little the other night. It totally jazzed her to have that kind of effect on him.

Hope felt sexy. She'd never felt that way before, but now she did, and she liked it. She'd already gone online and ordered a whole bunch of stuff from Victoria's Secret, lacy, silky, sheer stuff. She imagined Lucien's face when he saw her wearing the lingerie.

He'd only be drooling a little bit, she thought with satisfaction. Too much drool would be gross.

Her feet hadn't touched the ground since Monday. She had too many butterflies in her stomach to count. They moved around like they were riding little butterfly bumper cars. Try as she might, she couldn't keep Lucien off her mind.

She might as well be thirteen and boy crazy again. If she had an I in her name she'd dot it with a heart.

She'd always followed the rules. Now she was breaking a few of her own, and it felt fun. Naughty. Thrilling.

She was a *femme fatale*. Soon she'd have the underwear to prove it.

The kettle whistled, and she bustled to the stove to take care of it. She went through the motions of making the tea, flavoring it with milk and sugar, then took it into her office to enjoy it. She closed the door behind her, leaned back in her chair, and savored the moment.

She felt powerful. Feminine.

How long had it been since she'd felt this way? Had she ever?

Not with Cormac. She'd fallen in love with him before she even knew what sexy meant.

Well, she knew now.

She gave the tea a perfunctory stir as she wondered what Lucien would cook for their dinner next Monday.

Oysters would be in there somewhere. They were an integral part of the Cajun/Creole tradition and on the top of the aphrodisiac list. Just how he would fix them was the question.

It would have been so easy to give into temptation the night she cooked for Lucien. So easy. She was glad she'd stuck to her guns. The chase was romantic. Falling into bed for no reason, other than lust, was not.

She wanted romance, with all the hearts and flowers, with long slow kisses that spun on and on. Candlelight flickering. Soft music, Chopin or Debussy. Maybe Duke Ellington. Chocolate.

Lots and lots of chocolate.

Okay, maybe that made her a walking, talking cliché, but so what?

She wanted what she wanted. No shame in that. She brought the teacup to her mouth and blew across the hot brew before she took a sip. The next few weeks were going to be very interesting, that was for sure.

She couldn't wait.

****

Lucien stood in his home kitchen testing some new toppings for broiled oysters. He would name the dish Oysters Hope. He was thinking he'd try a more classical presentation. Right now he was leaning toward a tarragon-champagne infused, crème fraîche preparation.

It was a lovely place, his kitchen, all stainless steel, glass, wood, and marble. He needed to spend more time in it.

He'd dipped a spoon into the bowl of crème fraîche when his phone buzzed.

He sighed. A text from Angelique. She couldn't work tonight; she had a special review session for a mid-term exam, could he cover her in the front of the house, blah, blah, blah?

A cloak of uneasiness wrapped itself around him. This was feeling like New Orleans all over again.

He'd gotten her into Tulane University, and she'd promptly flunked out, preferring social life to attending class and doing homework. After that, he'd gotten her into LSU, and the same thing happened. Only that time she spent more time traipsing off to photographers and model agencies trying to start a career as a model.

That hadn't been what *Grand-mère* wanted. She wanted Angelique to get a college degree. Lucien would do whatever it took to honor *Grand-mère's* wishes.

At least he knew Angelique wouldn't be sneaking out with Shane Baker. Hope's was open and Shane would be at work.

Lucien didn't bother to text her back. He called instead, but went straight to voice mail. Of course. The message he left was curt and to the point. "Call me. Sooner rather than later."

He turned his attention back to the mixing bowl, but the fun of creation had paled. Why did she never do what she was supposed to? He'd given her every advantage, every chance and opportunity, within reason, that she could ever want.

Why wasn't it enough?

****

Shane stared at his phone screen. Those were some, uh, amazing photos she'd texted him. She took his breath away. She was also extremely high maintenance. And not very patient.

That being the case, all he had to do was figure out a way to get off work early. Maybe they wouldn't be busy.

He didn't want to leave Hope shorthanded. But Angelique…

His best friend on one side—the love of his life on the other.

He loved Hope but he was *in* love with Angelique. For the first time in his life he was head over heels in love.

Hope had just called him her partner in crime. He felt totally craptastic about playing her.

However, if he wanted to see Angelique it had to be on the down low. He didn't like it, but he liked not being with her less. He would do anything she wanted. Be anything she wanted. He loved her that much.

Chapter Twenty

Lucien smiled as he polished his kitchen counter. He had everything ready for his dinner with Hope, the best oysters, the freshest scallops, the finest chocolate. *La pièce de résistance?* His take on Bananas Foster.

Hope's dessert had been exquisite and a hard act to follow, but he rose to the occasion. He could hardly wait to see her face when he lit up the Bananas Foster and turned on the heat. He chuckled at the prospect.

Surely it would make Hope burn with passion for him. He intended for the evening to end with Hope in his bed. He shook his head. The no sex condition sucked. It needed to be ignored. Rescinded.

Laid to rest in a grave no one would ever find.

He'd taken care of every last detail of tonight's dinner, nothing left to chance. Not only would he seduce her with his food, he would also show her that he was the better chef. She was good, *c'est vrai*, but not as good as he was. Two birds, one stone.

He would own the night. Victory would be sweet. Very sweet indeed. He had no doubt about it. His doorbell rang and he smiled.

Magic time.

He ambled across the living room, expecting to steal her breath away. He opened the door to Hope, to let her into his life.

Instead she took *his* breath away.

Hope smiled. "Hi."

"Hi." He nearly swallowed his tongue. "Please come in."

Her eyes danced. "Thank you." With that, she stepped into the devil's den.

She looked breathtaking dressed in a soft cashmere sweater dress the color of butternut squash that hugged her body in all the right places. She made his mouth water. "You look lovely."

Hope gifted him with a generous lift of her lips. "Thank you."

She smelled like gingerbread and vanilla, seductive, with hints of darker spices. He couldn't wait to take a great big bite of her. He craved it, the taste of her.

Holding her small delicate hand, he brought it to his lips and brushed a kiss across her knuckles. "Your hands are cold."

"They usually are," she whispered.

"We'll have to do something about that." He pulled her into his living room.

"Wow! That's some view you have." She walked to the huge window and looked out at the lights of Addington as they blinked on in the early evening sky. Hope glanced back at him. "This is quite the apartment."

"Thank you. It suits my needs." He took her hand and pulled her away from the window. "Come sit down and let me make you my special cocktail."

She sat in the black leather and chrome sofa. "Special, eh?"

"*Oui.*" He moved to the wet bar he had made specifically for this room. When he entertained, he demanded everything to his exact standards. He brought two heavy Old Fashioned glasses and filled them with ice. Getting another glass, he dropped in a sugar cube and added just enough water to cover the cube. Deftly, he pulled out and mixed the other ingredients, absinthe, Peychaud's bitters, Angostura bitters, and some eighteen-year-old Kentucky Straight Rye Whiskey. The whiskey and authentic absinthe were difficult to find in this neck of the woods, but find it he did. He finished by rubbing two strips of lemon peel over the rims of the glasses.

Satisfied with his handiwork, he took the drinks to Hope. "*Sazerac au Lucien.*"

She smiled as she took her glass. "Thank you."

He sat next to her on the sofa and raised his cocktail. "To the most beautiful woman in the world."

Hope choked. "Aren't you pouring it on a little thick?"

Lucien turned the charm up to eleven. "Absolutely not. From where I'm sitting, *c'est vrai*. Take a drink of the *Sazerac* and let me know what you think."

She took a careful sip and made a face. "That's really strong. I've never had absinthe before."

"It's good, *non*?"

"It's different." She set it on the glass-topped coffee table. "Very sophisticated." She gave him a wan smile. "I guess it's an acquired taste."

What did that mean? No matter, he had lots of tricks up his sleeve.

Undaunted, he got close to her and tipped her head up for a long, seductive kiss. He ran his hands down the soft material of her dress, loving the feel of it underneath his hands, loving the feel of *her* underneath his hands. He wondered if her skin felt as soft as her dress.

Her mouth moved under his, inviting his tongue to come in. She wound her arms around his neck and pressed her body close to his.

Their lips broke apart, came back together, then broke apart one more time. He rested his forehead against hers. His breath sawed in and out of him. He knew he had to slow down his seduction of Hope fast. "Let me get something to have with our cocktails."

She nodded, her eyes heavy lidded, her lips red and swollen. Yeah, he needed to put on the brakes before they peaked too soon. "I'll be right back."

In the kitchen, Lucien pulled his pecan cheese crisps out of the oven. Golden, nutty perfection. He fussed with plating them, making sure they were total food porn. She wouldn't be able to resist.

When he returned to the living room he found her inspecting the framed photos of all the L'Enfer restaurants. He set the platter on the coffee table then approached her. He put his hands on Hope's shoulders and gave them a little squeeze. "That's my restaurant in Paris."

She turned to face him, and he dropped his arms around her lower back and pulled her closer. She lifted her face and parted her lips for a kiss. He didn't need more encouragement. He savored the flavor of her, the buttery sweetness of the whiskey, the pungent note of the absinthe, and the unique sweetness that was Hope.

Reluctantly he ended the kiss. "Come. I've brought you sustenance."

Hope took a deep sniff. "They smell lovely."

He led her back to the couch. "Here." He held a

crisp to her lips.

She took a bite. Her tongue snaked out to catch some flaky crumbs that fell as she crunched. "Mmmmm. This is very good."

"*Mais, yeah.*" Of course it was very good.

"The richness of the pecan pairs well with the Sazerac." She nipped the other piece of crisp from his fingers. His lips fizzed where her lips and tongue touched.

Suddenly thirsty, he picked up his cocktail. The alcohol burned on the way down his throat and didn't do much for his current parched condition. He coughed.

"Where is your sister tonight?" Hope licked at some crumbs that had stuck on her mouth.

Lucien nearly lost all power of speech. He shook his head to clear it. "She's working."

"Ah." She smiled. "So we're alone for the time being."

"*Oui.*"

She picked up another pecan crisp and bit into it. "These are addictive."

Just like he could get addicted to her. Or get her addicted to him, which was a much better plan as far as he was concerned. Time to proceed with the rest of his evening plans. "I'm glad you like them. Let me go and finish off the first course." He kissed her, another slow, sweet meeting of the lips. "Stay right here.

Hope smiled. "I'm pretty sure I'll be here when you get back."

"I'm counting on it."

****

Dear lord, Lucien's apartment was so streamlined and modern, with absolutely no sentimentality. She'd never been in a home so devoid of personal touches.

Except for framed photos of his restaurants. How sad. Rather than find him cold, she decided he kept things bottled up.

Well, except for his libido. He didn't keep that under wraps, that was for sure. She kinda liked that about him.

Actually, she really liked that about him.

He looked beyond handsome tonight in a gray cotton button-down shirt tucked into a pair of jeans that hugged him in all the right places. He'd rolled up the shirtsleeves giving a tantalizing view of his strong, capable hands. She could just imagine how they would feel against her skin. He had working man's hands, roughened and calloused from working in the kitchen. They would rasp across her sensitive flesh to tickle and to tease her. To arouse her.

She shivered at the thought of it. There was something different in the air tonight, something that made the air crackle.

To sizzle.

He returned with two plates laden with oysters, and placed them on a table next to the kitchen. "Come," he said. "You don't want to make them wait."

Trust Lucien to talk about making food wait, like the oysters were some type of royalty.

Another thing to like about him. They were adding up pretty fast.

If she wasn't careful, she'd end up in love with him.

She choked on that thought. No way would she be in love with anyone other than Cormac. Never, ever, ever. She could enjoy Lucien physically, but there was no way love had anything to do with it.

Who was she kidding? Of course she was falling in love with him. That's the way she was hardwired. The realization gave her a queasy feeling in her stomach. She definitely did not want to be in love with Lucien Durand.

He had set the table with an immaculate white tablecloth. Sleek, modern candlesticks were topped with long white tapers. His china was black and square and unadorned. He'd placed a platter filled with oysters in the center of the table.

He pulled out a chair for her. "Please, sit, while they are still warm."

"They smell delicious. What did you do with them?"

He sat. "I broiled them and created a new sauce. I call the dish Oysters Hope."

"Wow! Nobody's ever named a dish after me."

He placed a few oysters on her plate along with a seafood fork. "Here." He picked up a bowl with a white herb sauce. "Try the sauce. It's a brand-new recipe." Lucien winked. "If it's good, I'll put it on my menu."

She dipped the small serving spoon into the white, herb-y creamy sauce and topped the oysters with it. She inhaled deeply. Lovely. If it lived up to the promise of its aroma, this bite would be heaven. "It looks delicious." She used the seafood fork to pop it into her mouth.

Taste exploded on her tongue. The combination of tarragon and champagne-infused crème fraîche fizzed slightly and perfectly complemented the tang of the broiled oyster. "Oh. My." She licked her lips to get the rest of the topping.

"Does that mean you like it?" Lucien totally looked like he already knew the answer to his question.

"It's very good."

He offered her another oyster. "So it's okay to put it on my menu?"

She took an oyster and spooned on some of that amazing sauce. "You'd be foolish not to."

"I'll put it on the list of specials tomorrow." His mouth quirked into a lopsided smile. "Maybe I'll make it for the competition."

"I can still beat it. I've got something awesome planned." She sank her teeth into the next oyster.

"I just bet you do." He ate an oyster himself. "Forgot the rest of the champagne. Wait right here." Off he went to the kitchen.

Hope looked at the platter of shellfish. The fact that he'd named a dish after her made her feel all squiggly inside.

He came back with an open bottle of champagne. "Here we go." He poured the wine into a pair of flutes, then handed Hope one. He lifted his glass in a toast. "To a new dish on my menu. *Merci* for the inspiration."

Her eyes filled with sparkly, shiny stars. "You're welcome. But I have to say it's quite an honor to have Lucien Durand name a dish after me."

He should have looked humble when she said that, but he didn't. Was it possible for a man to explode with pride? Like, blow up into teeny pieces that would take archaeologists years to find?

He put down his glass and helped her to stand. Then, after taking the drink out of her hand, he wrapped her in a loose embrace and kissed her. "Are you ready for the next course?"

Yes. Yes, she was. She was so ready. She nodded.

He smiled, slow and wicked. "I'll be right back."

"I'll be here."

He chuckled as he left the room. It sounded promising.

Resisting him tonight would be difficult. She just didn't know how difficult it would be. She'd had X-rated dreams about him all week. She'd loved sex, and right after Cormac died she'd not missed it at all. She'd had enough just getting out of bed every day. But now...

Now she couldn't stop thinking about it.

At all.

Big time.

She also knew Lucien would pour on the charm, which he was. In spades.

So, what was a girl to do? Saddle up and enjoy the ride? She took a sip of champagne. Her mouth watered, and it had nothing to do with the amazing scents coming from Lucien's kitchen and everything to do with the way her host filled out a pair of well-worn jeans.

Time to stop playing games. The time for the no sex clause of the bet had come and gone. The time for a little world rocking had arrived.

She was done protecting herself from a physical relationship with Lucien.

Chapter Twenty-One

"And here is dessert." Lucien brought his version of Bananas Foster to the table.

Dinner had gone very well, as he had known it would. No one could have resisted the meal he'd concocted, especially the *Coquilles St. Jacques* with lime-infused Basmati rice and *asperges*.The dessert was just the icing on the cake.

"It smells delicious. Do I detect some pineapple and coconut in there?" Hope asked, scrunching her nose and cocking her head to one side.

He deposited the chafing dish filled with bubbling butter, brown sugar, cinnamon, and fruit on the table then flicked a finger across the tip of her nose. "You do. It's my take on Bananas Foster. *Bananes aux Lucien*. I don't want people to confuse my recipe with what they serve at Brennans."

"Of course not," she said on a laugh.

He loved the way her eyes sparkled when she laughed, how her mouth kicked up, how musical the sound she made was.

He suddenly found himself tongue-tied. That never happened, ever. He cleared his throat.

The sooner he got her into bed, the better. A man could only wait so long.

"So how are you doing this?" Hope leaned forward over the table craning her neck probably to see what he was up to. Looking at his performance. He'd give her a show. One she'd never forget.

Lighting the candle underneath the chafing dish, he said, "I've infused these chunks of pineapple and the bananas with coconut liqueur." He sprinkled cinnamon over the top, then grabbed a bottle of brandy he'd set on the table earlier.

Lucien splashed some of the brandy over the dessert. He picked up the lighter then he grinned at her. "Here comes the fun part." He touched the lighter to the dish.

It ignited with a whoosh, then yellow, red, blue-tinged flames leapt to life. They speared high into the room, crackling and sizzling bringing the aromas of butter, sugar, pineapple, coconut, and banana along with them.

Perfection, thought Lucien. Absolute perfection.

He couldn't have planned it better. *Bien sûr*.

He was The Man.

Capital T. Capital M.

Hope clapped. "Bravo, chef! You are a god among chefs."

"All this flattery will go to my head."

She laughed. "I hope the taste will equal the presentation."

He scooped up some banana, pineapple, and sauce and ladled it into a bowl. "It will." He set it in front of her, then offered her a spoon. "Try it."

Hope dipped the spoon into the dish, sliced into the banana, and covered it with the brandy sauce. She popped the sweet bite into her mouth and chewed slowly. She sighed. "It's amazing."

"*Bien sûr*," he replied. "I had to do something to

top that dessert you made."

"I wouldn't go so far as to say it outdid mine."

He cocked an eyebrow. "Really?"

"*Pffffftttt*." She pointed the spoon at him. "Anyone can set something on fire. It took a lot of finesse and skill to poach those meringue eggs."

"You don't say."

"C'mon, just admit it. I made the better dessert."

Lucien would admit no such thing. "*Ca c'est de la couyonade*." He grinned when her brow furrowed. "That's just foolishness, *chère*."

"I prefer to call it truth." She flipped her shiny auburn hair back over her shoulders and gave him a saucy grin.

"Sorry, *chère*." He shook his head. "I beat you and you know it."

She *tsk-tsked*. "You haven't won anything yet. You know the terms of the bet."

"You know that right now neither of us care about the bet."

"I certainly do care about who wins." Hope nodded. "And I know it's me."

"*Mais non, pichouette*," Lucien murmured. "But I have an idea how we both can win."

"Do you now?"

"Maybe even more than one." Which was true. He'd thought a lot about what the two of them could do together.

She licked her lips. "Maybe you can tell me about a few of them." She shrugged. "If you're not too chicken to tell me."

Chicken? Nobody had ever accused Lucien Durand of being a coward. He narrowed his eyes. "You've got a smart mouth on you, *chère*."

She turned up those bright green eyes of hers to stun. "What're you going to do about it?"

Oh, he had a number of very good ideas about what he could do with those soft lips of hers. "Got any suggestions?"

"I can think of one or two." Hope's voice got a little breathy, a little husky. She cleared her throat.

"I'll just bet you can. Want me to show you my ideas?"

"Maybe."

He chuckled. "There's no maybe about it, *chère*. He stepped closer to her and lifted her out of her chair. "You want me to do this."

Not caring what was in his way, he pulled her against him and kissed her.

Chapter Twenty-Two

He consumed her, Hope thought. He just up and took possession of her mouth, and there was nothing gentle about it.

Just the way she wanted him.

She stood on tiptoes and wrapped her arms around his neck. She opened for Lucien and returned his kiss with all her heart. His mouth was avid and warm and possessive. He tasted of rum and caramel.

The man was sex on a stick. Speaking of which—

His hands streaked down her back to cup her butt and pulled her in tight. He lifted her up so she could wrap her legs around him, then he turned, rested her bottom on the table, without breaking the kiss. His erection pressed the notch of her thighs, and she wiggled to get more contact.

He hissed, then slid his hands up her back and began to unbutton the row of buttons holding her dress together. He ripped his mouth from hers. "I need to see you," he growled.

Those amazing hands of his teased and tantalized as he undid one button after the other. He pressed kisses along her neck as he loosed her dress with annoying patience.

She brought her hands between them and started to take off his shirt. Her fingers were maddeningly clumsy, as she worked the tiny buttons. His skin was warm, so warm. He smelled of citrus, a clean masculine scent.

Hope wanted him, was greedy for him. Her body ached for him.

He pulled away from her and eased her sleeves down her arms. She shook her hands free and let her dress drift to her waist. He brought a finger under her chin and lifted her face, his gaze lit with passion, demanding her attention. "I've been waiting for a long time for this." He kissed her again, then moved those skilled hands behind to unhook her bra.

He didn't take his eyes off her as he removed the silky scrap of lingerie covering her breasts. He cleared his throat but still his voice was husky. "I feel like it's Christmas, and I'm opening my present." He gave her a long, slow kiss, full of the promise of things to come.

Both of them were breathing hard when he pulled away. "God, you're so sweet. I've got to taste you."

His eyes roamed south, fixed on her breasts. He cupped them and rubbed his thumbs across her nipples. "*Jolie. Très jolie.*"

"Oh, God," she moaned as the callouses on his fingers rasped and abraded the sensitive peaks of her breasts.

"You're so beautiful, *chère*. Pretty as a picture," he growled. "I need to taste you." He leaned over her and enclosed one aching tip with his lips.

She gasped as he sucked her nipple into his mouth, then lightly bit and scraped his teeth along it. She threaded her fingers through his hair, holding on for dear life while Lucien turned her world upside down. Her head swam with the thrill of it.

His head lifted, and he regarded her with heavy-lidded, mischief-sparkled eyes. "You taste good, *chère*, real good. But—" he reached over to one side and gathered up a couple of fingers full of *Bananes aux Lucien*—"I'm gonna guild the lily a little." He traced a line around the circle of her mouth then painted both of her nipples with the delicious, fragrant dessert. "Mmmmm. They look good enough to eat. *You* look good enough to eat."

Then he leaned over her and went to work.

And she lost her sanity.

Swamped with desire, drenched with longing, she gave herself up to him.

Chapter Twenty-Three

Lucien was drunk with the taste of her, the feel of her. Her breasts were the color of fresh cream, topped by large raspberry-colored nipples. They had gathered into hard buds, so responsive to his touch, to his lips and teeth.

She gasped as he pleasured her and dug her hands into his hair like she needed an anchor. He wound his tongue in a slow circle around a nipple and she whimpered.

The sound went straight to his cock, which hardened even more than it already was. *Le bon Dieu*, he was hard enough to pound nails.

Mais non. Hope was delicate. A real Irish rose. He'd put his own needs aside for the moment to make her feel safe and cared for.

Cherished.

He gathered up another couple of fingers-worth of the dessert and painted it down along her body, starting from her soft throat to her belly button. He pulled back slightly to inspect his handiwork. "Aw, *pichouettee. Si douce. Si bon.*" He hunched over her and laid the flat of his tongue to lap up the sticky trail.

Hope let out a long, breathy moan and pulled his hair more tightly. Her skin shivered underneath his tongue, revving his engine even more. Her skin was so soft, so supple. He liked softness in a woman. So different from the hard, skeletal models he usually escorted. He wanted to revel in Hope's body and find all her soft places, both inside and outside.

He craved to bury himself in her warmth, a sharp edge of longing that no one but Hope could slake. Desperate, his skin prickled with the urge to take her. Right. Now.

He reined in his desire because he wanted to make sure she was ready. So he forced himself to slow down, to take his time pleasuring her. Lucien devoted himself to her needs, feeding on the ripples underneath his tongue, her little gasps and hums of her excitement.

Her satisfaction.

He reached underneath her skirt and ran his fingers up her legs to cup her bottom. Delighted to find thigh-high stockings, he smiled and nipped her leg where the hose ended. Slowly, he rolled them down and pressed kisses along the flesh he bared.

Lucien reached her ankles and slipped off one stocking then the other along with each shoe. He rose up over her again and pressed avid kisses to the side of her neck. "*J'aime te faire l'amour avec toi.*"

She moved to catch his lips with hers in a soul-sharing kiss. "I don't know what you just said, but I like the sound of it."

"I want to make love to you, *pichouette*. Let me show you," he whispered, making his breath rasp along her skin. Her flesh quivered as he did so. He traced every ripple, eliciting sexy little whimpers from her.

He meandered his way down her body, licking here, nipping there, his hands roaming all over her warm, soft skin. She tasted like a treat he'd been waiting for all his life. He needed to taste more. He flipped up the skirt of her dress and cupped her firm little bottom with his hands and brought her closer to him.

She wriggled a little, like she was trying to get closer.

"Shhhh. Just relax, *pichouette*." He smiled. "Me, I'm gonna take you to heaven."

He kissed the delicate skin between her thighs and marveled at its softness. Unable to wait another moment, he lowered his mouth to her sex and used tongue and lips to her warm, wet core.

She nearly shot into space. Lucien had to hold on to her so he could continue to please her. "Like that, *chère*?" he whispered.

She gasped, then whimpered.

"How 'bout this?" He dragged his fingers to rim the entrance of her inner passage then slipped them to reach deep inside her.

She keened, the sound high as she flew apart against his mouth. He lapped at her clit as he brought her back to earth.

"Omigawd!" she panted. "What was that?"

He kissed his way back up her body. "If you don't know, *pichouette*, then I didn't do it right."

Her face turned an adorable shade of pink. "You did it right, trust me. I'm a little embarrassed that it happened so soon." She sat up.

"Nothin' to be embarrassed 'bout, *chère*." He gave her a quick, hard peck on the lips. "I can't wait to do it again."

"It's just that, well, it's been a long time for me."

"How long?"

"Ummm, since my husband died." She blushed

even more. "About ten years."

Le bon Dieu! He couldn't even begin to imagine that. "Not even one boyfriend?"

She shook her head. "No."

Satisfaction flooded through him. She chose him to be her first, as it were. "Well, you've got some catching up to do." He grinned. "Me, I can help you with that."

****

God, she didn't know if she could take much more of his help, although she was ready to try. Turnabout was only fair play, right?

She sat up and scooted to the edge of the table. Wrapping her arms around his neck and kissing him, she snugged her legs on either side of his hips and pressed herself against that obvious and impressive erection of his.

It had been so long since she'd been up close and personal with one of those bad boys. She ached to touch him.

She slipped her hands between them and grappled with his belt, her usually steady and skilled fingers shaking and clumsy. Finally undone, she turned her attention from his belt to the zipper of his jeans. Finally victorious, she rubbed the long, hard length of his penis through his black silk boxers.

He hissed as her hands freed his erection from his pants. So warm, pulsing with life, she ran her thumb over the dark, plum-shaped head, spreading the moisture that beaded the top of the tip. She petted the length of him, loving the effect her touch had on him.

He was at her mercy, and she really liked that.

A. Lot.

Lucien brought his hands and gently cupped each

side of her face as he brought his mouth down to kiss her. "How 'bout we take this party to the bedroom?" he murmured, his voice rusty and hoarse.

"God, yes."

"Wrap your arms 'round my neck, *chère*." He shifted her legs to circle his hips. He kissed her again as he put his hands under her butt and lifted her as if she weighed nothing.

Hope liked that too.

She pressed kisses along his neck and jaw as he carried her. She loved the way his muscles bunched and flexed as he moved. Once in his bedroom, he gradually let her slide down his body to her feet as he kissed her long and deep, his pants dropping with her. His hands rested on her bottom, his fingers flexed, then tugged her close. She gave her hips a slow swivel against his silk-covered erection.

He pulled her dress over her head and dropped his mouth down to suckle one nipple while he plucked at the other with those sand-papery fingers of his. Dear lord, the pleasure-pain of it swamped her. He made her crazy.

But she wanted to make him crazy this time. She just plain old wanted him.

Wanted him helpless and at her mercy. She kissed her way over to one of his ears and tugged at it with her teeth. "Take me to bed."

"*Avec plaisir.*" Lucien scooped her up and laid her on the bed. He shucked off the rest of his clothes then lay on his side next to her. The navy cotton duvet was soft and cool, which was good because he was so hot she was about to burn up.

He ran his hand over her stomach, causing her skin

to come alive with desire. She pushed him onto his back and straddled his lap. Leaning over him to kiss him, she rubbed her hyper-sensitive breasts across his chest.

"Looks like you got me where you want me, *chère*. What you gonna do now?" He grinned. "Should I be scared?"

"Maybe," she trilled on a laugh. "I've got a lot of ideas and a lot of time to make up for."

"Maybe you should get started."

She shook her head. "So bossy. You're not in charge here anymore."

"Talk about." He bumped up his hips, his arousal blatant and straining against her. "C'mon *chère*." His voice dropped to a low whisper. "Do your worst."

Oh, boy. She knew just where to start.

"First, let's get rid of these." She slid down a bit and went to work. "Lift up."

He obliged and she slid down the soft silky boxers. Finally she got to see all of the man.

He was beautiful. Even that word was too tame to describe his body. He had the lean muscular build of a swimmer, with broad shoulders, defined abs, and narrow hips. His chest was lightly furred, trailing down to a thin line indicating to where the good stuff was.

Again she stroked his straining shaft loving the hard strength covered by soft, sensitive skin. He pulsed against her hand, full of life and heat and promise.

"You keep that up and you're gonna get something you're not ready for." His husky voice grated low and made her sex clench with anticipation.

"I think I'm ready for a lot," she whispered. She licked her lips, leaned over, and took him into her mouth. Stroking his shaft, she tongued him around the bulbous head.

Lucien sucked in a breath and the muscles underneath that warm toast colored skin bunched and jolted beneath her hands. He reached down and held her hair off to the side while she slid on a condom.

Hope caught him watching her with hot, avid eyes. His gaze compelled her to keep her eyes open and connected to his.

She couldn't look away.

Then his eyes shuttered closed, and his breath sawed in and out of his lungs. He murmured something in French, but she didn't catch it.

Chapter Twenty-Four

"You okay, *chère?*" Lucien's sleep-laden whisper gusted across Hope's hair.

"Oh yeah." She smiled. She couldn't remember the last time she felt this good. Tucked in close to Lucien, her head resting on his chest, the thud of his heartbeat in her ear, their legs entangled, she felt warm, safe, and a little drowsy.

Not to mention nearly boneless after the incredible orgasms he'd treated her to. No doubt about it, right now it was pretty damn good being Hope Monahan.

"Are you hungry? I can go and grab us some of the dessert we didn't eat."

"No. I want to stay here with you right now, just like this." She used the hand she'd flung across his chest and traced little hearts over his pecs.

He pulled her in tighter and kissed the top of her head. "*C'est bon.*"

Speaking of French. "Did you know that you went into a real heavy Cajun accent when we were, uh," she searched for the right words, "fooling around."

His body stiffened a bit at this news. "I've never noticed it."

"Are you embarrassed? You shouldn't be." She lifted up and kissed the warm skin of his neck. "It's very sexy."

A long moment of silence. He cracked a smile. "In

that case, it's good."

"Why does it bother you? Your accent, I mean."

He blinked. "It doesn't. I'm proud of where I come from. It's only that no one ever told me before." He gave a quick little shrug.

"You're blushing." She laughed.

"No, I'm not." He looked at her, his expression stern. "I never blush."

"I'm sorry. You blush. You're doing it right now."

"I am far too manly to blush." He kissed her. "Don't forget it."

"Aye, aye, captain." She saluted.

Clearing his throat, he pulled her close. "How are you?"

"I'm good. Better than good."

"You had a long dry spell before tonight. I'm glad you picked me to break it."

She had loved her husband with all her heart, mind, and soul, but she needed to move on. And she was crazy drawn to Lucien, physically yes, of course. He was sexy beyond belief. But he also intrigued her on an emotional level. Pulled her in with some kind of electric voodoo that reached down low into her and spoke to the heart of her being. She trusted him.

Not that she knew or understood why. The man was a player, most likely it was encoded on his DNA. He could drop her without a second thought, but she didn't care. He filled her up. He watered all her dry places. He was the biggest risk she had ever taken, and he was the safest place she'd ever found after Cormac.

Totally crazy. She needed to have her head examined. So she said, "I was in love with my husband. I never expected to be with any man other than

Cormac."

"Yet here you are." His voice was soft and serious.

"Yes." She paused. "I *am* here. By choice." She drew another heart on his chest. "I choose you."

Again, he went very still. He even seemed to stop breathing. "You loved your husband very much."

"He was my life. My first love. My first and only." She sighed and smiled. "That was then, this is now."

"Hmm." He rubbed the small of her back.

Yum. She wanted to melt underneath his hand. "Don't worry. I don't expect anything from you beyond this."

He kissed her. "I'm glad you're here with me."

Her heart gave an extra hard thump. A wealth of emotions spread through her: happiness, relief, contentment. Desire. "I'm glad to be here with you." More than glad. Glad didn't even begin to describe how she felt. Delirious was more like it.

"I want you to stay with me tonight. All night."

She wanted that too. But she didn't want an audience. "What about Angelique?"

"What about her?"

"When is she coming home?"

"She's not. She has a big exam tomorrow and is going to study with a friend after she gets off her shift." He grinned. "Are you shy?"

Hope grimaced. "Not shy. Just…private."

"Then we'll keep things private. I feel the same way. I'm not ready for reporters to find out about us and plaster your picture on magazine covers, so I'll let my publicist know, and he'll take care of it."

The thought had never occurred to her, but it struck her as being silly. "Why would anyone want to take pictures of me? I'm not newsworthy."

"You would be. The public seems to really be interested in my love life."

"No way. I'm sure not any supermodel."

"That's right. You'd be the woman who replaced a supermodel. The warm, wonderful, amazing woman." He shook his head. "The paparazzi would eat it up."

"Paparazzi?" The thought made her laugh. "That's ridiculous."

His face looked so serious. "I'm afraid it's not. They've been leaving me alone here in Addington, and that's great, but I can't take the chance that this is a permanent thing. And I don't want them turning your life upside down."

Nobody could possibly be interested in a small-town chef running a small earth-to-table restaurant in Massachusetts.

Hope Monahan, to her own way of thinking, wasn't all that special. Certainly no celebrity.

Nothing to see here, folks, move along.

"We should also be careful because of the competition anyway. The paps will be there for sure."

Oh. She hadn't thought of that. Things were getting complicated.

"Looks like you're thinking some big thoughts there, *chère.*"

Hope shook her head. She didn't see the point of prolonging that particular discussion. "I'm thinking about how much you bring the sexy."

He chuckled and shifted their positions, so he was on top of her. He pulled her legs apart and settled them on either side of his hips. "That so?"

She nodded.

"Well then, I better make sure I'm up to that reputation."

Oh, yeah, Hope thought, *Lucien was up to it.* She wiggled her pelvis where his hard shaft met the sensitive skin of her core. "I guess you'd better."

He brought his hand down to caress her. She couldn't have kept up a conversation even if she had wanted to.

Lucien lay awake, watching Hope sleep. Her chest rose and fell as she breathed and she snuggled up to him, the hair on her head tousled, soft, and fragrant, and snagged on his beard stubble. He lifted a finger to disentangle her hair, then brushed a soft kiss to the top of her head.

He didn't think he could do much more than that. Who knew he could fall in love so fast and so hard?

Who knew he could fall in love in the first place?

****

Shane surfaced from sleep to find Angelique wrapped in a bed sheet, sitting up and texting like crazy. He shook his head to clear it. "What's up?" he asked around a jaw-cracking yawn.

She turned to him, her smile brilliant. "Did I wake you?" She didn't wait for an answer. "I've just gotten the most amazing news!"

He sat up and rubbed his eyes. "Oh yeah?"

"Oh, you won't believe it! Remember I told you about Cäcilia and her helping me get a modeling career?" She paused only to take a breath. "Well, she's coming here!"

Shane blinked. Maybe he wasn't awake yet. "Okay."

She smacked him on the shoulder. "She's coming

to help me convince Lucien that I don't need to go to school." She sighed. "That I'm meant to be a model."

Shane's stomach dropped to his feet. His heart twisted like it might break in two. He didn't want her to leave. Ever. "When does she get here?"

"Thursday. She's coming to watch round one of the competition." Angelique wrinkled her nose. "I think she's gonna try to get back with Lucien."

"I see." Shit. "What about Hope?"

"What about her? You don't like her dating *mon frère*. Cäcilia will take care of that for you." She smiled then pecked him on the cheek.

Very true. He didn't think Durand was good for Hope, but he didn't want her to be publicly humiliated when Durand was no longer interested in her. Not to mention, Cäcilia's presence at the competition would definitely disrupt Hope's concentration, to the point that she might lose. He had no doubt that when she was on her game, she'd easily win Addington's Tables, in spite of Asshole the Wonder Chef.

A very ugly suspicion crossed his mind. "Did your brother invite her here to sabotage Hope?"

"Oh no!" Angelique's eyes widened. "He doesn't know she's coming."

"I think I should at least warn Hope."

"Don't you dare! It's supposed to be a surprise!" She shook her head. "I don't want any word about this to reach Lucien's ears. He'll pack me up and send me to a convent." She scrunched up her nose. "Me, I don't think I'd make a very good nun."

Wasn't that the truth? But Shane couldn't shake the feeling that there was something wrong. It didn't all add up.

If Lucien was hellbent on keeping Angelique away from this Cäcilia, it wouldn't really make a difference if he knew about her coming ahead of time.

The love of his life was definitely keeping something from him. He rubbed his hand over his heart. Hope should know. He knew that beyond the shadow of a doubt. This was yet another time Angelique was making him choose between her and Hope, although she probably didn't think of it that way.

He closed his eyes. Maybe it would all go away.

Angelique's small hand sneaked underneath the blanket and stroked him. He didn't think about anything going away after that.

Chapter Twenty-Five

Hope's eyes fluttered open to find Lucien's room flooded with sunlight. Lucien was wrapped around her, fingers tugging lightly on her nipples, mouth pressing kisses to her neck.

She sighed. A girl could get used to this. "Mmm."

"You like that, *chère*?" His teeth scraped along her earlobe. "Maybe I can find something else you like."

"You can give it the ol' college try if you feel up to it."

He pressed his erection against her butt and rubbed it up and down. "Could be I'm up to it."

She wiggled back against him. "Prove it."

"*Avec plaisir.*"

And boy oh boy did he prove it. An hour later they were both totally wrecked and loving every minute of it. Hope struggled to suck in a breath.

Then again, all things considered, breathing was overrated. Way overrated.

He touched her breast. Her breath caught. Yes, she thought. Breathing was way, way overrated.

****

"How do you feel? Are you hungry?"

Hope painted a beautiful picture, Lucien thought. All pale skin, mottled with the pink blush of passion.

Colored with his passion. Pleasure he had brought her. He smiled against her skin. He'd marked her. She

199

was his.

His.

He liked the sound of that.

A man in love wanted to feed his woman. At that particular moment, his stomach growled.

"Are you hungry?" Hope lifted her head off his chest to look at him.

"I could be. Are you?" He would have happily died of hunger as long as he held her in his arms.

"I could eat."

Thank God. He was ready to eat a side of beef merely as a starter. "*Bien*. Is there anything you won't eat for breakfast?"

She pulled herself from his arms and sat up. "You cooked last night. I should at least help you now."

He chuckled. "My kitchen, my rules." Good lord. She was beautiful, all rumpled and messed up. She was beautiful anytime, anywhere, anything.

"I promise that if you let me help, I will follow your rules to the letter."

He cocked his head to one side and studied. "And if I cook in your kitchen?"

She laughed. "I will post a list of rules on the refrigerator."

He smiled. "And I will ignore them."

"Of course you will." She shook her head as she laughed. "It's the Lucien code."

"I have a code?" He was pretty sure he didn't have one.

"Of course you do. Not following rules you don't like is, like, at the top of the list."

He closed his eyes, gathered his energy to him. "Right now my code is telling me to make you some breakfast. Do you trust me?"

"Of course I do. But I know that this is not a long-term thing."

Or not.

"You can trust me."

Her eyes got very serious. "Can I?"

"Have I ever given you reason to doubt me? At least my feelings about you?"

Hope looked away, and her body tightened a little underneath his hand. Her silence stretched between them. Finally she looked back at him. "Look. I know who you are. I know what you are. I knew from the get-go that this wasn't going to be long-term. That you don't do long-term. So, don't worry, I'm not looking for it." She kissed him. "I'm happy just as we are." She sighed and snuggled back in close. "I'm grateful for you reminding me I'm a woman again."

Grateful. She was grateful?

Here he was, falling in love with her and she was fucking grateful. His heart thumped against his rib cage in hard, staccato bursts, painful as a round of bullets from a machine gun.

What a sap he was, a stupid, stupid sap. Not that he'd ever let her know that. "You're welcome. It was my pleasure." His voice didn't crack, *Dieu merci*, but it was a near thing. "I'm getting hungry." He sat up and disentangled himself from her. "How about you?"

She blinked. "What time is it?"

He glanced at the clock on the nightstand beside his bed. "Nine something or other."

"That late," she murmured. "I lost all track of time." She shook her head. "While I'd love to taste whatever you'd whip up for breakfast, I have to go. I've got to get to the restaurant and figure out tonight's menu." She smiled. "Rain check?"

"*Bien sûr,*" he said.

"I feel bad. I should help you clean up that mess we made."

"Don't worry. My cleaning lady comes today. I'll pay her extra to take care of it."

Hope bit her bottom lip. He'd like to bite that bottom lip too. Again. "If you're sure."

Lucien went into his closet and pulled out a bathrobe. "I'm sure." He held the robe out for her. "Here, you can put this on while I help find your clothes."

She took the robe, then tucked that gorgeous body of hers into it. She pulled the belt in and tied it tight. "Sure." She paused. "Thank you."

He supposed she was grateful for this too.

****

Hope stood in her shower, letting the hot water sluice through her hair and down her back. She flashed back to what she and Lucien had done in his Jacuzzi.

She remembered every pass of his lips and tongue on her breasts, her body. She remembered his rough palms finding, teasing and caressing every single erogenous zone she had. He even had found some new ones she hadn't known about. She liked that in a man.

She could lose herself in him if she didn't watch out. If she did lose herself, she'd never know the sexy, gutsy woman he'd awakened. She'd be about him and how she fit into his life.

She knew she'd pleased him, especially her taking the lead and calling the shots. She loved the way he'd responded to her touch. Hope felt full of her womanly power, like Cleopatra, Mata Hari.

That Kim girl with the enormous butt.

Hope shook her head at that one. If only she'd known that having a ginormous butt and dressing trashy would make her rich and famous, she'd have eaten anything she wanted and become a millionaire five times over by now. After turning off the water, she grabbed the towel she'd thrown over the shower rod. No, she thought, she was happy in her obscurity.

It was totally laughable that Lucien was worried about the paparazzi coming after her. She smiled at the thought that he believed her to be any kind of newsworthy.

It was also kind of flattering. Well, okay, a lot flattering, but she knew better.

It was sweet. So totally adorable.

She'd never had a boyfriend. She'd had Cormac. She'd been tied up for so many years.

Meanwhile, she'd keep saying what he wanted to hear. Maybe she'd start to believe it herself. But there was no doubt that Lucien had brought her back to life. She had no illusions he would stay with her, even though she wanted him to. She wanted a future, that's just the way she was hardwired. But she would always have a special place in her heart for him.

He woke her up, brought her out of the dark and into the light, treated her like the powerful woman she wanted to be. His equal in passion and desire.

God bless equality.

****

"What's got under your skin?" Hope walked into her kitchen to find Shane flinging pots and pans around.

Shane didn't look at her when he answered.

"You're late."

"Tell the boss to dock my pay." She leaned against a stainless steel counter. "Seriously. What's going on?"

Shane froze then very slowly and carefully turned to face Hope. "Did you have a good time last night?"

He looked bad. He hadn't shaved and there were bruise-like shadows under his eyes, like he hadn't slept in a month of Sundays. "Yes, I did. I had an amazing time."

Shane grunted. "Great. Just great." He turned his back on her.

"Are you getting sick or something?" She grabbed an apron and tied it around her waist.

"No."

Hope rolled her eyes. "I'm going to start the bread for tonight. Let me know when it's safe to talk to you." She smiled and hummed to herself as she put the dough together. Shane's sulking wouldn't ruin her buzz.

Her phone chirped so she hot-footed it over to her purse to get it. Please let it be Lucien.

She grabbed her bag and wrestled her phone out of it. Her hands shook a little. "Hope Monahan."

"Hey, *chère*." Lucien's elegant baritone sounded in Hope's ear.

She took a breath. "Hey yourself."

"I just wanted to know if you got home all right and made it to work."

"I got home all right, but did not manage making it to work on time."

"You're the boss, *bébé*. Whenever you arrive there is on time."

She sighed and slid a glance over to Shane. "You'd think so."

"Is that clown Baker giving you any trouble?"

"Not really. Nothing I can't handle."

"I've been thinking about you all morning, Hope."

"You don't say." She smiled.

"Have you been thinking of me?"

"You know I have. What about you?" Hope bit her lip.

"No, I don't think I've been thinking of me at all." He laughed when Hope sputtered. His voice lowered a couple of octaves. "I've been thinking of you and all the things I want to do with you."

Her breath caught in her throat. "And what would those be?"

"Well, let's see. I'd start by kissing you. Just a simple kiss. An *amuse-bouche* to whet your appetite."

Okay. She would like that. But…

"Yeah. And?"

"You don't fool around, do you, *chère*?"

"I might. Given the right incentive."

He laughed full out, and she felt his mood sizzle right over the satellite signals.

"What kind of incentive do you need?" Lucien asked.

"Let me think." She pursed her lips. "Maybe something along the lines of chocolate and champagne?"

"I'd love to paint every lovely inch of you with chocolate sauce and lick it off your body." His voice was low and kind of growly. "Really slowly."

Her breath caught. "That would be memorable."

"That it would."

"Especially if you let me return the favor with the champagne."

"I can do that. I'll meet you in your bar tonight after you're done serving, and I've tied things up here."

Hope heard a voice in the background and could tell he'd covered up his phone. "I've got to go," he said two seconds later. "I'll see you tonight. You bring the champagne, and I'll bring the chocolate."

"Can't wait. I'll see you later."

"*Bientôt.*" He ended the call.

Hope sighed. She had a boyfriend. How cool was that? She pocketed her phone and turned around, only to find Shane staring at her. "What?"

Shane pursed his lips, then looked down at the floor. "That Durand?" He brought his gaze back up to her.

"Yes. He's coming by tonight after he leaves L'Enfer."

"I see."

Hope sighed. "I really, really have feelings for him. I haven't felt this good in years." She walked over to Shane and put her hand on his arm. "Please be happy for me."

"I'm trying, Hope, I really am, but he's a player." He put his hand over the hand she'd placed on his arm. "I promised Cormac I'd take care of you. I'm going to keep that promise." He lifted her hand and kissed her knuckles.

"Oh, Shane. This is what I want. This is what Cormac would want." She smiled and gave her head a nod. "He wouldn't want me to be alone forever."

"He wouldn't want you with a guy like Durand, either." Shane dropped her hand. "He's into you right now, but as soon as a new woman walks in his life, you'll be out."

"I know who he is. And I like him just the way he is. I'm having fun, I'm looking out for myself. There's no bad here."

"I hope you feel that way when you have to see him with another woman on his arm."

"I'll deal with that when I have to. There's no need to borrow trouble."

He cleared his throat and opened his mouth like he was going to say something, then closed it, like he changed his mind. Shaking his head he said, "I'm here for you if you need me."

She gave him a quick hug. "I know I can count on you. You've been such a good friend to me." She stepped away. "Like the brother I never had."

Shane's eyes slid to the left and his face flushed red. "I just want the best for you."

"I want the same thing for you. Now," she said, "I better get back to the bread. It's not going to make itself." Shane was such a worrywart. His heart was in the right place, but he had absolutely no reason to worry about her.

No reason at all.

****

"How did your exam go?" Lucien stood at the hostess stand when Angelique showed up for work.

She tossed him a sassy smile as she arranged some menus. "I'm pretty sure I aced it."

He nodded. "Good. So, listen." He tightened the knot of his tie. "I'm going to take off after the rush, and I need you to stay."

She raised her eyebrows. "*Pourquoi?*"

"If you must know, I'm going to Hope's."

"Oh." She shrugged. "Sure. As long as I can get

Thursday off."

"Why do you need Thursday off?"

She frowned. "I just do…okay?" Rolling her eyes, she said, "You're my brother, not my jailer. I don't have to tell you everything."

"You do when it means I have to rearrange the restaurant's schedule to accommodate your wishes."

"Fine." She crossed her arms over her chest. "A friend of mine got dumped by her boyfriend, and I promised to spend some time with her to, you know, help her through it. She's really in bad shape." She flipped her hair back. "I'm worried about her."

"Hmm." Why not? But… "I'll need you to do an extra shift next week."

"*Oui*! *Merci beaucoup*!" She stood on her tiptoes and gave him a peck on the cheek. "You are the best brother ever."

"Of course I am." The front door opened, and he glanced over to it, smiled. "*Bienvenu à L'Enfer*. Angelique will take care of you."

Seeing that everything was going well, he went on his way to the kitchen to check on things there and to see what he could do to whip up some amazing chocolate.

Chapter Twenty-Six

Lucien took a seat in Hope's bar and soaked up the ambience. Warm and cozy, a fire blazed in the fieldstone hearth, candles flickered in antique sconces and low, soft Irish harp music filled the room. A lovely, gracious, and romantic space. Homey in the best sense of the word.

Much like the woman who owned the bar.

A pretty blonde bartender came and placed a cocktail napkin and a bowl of Hope's cheese straws in front of him. "Hi! Welcome to Hope's. Can I get you a cocktail?"

"Do you have a single malt scotch?"

She nodded. "Glenlivet."

"Sounds good. On the rocks, please."

"You got it." She turned away to get his drink.

He picked up a cheese straw, wondering if it was as delicious as the ones Hope had made when he had dinner at her apartment. He crunched into it and discovered it was as nice as he remembered. He'd have to see if he could replicate the recipe. Most likely improve it.

No way he'd ask her for it.

He had other *funner* things to ask her for.

"Here you go." The bartender set his drink in front of him. "Would you like to see a menu?"

Well, yes, he would. He had to check out what

Hope had going on with her tavern menu. "Please."

She reached under the bar and pulled up a hand-lettered parchment. "The soup is a Guinness, blue cheese, beef and potato soup. It's very good."

"Thank you." He dismissed her by turning his attention to the menu.

Very interesting. Creative, as expected. Beet chips with curried sour cream. Hazelnut and olive rugelach. Wild mushroom strudels. A green leaf lettuce, apple, and almond salad. But his bar menu would win over Hope's any time.

Imagine what the two of them could accomplish if they went into business together. They'd rule the world.

He smiled as he sipped his scotch.

"Well, look who's here, sitting at my bar."

Lucien felt a smile spread across his face. "I don't know. Who's sitting here at your bar?" He turned in his stool to face her. She'd changed out of her chef's smock but still had a little flour in her hair. He found it adorable.

"You." She leaned in and gave him a quick kiss on his lips. "What are you drinking?"

He toasted her with his glass. "Glenlivet."

Her brows crashed together over her eyes. "You're drinking scotch in my bar?"

"You sell it."

"Against my better judgment." She motioned to the bartender. "Sophie. Would you bring us both a shot of the Connemara single malt?"

Sophie grinned. "You got it, chef."

"Prepare to be schooled," Hope told him.

"I'm looking forward to it."

"Enjoy!" Sophie placed two shots of whiskey in

front of them.

Hope picked up her glass and toasted him with it. "*Sláinte*." She downed it in one swallow.

He lifted his own shot and sniffed at it. "Very smoky."

"It's the peat." She nodded. "Go ahead. Unless you're scared."

He laughed and swallowed the shot. It burned, but he was ready for that. "Very different. The finish is not as smooth as the Glenlivet; it's more scratchy."

"You say that like it's a bad thing." She grabbed one of his cheese straws. "I hope you've seen the error of your ways."

"Absolutely." He leaned in and kissed her. "I hope you've got an appetite, *chére*. Me, I brought a lot of chocolate."

"Well, then what are we waiting for?" She stepped away from the bar. "Sophie, put these drinks on my account. Lucien, let's take this party upstairs."

He pulled out his wallet and left a twenty-dollar tip for Sophie. "Sounds like a plan."

****

"Oh, that looks like sin," Hope cooed as Lucien opened the chocolate hazelnut liqueur ganache he'd cooked up.

"Tastes even better than sin, *chère*. Let me give you a little taste." He dipped his finger into the chocolate and held it out for her to taste.

She snuggled up to him and drew his finger into her mouth to lap up the chocolate with delicate swirls of her tongue. The dark richness of the chocolate combined with the tang and heat of the hazelnut liquor, the sweetness tempered by sea salt was pure heaven.

Doreen Alsen

"Mmm." She let go of his finger with a slight pop.

Lucien's eyes glittered. "You like?"

"I like." She dipped her finger into the bowl, gathered some of the ganache and held it to him. "Try some."

The heat of Lucien's mouth encircled her chocolate-covered finger. The gentle pull of his lips, the slight scrape of his teeth made her remember how those lips and teeth would feel on her nipple.

"I believe that the last time you were here I didn't show you my whole apartment. Want to see what you missed?" Hope asked.

"Absolutely." He cupped the right side of her face, then leaned in and kissed her. "I very much want to see what I missed."

She pressed her cheek into his palm, then turned her head and kissed it. "Come with me. And don't forget the chocolate."

"I wouldn't dare."

She took his hand. "Come with me."

He brushed his lips across her knuckles. "Anywhere."

A comfortable and intimate silence cloaked them as Hope drew him into her bedroom. She turned toward him and twined her arms around his neck.

He laid the dish of ganache on the table next to her bed, then wrapped his arms around her waist. Sitting on the bed, he dragged her on top of him and kissed her. "You taste better than chocolate, *chère*." He nuzzled her neck.

His evening beard rasped over every single nerve ending. Every place he touched sizzled. Her body wept for him.

No longer able to wait, desperate to feel his skin, she pulled at the buttons of his shirt in her haste to undress him. Then she went to work on his belt buckle.

He chuckled. "Aren't you going to wait for the chocolate?"

"The chocolate can wait. I can't." She liberated his erection from his pants and stroked him. He was hot and hard.

He hissed. "Well, then. Have at it."

"Oh, I will." She sat up and swiveled her hips against him while she took off her top. His eyes glittered as she bared herself for his view, for his touch.

"So pretty, *chère.*" He reached up to cup her breast. "*Si jolie.*"

She leaned forward into his hands, pressing her sensitive, erect nipples into his warm palms. Her breath caught as he began to rub feather light circles over the tight peaks.

"Oh, God," she exhaled noisily.

"You like that, *chère*?"

"Yessssss."

Lucien pulled her down and kissed her, long and deep. "I don't think I can wait much longer," he said.

"Me either," she sighed. A grin blossomed across her face. "Let's go for it."

They grappled with each other's clothes, hands shaky, mouths coming together in fierce kisses. Hope ended up on her back with Lucien sprawled on top of her, but not for long.

He rose up and joined their bodies with one long, glorious thrust inside her. She keened with the joy of it, of his possession of her. She wrapped her legs around his amazing butt. She raked her fingers down his back wanting to mark him. To make him hers.

This, she thought. This!

And then she couldn't think at all. His hips pistoned against her, driving him deeper into her core. She met him thrust for thrust, twisting her pelvis to drive him crazy.

Their coupling was hard and fast.

Epic.

"I'm not gonna last long, *chère*." His breath sawed in and out of his lungs as he covered his erection with a condom. He grabbed her bottom and changed the angle of their joining, and managed to drive even deeper into her, finding a spot she didn't know she had.

"Omigawd!" Exquisite sensations of violent pleasure consumed her. She trembled with them as they built and built, then broke. She screamed as they swamped her.

Lucien growled as he arched against her. "I'm coming, *chère*! I'm coming so hard for you!"

She felt him push into her, deep, so deep. It drove her to another peak, her womb spasming hard in new contractions. Her heart exploded with love for this man. How could she give him up when he moved on?

****

Lucien braced his arms to lift his weight off Hope's trembling body. "Are you okay?" he asked.

She sighed and opened her eyes. "Better than okay. I've never, ever had an orgasm like that."

"*Moi aussi*," he said. "Me too."

His heart lifted with the truth. His love for her, her hold on *his* heart made the difference.

He knew he could never have sex without love again. To have sex with anyone who wasn't Hope.

"*Je t'aime*, Hope." He dropped a kiss onto her forehead. "*Tu as mon coeur*." He leaned his forehead against hers. "You own my heart."

"Oh, God, Lucien." She cupped his face in her hands. "God help me, I love you too."

Joy exploded and suffused throughout his entire body. He rolled off her and pulled her on top of him. "Kiss me."

She laughed and obliged him.

Dieu, this felt...right. Inevitable. Like it was his destiny to love this woman, and he'd been waiting all his life to find her.

And now that he had found her, he didn't intend to let her go.

Chapter Twenty-Seven

Shane stood with Angelique in Logan Airport, waiting for Cäcilia to deplane. Angelique fidgeted and fussed, apparently super excited to see her friend again.

He didn't particularly want to be there but Angelique had pouted and wheedled until he agreed. He was certain that nothing good would come out of this visit, which was totally made of suck.

It was a distraction Hope couldn't afford, what with the competition happening this coming weekend.

"Oh, look!" Angelique bounced on the balls of her feet. "Here she comes!"

Oh yeah. Here came Cäcilia the Magnificent, surrounded by an entourage of adoring fans begging for her autograph. He tried to look away, stomach churning, but found it impossible. Cäcilia, tall, blonde, beautiful, Teutonic Cäcilia, was a force of nature.

She pushed through the crowd, aloof and seductive with the natural grace of a woman who knew she was all that and a bag of chips. The snaps and pops of an airport full of cell phone cameras sliced through the air.

Angelique waved and greeted Cäcilia, then moved to meet her halfway. The two grabbed hands and leaned in to kiss each other on each cheek. They immediately started talking volubly in French.

He casually strolled toward them, wanting to get out of the airport sooner rather than later. He cleared his throat. "Uh, Angelique? Do you want me to get Cäcilia's bags?"

The ladies stopped talking long enough to look at him. "That would be so nice!" Angelique said. "Let me introduce you. Cäcilia, this is my friend Shane." She stepped back and beamed.

Cäcilia, however, only gave him a slight upward quirk of her lips. She held out her hand, palm down. *"Enchanté."*

Angelique elbowed him in his side. She nodded in Cäcilia's direction. He bought a clue and lifted Cäcilia's hand and raised it to his lips to give it a little peck of a kiss. "It's nice to meet you."

She pulled her hand back, a superior smile on her face, then turned to Angelique and spewed some more French. The two started walking toward baggage claim, chattering all the while, leaving him no choice but to follow.

He pulled Cäcilia's bags off the conveyor belt, put them on a cart, and went to get the car. The girls stayed on the sidewalk waiting for him to bring the car around.

When he did, both of them sat in the backseat. He felt like a goddamn *chauffeur*; all he needed was the uniform and a jaunty little cap.

Again, they conversed in French. By the time he pulled up in front of Angelique's condo he was more than ready to drop them both off and take some time, some breathing space. He got out of the car, opened the door for them. He held out a hand to help Cäcilia out

But both of them didn't leave out of the car. Only Cäcilia did. And Angelique handed her a key ring. Alarm bells went off in Shane's brain.

He popped the trunk and hauled her bags out.

Cäcilia turned to him. "If you take the bags to the doorman, he will make sure they get to Lucien's condo." She gave him an imperious wave then walked away. Shane stood there, rooted to the spot.

"Come on, Shane. We can go now," Angelique called.

Right. He gave one last glance to the door, got back in the car, and drove off. His knuckles turned white with the force he held the steering wheel.

Yep, he'd been right. This visit was totally made of suck.

****

Hope's cell phone buzzed in her smock pocket. She wiped her hands and dug in to get it.

Lucien calling! "Hey," she said. "I was just thinking about you."

"I'm always thinking of you. What do you think I pick you up after you can get away and we take another turn in the Jacuzzi?"

Hope blushed at the mention of the Jacuzzi and what they'd done in there the first time at his home. "While I would love that, we're really busy, and I don't know when I'm going to be done here."

"The time doesn't matter. I'll wait for you at my condo."

"Okay. I'll call if I'm going to be really late."

"*A bientôt.*" He disconnected the call.

Hope slowly closed her phone and slipped it back into her pocket.

"Hope! We need two beer, beef, and bleu cheese pot pies."

She hustled to get back to work. They really were super busy.

"So, was that Durand?"

"Yes, and I don't want to talk about it to you. I know you don't like him and don't trust him, but I do."

Shane shook his head and plated the Dijon mustard chicken with rice pilaf he'd been working on. "Hope, there's some—"

"I love you, Shane. You're my best friend, but please no more about this. I'm *so* in love with him, and I'm *so* happy with him. Please be happy for me." She pounded the puff pastry dough so she could work the bleu cheese into it. "Apparently Angelique has the night off. You should give her a call, yourself. I bet she'd love to get with you tonight."

Shane looked at her as if she was smear on a lab slide under a microscope. He grunted and turned away. Reaching for the next dupe, he barked out, "I need two more pies and a stewed lentil casserole."

Hope breathed a sigh of release as she put the ingredients together. She hated being at odds with Shane, but it couldn't keep on if he was always putting down Lucien. She didn't want to have to choose. She really didn't.

Why couldn't the two men in her life get along?

Chapter Twenty-Eight

Lucien whistled as he walked to his condo door. He had big plans for the night. He couldn't wait until Hope got there. As he pulled out his keys to open his door, he heard music from inside. What the hell? He turned the key in the lock.

His jaw dropped. Sandalwood candles littered every flat surface in the room. A bottle of champagne chilled in a silver wine bucket that sat on the bar. Ravel's "Bolero" played slow, low, and clichéd. He knew only one person who liked the piece. He swore.

"Cäcilia? Where are you?"

A throaty chuckle came from his bedroom. "In here, *Schatzi*."

He crossed the room in two long strides. *Merde*! There she was, in his bed, swathed in his Egyptian cotton sheets, but clearly naked. "How did you get in here?"

She sat up and let the sheet drop so he got an up-close and in-person view of her breasts. At one point in their tempestuous relationship he would have relished the view. Not tonight.

Especially not tonight with Hope due to stop by any minute.

"Your sister, Angelique. She told me how you were pining away in this backwater little town. Besides—" she smiled—"you've got this absurd competition coming up, and though I don't know why you want to battle the yokels for culinary excellence, Angelique told me how much you want to win." She checked out her manicure. "And I've always been your lucky charm, *n'est-ce-pas*?"

Luck had nothing to do with it. Lucien made his own luck. Cäcilia had once been a convenience. Now she wasn't even that. He broke up with her because he had never been in love with her and because she had used Angelique to get to him.

"No, you're not. Please get out of my bed and put your clothes on. I'll wait in the living room." He turned on his heel and left the room. He thought about leaving the condo, but he didn't want to have an audience for this bad melodrama.

She followed him, naked of course, and wrapped herself around him and clung. Much like a leech. "Lucien," she purred. "You don't want me to do any such thing." She pressed a kiss to his neck. "Come to bed. It's been so long."

He grabbed her arms and pulled her off him. "Go get dressed, take your things, and leave."

Cäcilia's eyes shifted to a spot behind him. Then she focussed on him like a laser. She broke his hold and twined herself around him again. "You don't mean that, *Schatzi*. I'm here to help you. To make you happy."

"Am I interrupting something?"

Here he was, naked woman writhing against him, Hope walking in to see it all. He let loose of Cäcilia's arms to turn and face her. "This is not what it looks like."

Cäcilia stepped away from him in all her naked glory, a predatory smile on her face. "And who are you?"

Hope swallowed.

Lucien leaped toward Hope. "Everything. You are everything."

"This is obviously a bad time." Hope inched backward toward the door. "I need to leave."

"No, stay!" Lucien said. "She's leaving."

Cäcilia smiled an oily upturn of the mouth. "What are you talking about, Lucien? You asked me here, and here I will stay."

"Go get dressed and get out of here." He ran to catch Hope. "Hope, wait! She's leaving."

She stopped and turned. "I'm tired. I'm going home."

He grabbed her hands. "I didn't invite her here. I was surprised when I opened the door and found her in my bedroom. Please. Stay."

Her eyebrows shot to the top of her forehead. "You found her in your bed?"

Probably wasn't the best thing to say. "Well, yes. But that's not the point."

"You expect me to get into that same bed with you after she's been in it?"

"I'll change the sheets." Even as he heard himself say it, he cringed.

She scowled. "Are you kidding me? I am so out of here." She turned and practically ran away.

His stomach clenched, and he felt the blood fall out of his head. "Hope! Come back!"

She just went on walking.

****

Lucien growled as he crossed his own threshold. Cäcilia was stretched across his sofa. She had at least put a robe on. "Darling," she purred. "I thought you'd never get back."

"Why are you still here?"

She flashed her best siren smile. "You don't really want me to leave. You're just playing hard to get."

"*Tais toi!*" The very sight of her nauseated him. "You'll be quiet if you know what's good for you." His hands itched to wrap themselves around her neck and squeeze the life out of her.

"Lucien. *Liebchen.*" She shifted positions, giving him a good look at her skinny ass. "You need to be with a woman again, not a little farm girl."

He went around the room blowing out one candle after another. Cäcilia got off the couch and oozed her way across the room. "*Bitte*, Lucien." She grabbed his butt and squeezed.

His skin crawled. "That's it. You're leaving now." He turned, grabbed her arms and hauled her to the door.

"What are you doing?" She fought him as he dragged her across the room. "You can't treat me this way."

"*Natürlich kann ich das.* I absolutely can," Lucien told her in both English and German, so she would have no problem understanding. He opened the door and tossed her out into the hallway, lingerie and all. "Go away. Don't come back."

He slammed the door. Immediately she began to weep and carry on with the finesse of a two-year-old. She pounded on the door and wailed like it was her job.

Lucien ignored her as he turned off that god-awful Ravel. Finally, he called down to security.

"There's a hysterical woman outside my condo. She's a stalker and dangerous. You need to make her leave, and if she doesn't, please call the police." He hung up.

And waited. Soon there were some angry shrieks and obscenities howled in German. As the sounds abated, he let out a long sigh.

He grabbed his keys and strode for the door. He needed to talk to Hope and make her see reason.

****

Hope had a moment of light-headedness and eased herself into the driver's seat of her car. She forced herself to drag in one deep breath after another. She waited until her hands stopped shaking and pulled out her phone. She hit Shane in her contact list and listened while the phone went to voice mail.

"Hey, Shane?" She held back a sob that threatened to stutter out of her throat. She would not waste one tear on Lucien Durand. "I kinda need to talk to you right now. Can you call me back? Or come by my apartment?" She sighed and repeated, "I need you."

****

Shane shut off his phone and just sat there looking at it. He'd listened to Hope's message. His heart thumped painfully against his rib cage. She sounded so lost. He wanted to go get her, but Angelique had hidden his phone and he didn't get the message until it was way too late.

Angelique reminded him that it was only a matter of time before Lucien dumped Hope, and wasn't it better she found out sooner rather than later. While he believed that, the hurt and need in Hope's voice doused him in guilt. He should have answered the call.

He would make it up to her, he promised himself. Hell. He'd promised Cormac, a deathbed promise, that he would always look after her.

Angelique's phone blew up. "It's Cäcilia. I need to take this." She rose from the bed and moved into his bathroom. A couple of minutes later she came back into the room. "We've got to get dressed and pick up Cäcilia. Lucien tossed her out of his house, with her only in her underwear. *Cochon*!"

Shane thought he knew the answer to his next question, but he asked it anyway. "Where will she go?"

Angelique paused as she pulled up her jeans. "Here, of course."

Of course she was. "She can't come here." Shane shook his head. "This is my apartment."

"It's just for tonight, because Lucien threw away all her clothes, and she's outside in only her robe. The press would have a field day if they got hold of this. Tomorrow she'll move into a hotel. I guess it's going to take longer to peel Hope away from Lucien than I thought." She looked straight into his eyes. "I'm not lying when I say my whole modeling career hinges on getting her back together with Lucien. But can he ever make things easy for me? *Non*!" She gestured to him. "Hurry up and get dressed before the press finds her half-naked outside of Lucien's building."

"Uh, where's she going to sleep?"

"In your bed, silly. She and I will take the bed while you take the sofa."

Great. Just great. The whole situation was one giant FUBAR. "Give me a minute to get my clothes on."

"Don't dilly dally. We have to get her as soon as possible."

So, instead of helping his best friend, he was

helping some supermodel who had it in for his best friend. What was wrong with him? He'd had enough. "You know what? I'll take you to your car and you can deal with Cäcilia. I've got to take care of Hope."

She swung around and goggled at him. "Don't be silly, Shane! Hope will be fine!"

"Yeah, she will." He crossed his arms across his chest. "Because I'm going to take care of her."

"Shane!"

"The two of you can stay here tonight. I'll bunk on Hope's couch or in the restaurant break room."

"You can't mean that! I need you!"

"Hope does too." He finished pulling up his clothes. "Let's go."

"But…"

He opened the door and held it for her. "Let's go," he repeated.

Things felt right for once.

Chapter Twenty-Nine

"Hope! Let me in!" Lucien pounded on her apartment door. After Cäcilia had left, he'd wasted no time in getting to Hope.

Of course, none of this would be necessary if she'd just trusted him and waited until he got rid of Cäcilia.

Shane Baker opened the door. "Go away, Durand. She doesn't want to talk to you."

"Baker," Lucien seethed. "Get out of my way." He tried to push his way in.

Shane body blocked him. "I'm afraid not, *mon ami*." His tone dripped sarcasm.

"Shane, it's okay." Hope put her hand on his arm. "I'll talk to him."

Lucien gave Shane one last push before Shane stepped aside and let him in. "Hope, I had no idea—"

"I know you didn't plan it, but—" she sighed—"it brought up some issues that I need to think about."

"It's so simple, *chère*. There's nothing to think about."

"Please go. I'm tired."

His jaw clenched. She had to listen to him.

Shane stepped forward. "The lady said she'd talk to you later." He inclined his head to the door behind Lucien. "There's the door. Use it."

Lucien's hands itched to punch Shane Baker in his oh—so-smug face, but Hope was standing next to him, her eyes sad and tired. Though it went against every instinct he had, he said, "I'll go." He moved in to kiss her.

She turned at the last second so that he kissed her cheek instead of her mouth.

He stood back, his stomach churning. "I'll talk to you later." Every instinct he had screamed at him to stay. It took every inch of resolve he had to do what Hope wanted him to do. He left.

He looked up at her apartment before he got into his car. He saw Shane glance out a window, then close the blinds, shutting Lucien out.

****

"You okay?" Shane sat on the couch.

"No, I'm just tired." Hope tucked her feet beneath her as she sat on her favorite chair. "It was a shock, that's for sure." Yeah, like she couldn't breathe and the room spun for one horrible minute.

"I'm really sorry I wasn't there for you." Shane hung his head and slumped forward.

"That's okay. It brought a couple of things home to me."

"Like how he doesn't deserve you? How he's been lying to you all along?" Shane looked at her.

"No. I don't think he lied to me. I'm sure he was surprised by Cäcilia's visit." Hope sighed. "He wouldn't bring me to his home if his ex-lover was going to be there. Some things became crystal clear."

"Like what?"

"Shane, he had a naked supermodel wrapped around him like poison oak on a tree trunk."

"Bitch."

She laughed, 'cause Shane could make her do that.

"Preach it. She didn't say much, but everything she said brought home to me that he's going away and that I have to remember this is what I signed up for."

"You didn't sign up to be humiliated."

Hope ignored him. "And how he's never going to be happy away from the bright lights and big city. I can't live anywhere *but* here. I let myself dream that this—" she waved her hand in front of her face—"thing between us could last forever. I should have never forgotten Lucien and I have an expiration date. And I'm jealous! Now that she's here, I can see I'm no competition. Shoot, she even called me a name and he didn't call her on it."

"She called you a name?"

Hope grimaced. "She told me to hop away, little bunny. It's stupid, I know, but it bothers me just the same."

Shane was silent for a minute. He appeared to be wrestling with something. "You can end it now before he gets you more tangled up."

"I have to talk to him, but I really don't want to." Hope unfolded herself from the chair. "And I especially don't want to talk about it tonight. I'm mad. I'm tired."

Shane nodded. "I'll go." He stood.

Hope did as well. "Thanks for being such a good friend."

He hesitated then bent to kiss her cheek. "Get some sleep." He left.

Hope went around her front room turning off the lights. She walked into her bedroom alone, trying not to remember the amazing night she and Lucien had spent there.

She'd been alone before. She could deal with being

alone again.

She'd focus all her energy and attention to the competition on Saturday. No matter how things rolled out for her and Lucien.

Sleep was a long time coming.

****

Lucien sat in his condo with a glass of cognac and a bad mood. Why the hell hadn't Hope been willing to talk to him? Tired, his ass. Baker turned her against him.

"How dare you!" Angelique stormed into the condo she shared with Lucien, who was sitting calmly, sipping his cognac.

Inside he was about to explode out of his skin. He bit his lip. "How dare I what?"

Angelique threw her purse against the wall and rounded on her brother. "Throw Cäcilia out in just her underwear! Seriously, you are so mean! I had to work long and hard on her to come because you were pining for her. And you threw my whole future out the window."

Lucien shook his head. If only she knew what he'd thrown out the window. He'd enlighten her. "Actually, if you want to know what I threw out the window, you can find Cäcilia's clothes down in the alley next to the building." True annoyance took over. "What planet do you live on? If I wanted to be with Cäcilia, I'd be with her. I never…pine."

"Arrrrggghhhh!" Angelique paced the room like a caged wild animal. "You couldn't be polite to her? My modeling career is in her hands."

So many topics, so little time. But first, "Calm yourself down. I will not speak to you while you are so out of control."

As usual, the calmer he made himself, the crazier Angelique got. She picked up one of Cäcilia's candles and lobbed it at his head.

And missed.

He sighed. There were times he truly regretted his promise to *Grand-mère*. He'd truly love to drop-kick Angelique into life and give her a clue.

She wouldn't last a month. Two weeks. But how long could she keep away from the drugs?

Yes until now, she hadn't done drugs. For once in her life, she'd been smart. At least he hoped so. Práyed for it.

Cäcilia was the one who'd introduced Angelique to that scene. Angelique saw Cäcilia as the Good Fairy, the one who held the keys to all her dreams.

The angel perched on her right shoulder.

Lucien snorted. Cäcilia was nothing more than the devil.

Soon the men with all the promises would swoop in and take all that was good and sweet in his sister. He knew those men. He hated them.

Despised them.

And he didn't know what the fuck to do. He did know one thing. No way was he going to give Cäcilia control over his sister. He had one pull on his sister and it was financial. Once the money went away, so would Cäcilia. "You can stay in school and get an allowance and a salary, live here rent free, able to spend whatever you want on clothes, shoes, makeup, whatever. Or, you can follow Cäcilia and you get no support."

"Don't you understand? Without you, there's no Cäcilia to follow. You're the deal breaker."

"Then you're flat out of luck. I don't want Cäcilia. I want Hope."

"I hate you! You're ruining my life on purpose!"

"What are you—thirteen? Please. Control yourself."

Angelique stared at him. "Here it is. You pick Hope or you pick me." She tossed her hair back. "I'm going to get Cäcilia's clothes and then I'm leaving. You have until tomorrow to make the choice." She gave him a tight smile. "Hope or me." Her smile broadened. "Hope or *Grand-mère*. Totally up to you." She stalked off to his bedroom.

No one gave Lucien Durand an ultimatum. "Pack a bag yourself and make sure you gather up Cäcilia's clothes from the alley. If the bums haven't gotten to them."

Hate beamed hot and wild, out of her eyes. Her body vibrated with it. "Oh, aren't you it. Lucien Durand, the king of the world. How on earth do you live with yourself?"

"Very well. I'm not counting on my sibling to support me. I made my own way in the world and did a damn good job of it. I love you, but this is it." He sat in his chair and leaned back. Against all hope, he wished she'd change her mind. "You're on your own."

"What?"

"You heard me." He asked his *Grand-mère* for forgiveness. "Get out. I'm not saving you anymore."

He feigned a nonchalance he didn't feel. "I set you free." He looked at her, her tousled hair, her wild eyes. "You want to be on your own. Go for it. Right now I don't care what happens to you." He took a sip of cognac. He drew his mouth back into a facsimile of a smile. "You want your freedom? Here it is."

She was struck dumb. She shook her head.

He leaped out of his seat. "I love you, but I won't keep enabling you. I probably ruined you by supporting you this long."

"I'm so tired of hearing that. *Pauvre St. Lucien.* And then you can drag out your usual refrain about *Grand-mère* and how she wanted so much for me." Angelique laughed, the sound dry and scratchy.

His temper pulled at the leash. "You may not agree with her, but you can damn well respect her legacy."

"What legacy?" She laughed, the sound pointy and sharp. "Struggling to be dirt poor in some backwoods bayou."

"*Mais, ca c'est fou*! *Grand-mère* sacrificed everything for you." Not to mention what he himself had given up.

"I'm not crazy. None of this makes what you do to me right."

A red haze covered his eyes. "Yes, you poor thing. I pay your rent, food, give you a job, pay for you to go to college. Pay for everything! I'm a really a sad son of a bitch."

"Whatever."

"Okay. Your choice. I've washed my hands of you."

"I don't believe you!"

He sat back into his chair. "That's your problem." He studied her, so like in appearance to their *maman*. It was like a knife wound to his heart.

He swiveled in his seat. Her attachment to Cäcilia was a mistake. Worse than a mistake. He simply hadn't been paying enough attention and let it get out of hand.

He'd failed her.

He still needed to teach her a lesson, no matter how hard it was.

"I hate you!"

"I think you've said that before. I'm tired now, so please gather what Cäcilia needs and take it to her. Take what *you* need for tonight. I have no desire to deal with female foolishness anymore."

"I won't be back!"

He gave her two days, tops, to come running back. He hoped like hell he was making the right decision.

For once he had his own life to take care of.

Chapter Thirty

"I need to talk to you."

Hope flicked her eyes up to find Lucien standing in her garden. She'd been on her knees laying evergreen fronds over her herbs so they'd survive the winter, enjoying the sunlight on a chilly autumn day. Leaves dipped and danced away from their summer branches as a light breeze coaxed them to come out and play.

Foolish leaves. That breeze was not their friend. It lured them to their death. Just like the man looming over her. Lucien Durand was not her friend.

He'd been her enemy and then her lover. But he'd never been her friend. Not in any sense of the definition.

She stood and nodded. They did need to talk. "Okay."

Hands shoved into the pockets of his brown leather bomber jacket, sunglasses shading his eyes, he nodded. "Let's go get coffee."

"I don't want coffee." Hope hadn't been able to eat since Cäcilia waltzed naked into her life. "We can talk right here." She took off her gardening gloves and tossed them on the pile of pine tree branches on the brick walkway.

A sour look crossed his face. "I really want to talk to you someplace private. Maybe we can go up to your apartment."

"No." Absolutely not. He had no place in her apartment. She didn't need more memories of Lucien's presence in her little refuge over her restaurant. The ones she already had were like to kill her. "Just say what you have to say and get it over with."

Lucien scowled, his mouth a severe line creasing his face, his eyes glittering. "We need some privacy."

Oh, no. "Maybe you do, but I don't." She flung her arms out. "This is my garden. No one is going to interrupt us."

"Baker—"

"Shane has nothing to do with this." With us. "He's not here yet. I imagine he's off somewhere waiting on your sister hand and foot."

Just like that, curtains came down over his eyes. "I cut her loose last night, so that is a likely scenario. She had no business bringing Cäcilia here, never mind giving her a key to the condo." He pulled his hands out of his pockets and made a move to grab hers.

She shoved her hands into her own pockets, well out of reach. "Okay. Is that all?"

"I didn't want her here. I don't want her here at all."

"It doesn't matter." She shrugged, trying for nonchalant. "You'll be gone soon, off to other places in the world."

"You can come with me."

"No, I can't. I won't. My life is here."

Lucien pulled back. "You think so little of me."

She finally dared look at him. "I don't. I admire you. I might even be in love with you, even though I've tried not to. But I can't deal with your lifestyle, I can't travel, and I won't deal with the women who think you've done them wrong."

"Hope." He took another step toward her and again she backed up, her heels slipping off the brick path into the nurturing mulch she'd been spreading around the rosemary plants.

As she windmilled her arms, he grabbed her then gathered her into his embrace. She took a second to revel in the warmth of his body, the strength of his arms. After coming to her senses, she pulled herself out of heaven. "I thought I was up for a fling with you. That we could have a relationship, and I would be okay when you went away, and I saw you with other women in *People* again after we're done."

"Fuck that, Hope." His eyes flashed bright fire at her.

"Let me finish."

He closed his mouth and banded his arms around his chest. "Go ahead."

She dragged in a breath to stall for time. This might be more intimate than giving her body to this man, than making love with him. "I knew this would end when it all started. I prepared for it." She chuckled at herself. "I didn't expect for it to end so soon and with such a blatant reminder that we can never be." Taking two steps toward him, she reached out on her own and pulled his hands out of his pockets. "You've given me more than I ever thought I could have again. So thank you."

He jumped back out of her touch like she'd scalded him. "Do you think this was a fling for me? That I've been playing with you while I'm stuck here in Addington?"

The words "stuck here in Addington" stabbed her

in the heart. "Yes. What else could I think? You are an international superchef." She shook her head. "I'm the definition of a homebody. If we got together, you'd be, as you said, stuck here in Addington, because I don't travel to anywhere I have to get on a plane to get to.

"But—"

"Shhhh." She put two fingers against his lips. "Nothing you can say will change anything." Regret bubbled up from the tips of her toes to the tip of her nose. "I have so loved being with you, but as much as I want it to, this thing between you and me just won't work."

"I don't accept that."

"You have to." Dear Lord, how could one person survive all these shallow knife cuts to her soul?

"No, I don't." He flung her from his arms. "All I know is that the only woman I've ever loved is being unreasonable."

"Unreasonable?" You jerk.

"Yes, unreasonable." His chest rose up and down. "I love you. I want to be with you. Only you. Why don't you believe me?"

A brown leaf floated down and across the brick walk. "I think you believe you're in love with me, but when you get a little distance, you'll feel differently."

"Don't tell me what I feel and what I don't feel."

She willed herself to calm. "You will never be happy stuck here, and I won't be happy anywhere else." She took a deep breath. "Please go. Go back to your life. Your jet-set, supermodel, tabloid magazine life. Maybe Cäcilia isn't the one but there are so many other women who you can love and are suited to your lifestyle."

238

"This is so much bullshit. I told you how I feel."

"No, you didn't. You told me how much you wanted to have sex with me—"

"We made love."

"No matter. You belong with someone like Cäcilia."

"I don't want someone like Cäcilia." He cupped her chin. "I want you."

Hot tears pricked behind her eyelids like so many little claws. She wanted to believe his words, so much so that she could barely breathe and hear over the pounding of her heart. But she couldn't.

Not after Cäcilia had shown up. What a wake-up call.

"It'll never work." She sniffed. "Please go. I've got a lot of work to do out here before it gets too cold and too dark."

"Well, I'm not going to beg. Good-bye, Hope."

"Good-bye." Her voice came out ragged and gritty, like she'd swallowed a bucket of sand.

He turned and left. She didn't watch, choosing to turn her back and drop to her knees in front of her herbs. Her hands shook as she tried to put her gloves back on.

She'd done the right thing, though it had broken her heart. After Saturday she wouldn't have to see him again. Most likely he'd pull up stakes soon and go back to gallivanting all over the world.

She'd have her friends and her work and go back to her quiet and safe life.

And she'd get over Lucien Durand.

****

Damn, Shane wanted earplugs and a beer in the

239

worst way. Angelique and Cäcilia chattered away in French, their voices sounding just like that fire engine red muppet Elmo on *Sesame Street*, every word like an ice pick going through one ear and exiting out the other.

He didn't understand everything they said, except for two words: Lucien and Hope. And he didn't like the tone of voice they used when they were talking about Hope.

With every hour that ticked by, he watched the woman he adored trash his best friend. She knew how much Hope meant to him. Apparently she just didn't care. So where the hell was his pride and why the hell was he still holding on to the hope that one day she'd love him the way he loved her?

His chest constricted, and his heart thumped hard. He dragged in a breath and had trouble swallowing. Sweat popped out of his forehead. Fuck this. "Angelique." When she didn't bother to answer him, he repeated, "Angelique!"

"What is it?"

"I'm not comfortable hearing the two of you tear Hope apart, and I'd like you to stop."

Angelique laughed. "Don't be so sensitive."

A frigid sheet of ice grew around his heart. "Well, either you stop trashing my best friend or else we're done."

"You are such a drama queen. You would never choose your precious Hope over me."

"You think so?" He couldn't believe she wasn't taking him seriously. "If you don't stop, I'm leaving, and I'm not coming back as long as you two are here in my apartment."

She barely turned in her chair to say good-bye.

"Okay! I'll see you later." She went back to her conversation with freaking Cäcilia, obviously not giving him a second thought.

"Right." No, she wouldn't see him later. He'd finally bought a clue.

****

"What are you doing here?" Lucien asked his sister.

Angelique's eyes were wide and wary. "I'm showing up for my shift."

"I'm taking your shift. You don't work here any more."

"What? Of course I work here."

"When I said you were on your own, I meant it." Especially since she was responsible for tanking his relationship with Hope. "Cäcilia can support you."

"Lucien, *mon frère*, I need this job."

He knew. With her allowance cut off, she really needed to work.

Tant pis. Just too damn bad.

"You made your choice. You demanded your freedom, and I got out of your way. You're on your own so get another job. You don't have one here any more." Every word ripped his heart into little pieces. "You. Are. On. Your. Own."

"Lucien, please—"

"Don't *please* me. If Cäcilia won't take care of you, go to Shane Baker."

"But you hate Shane. You think he's not good enough for me."

"Right now I don't think you're good enough for him." God forgive him, but that was true. He'd failed. He'd failed Angelique. He'd failed *Grand-mère*.

241

He'd failed himself.

But, no help for it. She got what she wished for.

Be careful for what you wish for. You might just get it. He added another layer of ice over his heart.

"I need this job right now."

"Where's your bestie Cäcilia? You told me she was going to put your modeling career into high gear. She'll get you a job, *sans doute.*"

"You are so hateful!"

He ran a hand down over his tie. "I get that a lot."

"*Cochon*!" She tossed her hair over her shoulders. "I'm sorry you're my brother."

An arrow flying through the air hit its target, his guilt. Score one for Angelique. "I know. I hope that will change."

"It will never change," she spat.

He wanted to cry, but he was Lucien Durand, and he never cried. Ever.

But, dammit to hell, he wanted to bawl like a baby. He hid his emotions like he was used to doing. He dug deep and pulled out the cold detachment he used as his default setting. "I wish you luck."

Angelique stared at him, her eyes wild. "You really are a bastard!"

A couple entered the restaurant. "Please keep the dramatics to a minimum." He forced himself to look at the newcomers to the room. "Do you have a reservation?"

He checked the book and summoned one of the wait-staff to seat the new party. When he looked up, Angelique was gone. He didn't know whether to rejoice or to mourn.

Mourning won out.

****

"You are Hope Monahan?" a heavily accented voice said as its owner entered Hope's kitchen.

Hope closed her eyes before she turned. There was one person with that voice who would want to talk to her. Cäcilia No Last Name.

Hope turned around. Yep. There she stood, Cäcilia in all her blonde Teutonic glory. Hair perfectly done, makeup perfect, body perfectly clad in the latest designer fashion made of silk.

Hope spread a smile across her face. "Cäcilia. What can I do for you?"

She beamed at Hope with an equally fake smile. "You remember me! I'm so flattered."

And pigs flew.

"Your reputation precedes you. Why are you here in my kitchen?"

Fingers be-ringed in gold and sparkly precious gems fluttered in the air in front of her. "I'm here because I want to save you embarrassment."

"Oh, really."

"I know Lucien was very angry with me last night, and I'm so sorry you had to witness that little lovers' spat. I left him, after all, and a man like Lucien has a very healthy ego, and my leaving dealt him a severe blow."

"I can imagine." Hope couldn't help a little wiggle of uncertainty. It was Lucien's word against Cäcilia's.

"He'll come back to me. He always does. There have been many women just like you who only got their hearts trampled on when he left them for me. You should break things off with him before he breaks your heart. There's no way you could ever fit in his world."

243

Now there was a news flash. "I already have. Last night. Have at him."

Cäcilia smiled a genuine smile. "*Sehr gut*. It's for the best." She looked at her watch. "I need to run. I'm glad we had this little chat. *Tschüß!*" She left on a cloud of Dreams by Cäcilia, her signature scent.

Not that Hope had ever worn it. At one hundred dollars an ounce, the closest she'd ever gotten was a spritz at the perfume counter at Macy's. It didn't smell all that good anyway, a cross between dead flowers and poison.

Still, Cäcilia had given her a lot to think about. Lucien said that he didn't want Cäcilia anymore, that he loved her, but could she trust it?

No. She couldn't trust it.

Shane finally made it into work. "Sorry I'm late."

He looked like death warmed over. Purplish bags under his eyes, chin, and cheeks covered in blond whiskers, his face gray, clothes stained and rumpled like he'd pulled on the stuff he'd dropped on the floor last night. This had to be Pod-Shane, because no way her best bud ever left the house looking like this.

He swung his head around and peered at her with bloodshot eyes. "I broke it off with Angelique last night."

"Oh, Shane. I'm so sorry."

He shook his head. "Don't be. We were all at Cäcilia's hotel suite, and I realized she doesn't love me as much as I love her. She probably doesn't love me at all." He sniffed and studied his shoes. "I was just a distraction until she got back to her real life."

"She's young, Shane. Immature. Maybe you should give her another chance."

"No fucking way in hell." He thumped his fist on a stainless steel counter. He might have dented it. "Even if she wanted a second chance, I'm not letting her use me like that. She had to choose between Cäcilia and chasing fame with the jetset—" his chest heaved—"and me. She chose fame and the jetset. I'm going to go change for prep work."

Hope thought of her breakup with Lucien, if you could call it breaking up, relinquishing him for his own good. So he could go back to the world he thrived in. Cäcilia's visit had only reinforced the rightness of her decision, not just for Lucien, but for herself.

It had been fun. He'd wakened the sensual woman in her, and she was grateful for that. Someday she'd meet a man with whom she wanted to have a physical relationship.

One thing was sure. She'd never forget the time she'd spent with Lucien Durand. As much as she wanted to.

A different emotion blared in her breast. She didn't want to forget it. Forget Lucien and their time together. She'd push past loving him, but she would love the times they had for the rest of her life.

Chapter Thirty-One

"Dammit!" Lucien growled after he tasted the sauce for his Crawfish Vermouth. It just wasn't quite the flavor profile he wanted.

As he dumped the contents of the pan into a garbage bin, he pondered what ingredients to try next. He really should have the recipe perfect by now, but he wouldn't let that thought tear him down. He still intended to kick contest ass.

He'd roll over anybody who got in his way. Including Hope.

He'd just finished adding chili-infused vermouth when someone stomped across the kitchen. He turned and immediately someone punched him in the face. He covered his nose as blood rushed out of it then shook his head to clear it.

And saw Shane Baker pulling his fist back, ready to hit him again. What the hell?

"Punch me again, Baker, and I'll have you arrested for assault," he spat out.

Baker had murder in his eyes, but he lowered his clenched hand. "Might be worth it, but I don't want to leave Hope stranded tomorrow."

"Jesus. You're a crazy man. *Fou!*" He grabbed a paper towel to staunch the bleeding. "What did you do that for?"

"I told you that if you hurt Hope, I'd go after you

and leave you in a world of pain. You know what, Captain Asshole? You hurt Hope."

"Hope broke up with me, not the other way around." His pride took a hit as he admitted it.

"Do you think she wanted to dump you? If you do, you're stupider than you look."

"She didn't look like she was having a hard time laying down the law," he gritted out. He checked out the paper towel and knew he needed to get some ice. He stepped around Baker to go to the ice chest. "All over this bull that we are such different people with such different lives."

"You are different people, and you do lead different lives." Shane crossed his arms over his chest.

Lucien wrapped the ice in another hunk of paper towel and pressed it against his nose. He hissed as it made contact. "I fell in love with her because she is so different than the women I usually meet. We could make it work if she wanted to give us a chance."

Shane stared at him. "You're in love with her?"

"*Oui!*"

"Like I'd believe a word coming out of your mouth." He hooked his thumbs in his belt loops. "Because from where I'm standing, both you and your sister are a couple of lying users."

"What's this about my sister?" His heart sank. "What the hell did you do to her?" He may have cut her loose, but he still cared about her welfare, and if this *imbécile* had done anything to harm his sister, Lucien would make him pay.

"The better question is what she did to me." Baker shook his head. "But this isn't about me and Angelique. It's about you messing with Hope."

Lucien felt smoke come out of his ears. "I don't answer to you. What happens between Hope and me is none of your damn business."

"The hell it isn't. Know this. If you do anything to sabotage Hope in the competition tomorrow, I will reach down through your mouth and rip your nuts out." His nose flared. "Count on it." Baker turned on his heel and stomped out.

Who does he think he is? Lucien threw the saucepan with his revamped vermouth sauce against the wall. If Shane Baker entertained the idea that he had any control over what Lucien did or didn't do, he had another thing coming.

Why didn't anyone see that he was the injured party, not Hope? She hadn't believed him. She'd dared to break up with him, when he was baring his heart, his soul, for the first time in his entire life. He had to make her see reason.

He wanted Hope back, but on his terms. He'd mount a charm offensive to coax her back into his arms, into his bed. Into his life.

Oui. Charm. No woman could hold out against him when he turned the charm up to eleven. He'd make sure Hope couldn't resist him.

****

Hope got to the competition venue early. Too early. Her eyelids felt weighted down with lead, and fatigue dogged her. She hadn't slept, really slept, since Wednesday night, the night before God's gift to the world—also known as Cäcilia—had shown up naked in Lucien's bed.

Lucien claimed to love her, but she didn't believe it anymore. Not after Cäcilia's little visit yesterday. The more she thought about it, the angrier she got, which felt way better than moping around acting like a sap.

She was totally going to beat him in this competition.

"Hey! You're here early."

Hope turned to find Ainslie bustling toward her. Ainslie was overseeing the whole event. "I wanted to get the lay of the land."

"You've got to come with me into the audience café and take a look at the tables the artists have donated for the auction. They are so amazing!" Ainslie grabbed Hope's hand and dragged her to the display area.

Amazing didn't come close to describing the tables. One had a breathtaking mosaic made of different sizes and colors of tiles. Another had been antiqued and decorated with Peter Hunt designs painted on the tabletop, the colors brash and brilliant. Another had all kinds of buttons covering the edges of the top and the four splindly legs. "These are brilliant."

Ainslie nodded. "I know!"

"I know you'll make a fortune for the ballet guild."

"That's the plan." Ainslie blew out a breath.

Who needed Lucien—the Liar King—when you had a bestie like Ainslie? Hope didn't want to examine that thought too closely.

She'd get over him sooner or later. She hoped it would be sooner. It *would* be sooner. She'd make sure of it.

But, today—that whole being over Lucien thing? Wasn't going to happen.

And if he brought Cäcilia to watch the competition... It would hurt almost as badly as

Cormac's death.

No! She would not harbor any more feelings for that man. Never, ever, ever!

Oh, hell. She didn't know. All her emotions collided around in her stomach, making a nasty, stabby, pain stew.

"Well, I've got to get back to my work area. I need to make sure that everything's in place. Don't want to take any chances!" She hugged Andi and Ainslie. "Good luck on the auction!"

She made her way back to her station in the competition kitchen. Her jaw dropped. Sitting on top of her workspace was a huge bouquet of flowers. Riotous colors spilled from the enormous display, brilliant red roses and sunny yellow lilies. Exotic Bird of Paradises with their blue, orange, pink, and yellow birdlike blooms.

Humph. Nothing local or seasonal. Pretty much over the top. Who could have given it to her? She didn't have to read the card to figure it out.

Just another sign that he just didn't know her. Understand her.

And, of course he had to pull a stunt like this on the morning of the contest. Was he trying to fake her out? Get her off her game?

She waited for some anger to bubble up, but it didn't come. Instead, a heaviness settled over her shoulders like a cloak made of those Acme ton weights they always dropped on Wile E. Coyote. After reading the card, which told her that he loved her and only wanted to be with her, she picked up the vase of flowers and dumped them into the garbage, vase and all.

Let him try to distract her.

If he really loved her, he'd respect her wishes and leave her the hell alone.

****

Lucien walked into the competition kitchen all ready to rock and roll. By now Hope should have gotten his flowers and she'd listen to him. The frosting on his contest cake, so to speak.

He looked around and saw Hope.

Just Hope. No flowers.

What in hell had happened? Did the florist mess up the delivery? He guessed he should figure it out. He crossed the floor to Hope's station in three big steps. "Hope."

She turned to face him. "Lucien." Her face looked totally blank.

"Did you get my flowers?"

"Yes, I did. Thank you."

Okay. This was not the reaction he usually got when he sent a woman flowers. The Bird of Paradise always got 'em. "Did you like them?"

"Yes, they were very pretty. Anything else?"

"I'm glad you liked them." He glanced over her head to see Baker shaking his head at him. "*Bonne chance*." He didn't know what went wrong. "Good luck."

"Good luck." She showed him her back, furiously stirring some batter in a bowl she carried.

He took his place in the station next to Hope's and saw the flowers, vase and all, in her trashcan. There was something very wrong with this picture.

Chapter Thirty-Two

"Good afternoon and welcome to the first annual Addington's Tables competition. I think it's going to be a great day, right Gloria?" Byron Callahan, lead anchor for Addington's local news station, flashed his pearly whites at the camera as he opened the broadcast of the contest. He passed off the microphone to his colleague, Gloria Silva.

"It is! The best chefs in town are here, and they are ready to rock and roll!"

"You can tell! The energy here is amazing. We've got quite a prestigious lineup of local talent today."

"We do, Byron. We really do. We've got Isadora Costa, owner and head chef of The Costa's Cozy Cottage. She serves up Portuguese cuisine that tastes like it came straight from The Azores. From Esmeralda's we have Sam Mason, who specializes in French bistro fare."

Byron smirked. "I hear we will also get food from Theo Chalkias, owner of Pizza Plus. His Greek take on everyone's Italian favorites is legendary." Byron patted his stomach. "I can attest to that."

Gloria twittered. "Oh, Byron."

"Who else is here today?"

"We've got Ruth Rawson, the genius behind the grill at the Pilgrim Steak and Rib House and Joe Cook, owner of the Clam Shack. You can count on him to present some spectacular seafood."

"Did I see Bobby Santos from The End Zone back there in the kitchen?"

"You sure did. He's so adventurous with his food. You never know what he'll come up with."

"Do you think there might be some onion rings in our future?"

"Along with a Bobby Burger? We can dream, Byron. We can dream." Gloria sighed. "And speaking of dreams, international superchef Lucien Durand is competing today, representing his latest restaurant, L'Enfer Addington. Cajun cuisine never looked so good." She winked at the camera while she fanned herself.

"Cool your jets, girlfriend." Byron guffawed. "Last, but certainly not least, is Hope Monahan, the darling of the earth-to-table set." He put a hand on Gloria's shoulder. "I'm set for an awesome day of eating."

Gloria moved slightly, and Byron's hand fell away from her shoulder. "Why don't we fill in the TV audience with the rules about today's competition?"

"Good idea. The first elimination happens during the Table silent auction. All the competitors have to supply their best *amuse-bouches*, those little compact bites that make or break a party. The audience will vote for which ones they like best. The four chefs who have the least votes will be eliminated. The other four chefs will go on."

Gloria took over. "The next four chefs will have to make their best dishes, an appetizer, an entrée, and a dessert for our panel of three judges. The judges will decide which chefs will go on to the next courses. The chef who has the best overall meal will be the champion."

"Let's go over to the auction and check out the canapés. I'm hungry!" Byron rubbed his belly.

"I'm right there with you," Gloria commented. "Let's go!"

As they walked into the auction area the camera panned over the tables loaded with the *amuse-bouche* offerings from the seven chefs. Servers from each of the restaurants manned their battle stations, accepting the tickets that served to determine the winner of this part of the competition.

"Here we are at Chef Lucien's station where he's offering us some Crawfish Vermouth," Byron stated as Gloria popped a toast point covered with a creamy crawfish mixture into her mouth.

"Mmmmm. Delicious!" She licked her lips. "And I don't mean just the canapé, if you get my drift."

Byron guffawed. "You bad girl."

They moved to the next station. "What does Chef Joe have for us today?" Gloria smiled at the waiter.

"Some Rocky Point Clam Cakes." He held out a plate with a golden brown, crispy ball to Byron.

It crunched audibly as Byron bit into it. He closed his eyes as he chewed. "These are just as good as I remember from when my parents took us all to the Rocky Point Amusement Park in Rhode Island. Well done."

"Next up is Chef Ruth's offering from The Pilgrim Steak and Rib House. Something smells very good, chef. What do you have here for us?" Gloria stepped to the Pilgrim table.

The server grinned and offered Gloria a bite of

barbecued pork on a toothpick. "Mini boneless ribs with her special sauce on them. Here…" The girl held the little sauced piece of meat skewered by the deadly toothpick. "Try it."

Gloria took the skewer, held a napkin under it, and stuffed it into her mouth. "Very good," she gushed around the food in her mouth. "Messy, but good."

They moved on to the next presentation from Esmeralda's. "Hello," Byron schmoozed. "What did Chef Sam cook for us today??"

"French ham, Dijon, Cornichons, and fresh thyme on house-made French bread."

"Sounds yummy!" Gloria picked up a fragrant thyme and ham-covered bite and nibbled on it. She nodded as she chewed.

"I think she likes it!" Byron chuckled for the camera.

They moved down the line tasting garlic mussels from Chef Theo, linguiça wrapped in Portuguese bread dough à la Isadora, and Bobby Burger sliders from The End Zone. They ended up at the final presentation. "These are the legendary Shrimp in Puff Pastry from Hope Monahan," Byron gushed.

"Mmm hmm," Gloria agreed. "Everybody's favorite!"

"And it looks like the votes are in! Let's listen."

****

Hope bit her lower lip as she waited to hear the results of the *amuse-bouche* part of the competition. The other chefs were formidable. She felt Lucien's eyes boring a hole through her back.

She wished he would just go away, so of course he had to have the station right next to hers.

Still her stomach clenched in anticipation of the results. She thought she'd go on to the next round, but everybody's bites looked delicious and very appealing. The other chefs were quite capable and creative, so she didn't dare think of it as a sure thing. Her heart thumped hard against her ribs.

The mayor of Addington moved to a stage holding up a podium. "Good afternoon, ladies and gentlemen! Welcome to the first annual Addington's Tables. As you know, you voted for the four chefs who will go on to the next round. Unfortunately, four very talented chefs will be eliminated. Let's see who moves on."

He extracted a white piece of paper from his jacket pocket, pulled out his glasses, and put them on. "I won't keep you waiting. The four chefs moving on to the next phase of the competition are Theo Chalkias from Pizza Plus, Bobby Santos from The End Zone, Lucien Durand from L'Enfer Addington, and finally, Hope Monahan from Hope's."

Relief washed over Hope like a typhoon. She was in the final four, and she'd be sure to serve up Lucien's butt on a platter. She slid a glance to Lucien, standing next to her.

He might have been a cat with feathers sticking out of his mouth. Cocky jerk.

The mayor turned to Isadora Costa, Sam Wilson, Ruth Rawson, and Joe Cook. "I'm sorry, but the audience has spoken. Thank you for sharing your wonderful food with us!"

He turned to the four chefs going to the next round. "So here are the rules. The four of you will go on to create your best appetizer. You'll serve it to our panel of expert chefs and they will decide who will go on to the entrée round and who will be eliminated. Let me introduce our panel of judges."

Hope barely heard anything, given the buzzing in her ears. She was going head to head with Lucien. And she would beat him.

Oh, yeah. Good times.

****

Lucien held his breath because he wanted to go up against Hope in the final round of the contest. He considered her his only true competitor. He'd pull out all the stops to defeat her.

He'd be kind. He certainly would not humiliate her. He wanted his competition hard fought so that there could be no doubt that his victory was real. He put his *sous-chef* to work shelling shrimp for his *Quenelles des Crevettes* appetizer. He glanced over to Hope's station. She was putting together pastry dough for some individual tarts. She already had flour in her hair.

He shook his head. Her sloppiness had grown on him. He now found it adorable.

He needed to stop watching Hope and pay attention to his *Quenelles*.

****

Hope looked up at the clock, then down at her Smoked Mackerel Mini-Tarts and liked what she saw.

"They look great, Hope," Shane murmured in her ear. "It's a winning appetizer."

"From your mouth to God's ears, buddy." She followed the other head chefs over to the judging panel. Her stomach jumped around like Ricochet Rabbit off his ADHD meds.

The judges tasted Theo's appetizer first. "I've prepared for you today battered and deep fried zucchini and eggplant and paired them with a *Skordalia* sauce."

They liked the crunch of the vegetables, thought there was a little too much garlic in the *Skordalia*.

Lucien was up next. He smiled his best come-hither-you-know-you-want-to grin. "You have before you Creole-inspired *Quenelles des Crevettes*. Enjoy."

Hope thought the female judge would fall off her chair in a full swoon. Of course the judges loved Lucien's appetizer.

Bobby Santos presented his offering to the panel, Peanut Crusted Thai Chicken Wings with a tamarind dipping sauce. The judges liked those too.

Hope stepped up to the plate. "What you have before you is a mini smoked mackerel tart, with a tomato *concassé* and fresh herbs from my garden. I hope you like it."

"Very creamy, very smooth. I like it," one of the male judges told her. "The tomato *concassé* is delightful. Did you smoke the mackerel yourself?"

"I did, thank you." Hope took a deep breath. She started back to her cooking station with the others to clean up and get ready for the next course, as long as she wasn't eliminated. Catching a glimpse of Lucien standing in her way, she veered and took another route.

Damn the man. She would not let him shake her concentration or her confidence. Even though he did, big time. She clenched her hands into fists.

A huge commotion came from the front of the hall. Hope looked around. Lots of noise and flashes from cameras the size of HumVees. Oh, goody. Cäcilia was in the house.

The press flocked around her of course. She looked absolutely beautiful and put together like a Teutonic

Barbie.

Hope kept her gaze lowered while she wiped down one cutting board. It didn't stop her from hearing what Cäcilia had to say.

That shrill, brittle, little fake laugh hurt Hope's ears. But the words following that laugh cracked the fragile barrier Hope had placed around her heart. "I'm here to support my fiancé, of course!" She blew a kiss to Lucien.

Hope slid her eyes over to him; his face was a total blank. Tears sprang to her eyes, and she blinked them away. After all, hadn't Cäcilia told her that Lucien always came back to her? She had no right to be surprised, as she had been warned.

Well, what didn't kill you made you stronger.

Or at least that was the adage.

****

Lucien clenched his jaw so hard he nearly grated his teeth into rounded stubs. Why was Cäcilia here pretending to be his fiancée? He thought he'd made it clear that they were over and done. Why the hell wouldn't she leave him alone?

He shot a glance at Hope. She stood with her head bowed, swallowing hard. He ached to go to her, take her into his arms, and kiss her so that everyone would see that Hope was the one he wanted to be with, not Cäcilia.

But her earlier coldness made him give that idea a second thought. Maybe she wouldn't welcome his gesture of love. He had to think of something.

The mayor stepped back up to the podium with the results of the appetizer round. Unfortunately for him, Bobby Santos was the first one to go.

259

Lucien didn't hear a single word they said other than the announcement of who would go on to the entrée round.

He studiously ignored Cäcilia's attempts to get his attention and immersed himself in his carefully planned second course, *Veal Grillards* and three cheese grits with some Southern Fried Okra.

He'd ignore Cäcilia until after the competition and let her know, in no uncertain terms, that she needed to go and stay away.

He snuck a sideways glance at Hope and watched her chest rise and fall, watched her ball her hands into shaky fists. He wished he could reassure her that he had nothing to do with Cäcilia's being here.

He had to make her believe it.

Chapter Thirty-Three

Hope did her best to block out the presence of T.B., a.k.a. Teutonic Barbie, but the woman didn't make it easy. She had to focus on her menu and knock it out of the park. She went about the business of concocting Roast Pheasant with Apples and Calvados, Colcannon potatoes with bacon, shaved brussels sprouts, thyme, and chives with an heirloom beet salad sprinkled with clumps of blue cheese and toasted, salted sunflower seeds.

She caught Shane staring at her every now and then, concern in his eyes, but she couldn't dwell on it. All he had to do was work on the elements of the dish just as they had rehearsed.

Hope, however, had to deal with shaky hands and trouble with her knife cuts. If she didn't get her head back in the game, she was going to lop off the tips of her fingers.

The time flew by; she sure hoped the pheasant was perfectly executed. Next thing she knew, she was up in front of the judges. Lucien's spit grilled veal looked delicious, as did Theo's *Moussaka*. They presented their meals and went back to the kitchen area to wait for them to announce who would go on to the dessert round.

In the meantime, Cäcilia held court and told anyone who would listen, even a few people who didn't want to hear it, about how Lucien had this contest in the bag.

"Hey, Hope?" Shane put his hands on her shoulders and started to knead out some of the stress. "Don't let her bother you. Just do what you need to do to win this thing."

"No problem, buddy." Her gaze slid to Lucien's station. He looked very grim.

"Good girl." Shane moved away.

Hope closed her eyes and focused on the breathing she'd learned in her yoga class, trying to create a little bubble of peace around her.

Too bad it didn't work.

****

Lucien grew more and more concerned about Hope. At least she was attempting to put things in order. Her hands were shaking. She dropped things. Almost cut off the tip of her finger.

A dark cloud of guilt and misery rose up around him. This was all his fault.

"Lucien, I'm here to give you a kiss for good luck."

Damnation. He shook his head as he turned to face the person he least wanted to see. Cäcilia stood right across from him, with only his work area between them. "I don't think so."

"Please, Lucien. All the press is here, ready to document our reunion."

"There is no reunion. *S'en aller*. Go away."

"That's no way to speak to your fiancée, *Schatzi*. Let me give you a kiss."

"I'd rather eat at a McDonald's. *Va-t'en*, before you embarrass yourself."

"But Lucien, you invited me. I'm here at your request."

The woman was insane. He moved around his station and grabbed her by the shoulders. "You are not welcome here. Not now, not ever. Now go, before I call security to drag you out."

She hissed as she pulled out of his grasp. "You are going to regret this. I'll ruin you and that precious sister of yours."

"You can try."

Cäcilia brought her hand up to slap him across his face. He caught her arm before she could connect. "Just go and take your side show with you." He let her loose.

She threw him one last, out of control look before she turned and hurried as fast as her four-inch high, red-soled stilettos would take her.

He risked a glance at Hope. She was staring at him, her eyes devoid of emotion.

"Hope, I can explain all of this."

"Don't bother."

Why wouldn't she listen to him? A big barbed-wire ball clogged his throat. And more than a little panic. He actually might not be able to get Hope back.

He might lose the best thing that had ever happened in his life.

After some confusion and a more than a little bit of soul searching, the answer came to him. It went against every instinct he'd ever had. But in the end, she'd never doubt his love for her if he could pull off this plan.

Nerves banged against his stomach walls, like rabid bats. If she didn't believe he loved her after he did this, she'd never believe him.

And he'd have to respect that and move on. Simple

as that.

He sent a brief prayer to *le bon Dieu* for help.

****

Hope heaved a huge sigh of relief when the mayor announced that she and Lucien were the two chefs going into the dessert round. She had to pull herself together. She loved the mini pomegranate cheesecakes and hoped the judges didn't take offense about her doing another individual portion thing.

And she knew—even better than she knew her own name—that Lucien would pull out all the stops. She had to be at the top of her game.

He would do anything he could to win. Winning this competition was crucial for him.

Well, it was crucial to her too.

She took a chance and looked over to Lucien. He watched her with an expression on his face that she'd never seen before. And grabbed for the salt.

What the heck? Was he actually going to throw the contest so she would win? That she couldn't win on her own?

Like he was God. Oh, no, no, no, no. "Don't you dare," she hissed at him.

He blinked. "Dare what?"

"You will not sabotage yourself so I'll win. If I beat you, when I beat you, it'll be on my merits, not because you give up."

He very slowly lifted his hand away from the container and gave her a brief, sharp nod.

Hope turned back to her own work. She had a dessert course to knock out of the park.

****

Hope rejected Lucien's big sacrifice. He was

totally out of ideas on how to soften her toward him. He'd lost control of the situation, and he still wasn't quite sure how. That never happened, not to Lucien Durand.

He inwardly cursed Cäcilia for her trickery. He cursed Angelique for being gullible and selfish. He cursed whatever damn fate that caused him to fall in love so hard and so fast with this amazing woman.

She stood next to him, flour in her hair, red pomegranate stains on her tunic, and she'd never looked more beautiful. She was as beautiful on the inside as she was on the outside. How could he live without her?

It just wasn't an option. To convince her that he loved her more than anything. The longing grabbed him, poured over him, filled him and spilled down around him.

He took a deep breath as the judges started on Hope's pomegranate miniature cheesecakes. The presentation was masterful, little creamy red-streaked cakes studded with pomegranate seeds, each one topped with a streusel of toasted, chopped, and sugared chestnuts.

Lucien had to hand it to her. She made desserts like no one else. She put Pascal, his pastry chef, to shame.

"So pretty! Almost too pretty to eat," one of the male judges told her.

"Thank you," Hope said.

"The cinnamon is just the right amount. A little more would have been too much."

Why, Lucien wondered, had he thought he had to screw his dessert up so that Hope could win? She was gifted with the skill to make a sublime dessert.

Lucien had to acknowledge that he didn't have that skill, which was the reason he'd hired Pascal to make the desserts for L'Enfer. He caught a breath and held it.

"It's the perfect fall dessert. The texture and taste are superb."

"I'm glad you enjoyed it." Hope gave each of the judges that warm, friendly smile of hers. The smile he hadn't seen in a while. The desire to see that smile aimed at him clutched and squeezed his heart.

Dammit.

"And Chef Lucien, what do you have for us?"

"Tonight you have before you a New Orleans Coffee Bavarian Cream. I've kept the dish whole so you can see the presentation, but have also individual slices for you. *Bon appétit.*"

His Bavarian Cream looked good. He'd glazed the top of the mold with a delicate chocolate ganache and chocolate-covered espresso beans. He knew it tasted out of this world.

But did it look and taste good enough to rival Hope's? He thought so.

"I like this. It really brings a touch of New Orleans into the flavor profile."

"I agree with that. I wonder, though, if the ganache is a little too heavy for the whipped cream and gelatin of the Bavarian cream."

"You've got a point," the last judge said. "The Bavarian cream is exactly the right texture and mouth feel, but the ganache is a little thick. Perhaps a fruit note, like an orange glaze for a bright hint of citrus."

"I so agree! Orange would be a wonderful addition! Just a little lift from some candied zest."

Lucien kept his expression blank, but every word

from the judges zapped him like a hornet sting. Orange, schmorange. The chocolate ganache worked plenty well.

"Thank you Chef Hope, Chef Lucien. Please go back to your stations and we'll call you when the judges have made their decisions."

Lucien nodded, first at the judges, then at Hope.

His nerves twitched as he walked back to his station, along with Hope. He wanted to win; he wanted her to win; he didn't know what the hell he wanted.

Except for getting Hope to believe in his love for her.

Nothing else mattered.

****

Hope held back the fist pump she wanted to do after the judges raved over her dessert. She replayed every comment in her mind. She'd meant to take the dessert round and she had.

Of course, winning wasn't a done deal. They had to take into account how many votes they'd gotten on the *amuse-bouche* part of the day, then the overall meals they'd served the judges.

She gave Lucien the side eye as he cleaned his knives. She simply could not believe that he'd been about to throw the competition so she could win. Like she couldn't beat him on her own. Puh-leez.

But then...why would he do that? Winning and being declared The Greatest Chef in All the Land defined his life. For him, failure was never an option.

That he'd actually considered letting her win, well...the mind boggled. He said he loved her and oh, dear Lord, every cell in her body wanted to believe him. That big scene with him throwing Cäcilia out so publically was a thing of beauty. That, added to his willingness to lose the contest added up to only one thing.

Lucien Durand was in love with her.

He would have thrown the contest to get her back. The only thing keeping him from doing so was the fact that she told him not to. He respected her wishes. He respected her. Saw her as an equal.

Euphoria whooshed over her, pulling her out to sea on a riptide. She drowned in the pools of love she'd been trying to ignore. She turned to find him watching her. His eyes sparked with intensity as he stared at her. Caught in that laser-like gaze, she could barely breathe, much less think.

Given the way he was looking at her, though, Hope felt that thinking was overrated. All she had to do was open up and feel. Feel? Every nerve ending felt raw and beyond sensitive, so much so, she could barely stand it.

For once, she wondered, all she had to do was reach out and all her dreams would come true.

The judges took that moment to call Hope and Lucien back to the stage.

Chapter Thirty-Four

Lucien faced the judges, his heart banging around in his ribcage. Would he win? Would he lose? Would Hope understand what he'd tried to get her to see?

The third one was the most important question he'd ever faced in his entire life. Nerves crawled all over him like fire ants.

He swallowed hard, trying to clear a huge ball of anxiety out of his throat. He didn't like it, not one little bit. Lucien Durand always knew what came next, simply because he made it happen. He'd totally lost control of his life.

Hope Monahan held his future happiness in her small, French-manicured hands. He wanted to take one of those hands and press a kiss onto it.

She turned to him and smiled. "Good luck."

"*Bonne chance.*" That smile of hers was worth a million bucks.

The mayor came back to the podium. "Chef Lucien, Chef Hope, the judges have reached their decisions based not only on your desserts but also on the entire meal. Judges?"

"Chef Lucien, we were overwhelmed by your mastery and inspiration. Truly, you brought all the flavor and color of New Orleans to our little town of Addington, and every dish was delicious."

Lucien's palms began to itch. He didn't like the

sound of this. "*Merci*. Thank you."

"But in the end," the second judge said, "we felt that Hope's dedication to local ingredients and commitment to seasonal eating made her the person best suited to represent Addington's cuisine."

The woman judge smiled at Hope. "Congratulations, Hope Monahan! You are the winner of Addington's Tables."

Hope gasped. Her mouth opened and closed, then opened again. Her chest rose and fell in what had to be painful bursts. Lucien watched absolute joy roll over her and it flowed to him. Rather than feeling disgust at losing, a strong sense of pride and pure, absolute love burst out of him.

He'd never known the like. A newborn. He felt truly made over in that one moment. Hope's happiness was his.

Hope was his everything. The knowledge burst along every synapse in his body. He didn't waste one more moment. He snatched her up in his arms and soul-kissed her. She fizzed against him like fine champagne. They broke apart, and he cupped her cheeks with his hands. "I am so proud of you!"

She grinned. "Thank you!"

He grabbed her against him again and spun her around. "*Dieu, je t'aime. Je t'aime pour toujours.*" A little dizzy, he stopped. "Marry me."

"What?"

"I love you! Marry me."

"I don't know." She frowned. "We've still got a lot to work out."

He looked around and saw the entire town staring at them with their mouths hanging open. "We're going to do this without an audience." That said, he picked her up, tossed her over his shoulder in a fireman's hold, and marched off the stage while the crowd cheered.

"What are you doing?" She pounded her fists on his back and kicked her legs in the air. "Put me down!"

"Wait! Bring her back! She didn't get her trophy yet," the mayor yelled, but Lucien ignored him. He marched her to the backstage area and closed them inside the walk-in refrigerator, then he put her down.

"You are a crazy man!"

"I am. Totally and absolutely crazy in love with you." He grabbed her hands. "After today you have to know how much I love you. I sent you a boatload of flowers. I publically humiliated Cäcilia." He went in for the kill. "I was ready and willing to sabotage myself and lose the contest so you could win."

"Yeah, about that. I'm less than excited about the fact that you thought you had to mess up for me to win." She pulled her hands out of his and wrapped her arms around herself. "Damn, it's cold in here."

"I'm sorry about that, but I've got this ego thing going on. I promise to work on it. But doesn't that show you how much I love you?"

She sniffed and looked into his eyes. "I want to believe you, I really do."

"Then believe me! Do you love me?"

"I do."

"Then trust me. Let me love you and take care of you. Marry me."

She raised her eyebrows. "Are you asking me or telling me?"

"Begging you, if I have to. I don't want to waste one more minute of my life without you."

Doreen Alsen

Tears sprang to Hope's eyes. "You'd beg?"

He dropped onto one knee and grabbed her hands. "*S'il vous plaît*. Please."

"You want to stay here and make a home with me? Raise children with me?"

His eyes kind of crossed at the word children. "How many do you want?"

A gentle smile crossed her face. "One is enough to start with."

"So, that's yes? You'll marry me."

"I'm not sure. "

Lucien's heart just about shattered into one big gooey mess as he stood and banded his arms around her again and kissed her.

"I'll never give you another reason to doubt how much I love you. How much I need you," he told her as he rested his forehead against hers. "You're my family now. My life."

"I love you," she whispered, "with all my heart and soul."

"I don't deserve you, but I'm going to spend the rest of my days making you the happiest woman on earth."

"I'm going to hold you to that." She laughed.

He watched her, his perfect Hope, the light to lead him out of the lonely hell he hadn't even known he'd been in. "Let's go. I've got a big diamond ring to buy."

She shook her head back and some of the flour in her hair flew off and tickled his nose. "Sounds like a plan."

He kissed her, putting all the love he felt for her into the kiss. They were both breathing heavily afterward.

"We should probably go out there and let everyone know the good news," Lucien said.

"And I've got a trophy to get."

"That you do. Only one thing."

"Only one?" Hope raised her eyebrows.

"I think we're locked in here."

The door opened and Shane popped his head in. "Things okay in here?"

"Oh, yeah," Hope said. "Everything is perfect."

Lucien picked her up in his arms and carried her out of the walk-in. "Everything's better than perfect. Let's go get you that trophy."

Epilogue

Hope and Lucien got married in her restaurant and held the reception in his. They served Cajun-inspired local cuisine. Shane was there, and in a world-shattering surprise, was Lucien's best man. Ainslie was her matron of honor. Hope gave herself away. Angelique wasn't there, as she was trying to make it on her own as a model in Europe and chose to have no contact with Lucien.

Hope trembled past her fear of flying on a plane and went to New Orleans with Lucien for their honeymoon. New Orleans was everything it was cracked up to be, but Hope fell in love with the swampy bayou upon which Lucien had grown up.

He took her to the gas station/grocery store where he'd helped *Grand-mère* sell gas, beer, cigarettes, and sandwiches. Though it was a hot and oppressively muggy day, while Hope moved around the store a cool breeze kicked up and wafted over her. Being Irish, she figured it was the spirit of *Grand-mère* welcoming her into the family.

He even took her fishing.

She looked around to see Lucien standing away from her, with the refreshing, cool breeze ruffling his hair. "I think she likes you."

"I think she does. Will it embarrass her if I kiss you while she's here with us?"

That pirate grin bloomed across his face. "Only one way to find out, *pichouette*." He walked to Hope, put his arms around her, and proceeded to kiss the bejeezus out of her.

A throaty chuckle floated on the cool wind that swirled around them. Lucien broke the kiss and looked at her. "I think she likes you, *chère*. I think I like you too. At least enough to keep you around for the next fifty years or so. That okay with you?"

Hope grinned. "*Bien sûr*," she whispered against his lips. "It's a dirty job, but somebody's got to do it."

"Speaking of dirty jobs," Lucien lifted her in his arms, "I think it's time to go back to the city. Me, I have a couple more naughty tricks to teach you. What do you think, *pichouette*?"

"*Oui*," she murmured against his lips, shivering in anticipation of what he wanted to show her. "*Absolument oui*."

A word about the author...

Doreen Alsen has wanted to be a writer all her life but took a brief detour into becoming an opera singer and choral conductor. She realized that she should spend more time writing when creating the backstories for her operatic characters was more fun than actually singing the roles. Plus, her romance-lovin' heart couldn't take all the dead bodies littering the stage at the end of the performance. She is still an active conductor and is regularly found waving her arms around in front of singers.

www.doreenalsen.com

Thank you for purchasing
this publication of The Wild Rose Press, Inc.

If you enjoyed the story, we would appreciate your
letting others know by leaving a review.

For other wonderful stories,
please visit our on-line bookstore at
www.thewildrosepress.com.

For questions or more information
contact us at
info@thewildrosepress.com.

The Wild Rose Press, Inc.
www.thewildrosepress.com

Stay current with The Wild Rose Press, Inc.

Like us on Facebook

https://www.facebook.com/TheWildRosePress

And Follow us on Twitter
https://twitter.com/WildRosePress